Alfred placed the candle back on the wall and reached for a clean blanket. He covered the man. “There is something familiar about him. Did you learn anything?”

“I know how he came to be here, but not who he is,” Jane murmured. “It was the strangest thing, Alfred. When I touched him, I saw what happened. It was not a whisper in my mind.” She gazed at the stranger.

He shall be your lover…

She jerked back as if she were burned. “He cannot stay. He is to leave as soon as he can travel.” Jane rose and turned toward the door, easing her twisted leg before her.

“My lady, I thought you were urged to help him. What changed?”

Your lives are twisted together as your bodies shall…

Jane stopped in her tracks. “We have little enough to eat as it is. We do not need another mouth to feed.” She turned to Alfred. It was a feeble excuse, but it was all she had. She would not reveal the reason for her anxiousness.

Praise for Virginia Barlow

The Wicked Sister
A Fallacious Seduction

"I thoroughly enjoyed this unique take on a classic fairy tale. The villainess was so wicked. The heroine was adorable and admirable, and the hero was dreamy. Some humor and some nice twists thrown in, then a perfect ending, made this unputdownable."

"This book will have you wanting more! Steamy, hot romance! Takes you back in time with a plot that keeps you reading and characters that make it hard to put the book down! A highly recommend book!"

"*A Fallacious Seduction* is a fantastic historical western romance I couldn't put down."

A Fallacious Seduction won the Crowned Heart of Excellence Award from InD'tale Magazine

A Fallacious Seduction was nominated for Book of the Year at N.N. Light's Book Heaven

The Witch of Rathborne Castle

by

Virginia Barlow

This is a work of fiction. Names, characters, places, and incidents are either the product of the author's imagination or are used fictitiously, and any resemblance to actual persons living or dead, business establishments, events, or locales, is entirely coincidental.

The Witch of Rathborne Castle

COPYRIGHT © 2021 by Virginia Ann Barlow

All rights reserved. No part of this book may be used or reproduced in any manner whatsoever without written permission of the author or The Wild Rose Press, Inc. except in the case of brief quotations embodied in critical articles or reviews.
Contact Information: info@thewildrosepress.com

Cover Art by *Jennifer Greeff*

The Wild Rose Press, Inc.
PO Box 708
Adams Basin, NY 14410-0708
Visit us at www.thewildrosepress.com

Publishing History
First Edition, 2021
Trade Paperback ISBN 978-1-5092-3796-8
Digital ISBN 978-1-5092-3797-5

Published in the United States of America

Dedication

To Eda, for teaching me to listen to my heart.

Chapter One

England, 1739

It all started with the wind.

The gentle autumn breeze picked up speed and switched direction. Lady Jane Lenwood glanced up as storm clouds darkened the sky. The air turned frigid. She shivered and tucked the ends of her shawl tighter around her. Gripping the head of her cane, Jane continued her walk, focusing on the cobblestones beneath her feet instead of the pain.

The wind tugged at her hair and long woolen skirts, making an already difficult situation harder. The colder it got, the more strenuous her walk became. She would finish despite the opposition. Jane glanced toward the castle. Where was Thomas, her footman? She required her cloak if she were to stay out much longer. She clasped a hand to her bosom to hold her shawl in place. The end of her nose was numb, and her eyes watered from the bite in the wind. Jane slid her foot forward, leaning heavily on her cane.

Winter comes, the voice in her head whispered.

Jane frowned. It was the first week of October and too early for snow. She sniffed the air. The crisp scent of frost filled her nostrils. With a sigh, she continued her walk. She thought she had a few more weeks to enjoy the sun before winter forced her indoors.

Danger approaches…There is blood and death. Take caution.

Jane stopped. Where? Chills raced down her spine. She searched the courtyard carefully, listening for any unusual sounds. Gray stone walls rose high above her on every side, gleaming in the dimming light. Gray cobblestones lie beneath her feet. There was silence. She was alone like she was every evening when she walked. The scene was familiar, solid, and safe. Jane trembled despite the comfort her surroundings provided. The voice in her head was never wrong.

A stranger enters your world.

She waited. Dried leaves scratched the cobblestones as the wind twirled them in tight circles at her feet.

He comes through the gate.

Jane turned toward the front of the castle. Strangers were no longer welcome. She would cast this one out the same as the others. The rusty scent of blood drifted past on the breeze. Her breath hitched. Just what she needed. The wounded stranger must be dealt with. She moved forward. Her lips pinched together as pain raced up her leg.

The stranger is dangerous and determined.

Approaching footsteps drew her attention. Jane turned sharply toward them.

Alfred, her gray-haired butler, appeared beside her with her heavy fur-lined cloak. "Here, my lady. I thought you might need this."

"Thank you, Alfred." Jane sighed with relief and threw the cloak over her shoulders. She tied the strings beneath her chin.

Death approaches from the forest.

"Will you be coming in now, my lady? It looks like a thunderstorm." Alfred gazed up at the sky.

"No. Come with me." She hobbled forward.

Alfred paused. "Is something wrong?"

Nothing will be the same.

Jane looked up at the darkening sky. Already things were different. "There is danger. It comes from the gate."

"Should I fetch a sword, my lady?" He stayed close to her side, glancing around them with concern.

Her leg ached, and the wind grew stronger. Jane leaned forward. The voice urged her toward the front of the castle.

Hurry. Hurry.

"No. We have not the time." Jane gritted her teeth and took another step. The wind blew her hood from her head. She reached for it as Thomas, her footman, hurried toward them.

"My lady, there's a man inside the castle wall." Thomas waved his arms to get their attention. He was a stout man with red hair and freckles in his early twenties. He came to them from the village as a lad.

The stranger is dark and full of secrets.

"What does he want? Did you ask why he trespassed on Rathborne property?" Jane asked when Thomas stopped beside her, breathing heavily from his run.

"He would not answer me if I did. He is wounded, my lady. There is blood everywhere."

Death waits beneath the trees.

Jane stopped. "Is he alive? How bad are his injuries?" She glanced toward the gate.

Thomas shuffled his feet. "I don't know, my lady, I

didn't get close enough to see."

"Why not?" Jane took another painful step and waited. The wind whipped her skirts against her legs. "If he can stand on his own, he can leave on his own. I do not want him here." Fear pricked the hair on her neck.

Thomas gazed at her with wild, terrified eyes. "He was not standing, my lady, and I do not think he will be going anywhere. There are wolves outside the gate."

Jane's gaze snapped to his. "Wolves? There have not been wolves in England for years. You must be mistaken."

Thomas glanced nervously toward the gate. "There's no mistake, my lady. I saw them."

"There was talk in the village, Lady Jane. A huntsman said a pack migrated from Scotland recently. He tracked them through the forest." Alfred stood by her side. He, too, glanced toward the gate in the wall.

They are hungry.

Jane shuffled forward. "Show me." Her apprehension increased with every step.

Thomas nodded.

As they made their way toward the front gate, Jane's gaze caught on the form of the man on the ground—Jane frowned. It was as Thomas said. He was not on his own two feet. She clutched the head of her cane. Indecision furrowed her brow.

He requires your help.

Jane grimaced. She detested visitors, especially those who reeked of secrets. Who was this person, and why was he in her forest? She shuffled down the long cobblestone drive to the heavy front gates, ignoring the throbbing in her knee.

“Is this man the danger you fear, or is it—?” Alfred stopped short. His mouth gaped open as he pointed in front of them. “Good lord!”

A movement across the road beneath the trees caught her attention. *Wolves!* Jane froze, her heart thumping wildly in her breast. *Thomas was right! There were wolves in her forest!* Why were they so close to the castle? Her gaze caught on the figure on the ground.

They have many mouths to feed.

“The wolves smell the blood!” Jane lifted her gaze back to the trees. Several sets of yellow eyes stared back from beneath the dark, twisted branches. A large male stepped out onto the stark, overgrown road in front of the gate. He bristled and snarled, warning her to stay away. Jane put a hand over her stomach to quell her nervousness and motioned for Thomas to come closer.

“See if the stranger is alive. Be vigilant. The gate appears to be latched shut. The beasts cannot enter the grounds if it is. If he is alive, bring him along. We must get him inside before nightfall.”

Thomas nodded and made his way toward the figure on the ground. He kept his attention on the large alpha challenging him from across the road.

“Are you sure we should bring him in, my lady?” Alfred asked quietly.

Jane nodded. “I am urged to do so. Whatever threatens us, it is not this man. We must help him.” She shivered as Thomas bent over the man.

Thomas waved a hand at her and grabbed the figure by the arms. He pulled the stranger toward them, keeping his gaze on the wolves.

Alfred hurried forward and grabbed the stranger’s

other arm. Together they pulled him toward the castle.

Clutching her cloak closer, Jane motioned for them to go ahead of her.

The large alpha howled, and several pack members joined in.

Ice trickled down her spine. Jane looked up as more of the pack joined the alpha in the road. The ground vibrated with their snarls. Fear clutched her heart like the twisted branches of the dark forest before her. The giant beasts were not happy to see their prey taken away.

They cannot get in.

The pack charged the gate, and Jane's life flashed before her in slow motion. She cried out as the mctal gates clanked and groaned with the force of the impact. The sharp sound shot across the empty castle grounds.

"It held. The gate held," Jane whispered, as she wiped the perspiration from her forehead.

The wolves paced back and forth on the empty forest road. Their haunting yellow eyes glowed in the semi-darkness of the evening. Coarse hair on their backs stood on end.

The temperature dipped lower with the setting sun. Jane held her cloak together with one hand while she gripped her cane with the other. She followed the men as swiftly as she could.

The wolves howled. Their eerie cries filled the silence of the night. Jane glanced over her shoulder. The beasts congregated in front of the castle gate, showing their razor-sharp teeth, and following the trio's progress toward the castle with their strange yellow eyes.

Jane turned her attention to the path in front of her

and the stranger. The intruder was a large man, half again as large as Thomas, and equally so of Alfred. He had a broad chest and heavily muscled thighs. Blood covered the side of his face and poured from a wound on his leg. An arrow protruded from his upper chest. Blood soaked the front of his clothing. Jane's gaze narrowed on the shaft of the arrow. He brought trouble with him. Who was he? He was not a nobleman, or he would have servants with him. He was not a servant either. The quality of his clothing was too fine. The only assumption she could make was he must be a merchant or a scholar.

He comes to Rathborne searching.

Jane frowned. Searching for what?

Both men struggled as they dragged the man toward the castle. The going was slow.

The brisk pace she forced her leg to make made it difficult to breathe. She required all her strength to keep up. The wind plastered her skirts against her legs. The smell of death disappeared, but her fear did not. She stopped. It was not the wolves causing her anxiety. When she directed her thoughts toward them, there was nothing. Jane frowned. What then?

The pack would leave as soon as the smell of blood disappeared. Jane glanced at the stranger again. She would have to allow him to stay long enough to heal. Her lips twisted. The last thing she required was wolves or visitors.

Her nose twitched. The scent of danger rode high on the evening air, but it did not come from the stranger or the wolves. Did another come? Or was it the people in the village?

The tension between the villagers and her was

high. Ever since the incident with the young boy, they feared her. They believed Jane was a witch, cunning and evil. She looked the part with her dark cloak, bent over form, and crooked cane. Rathborne Castle itself was menacing and sinister. With no coin to buy candles, the tall, impressive structure loomed darkly over the village below. Jane could not afford workmen to cut the forest back, so it grew thick and gnarly right up to the castle walls. It was black, overgrown, and a perfect backdrop for the superstitions the villagers harbored about the haunted castle and the witch who lived there. Jane grimaced.

Several times she journeyed to the village, hoping to settle the differences between them. It proved a futile effort. As soon as Jane's carriage pulled onto the main street, there was a flurry of activity. The villagers grabbed their offspring and their spouses and disappeared. The only sound was running feet and the slamming of every door and shutter.

Jane shook her head. They threatened to burn her on more than one occasion. The last legal execution of a witch was in Scotland seventeen years prior. Since then, all witch trials stopped. But it did not put an end to the superstition or the rumors. There was no local militia or army to keep the villagers from taking justice into their own hands. Thank the gods a few of the merchants were levelheaded. They demanded proof of Jane's wrongs before they allowed her to be arrested or tried for witchcraft. Those sane individuals kept the rabble at bay.

The trio reached the steps of the castle as darkness settled around them.

Jane pulled the latch on the heavy oak door and

stepped back to allow Alfred and Thomas to carry the stranger inside.

"Put him in the dungeon," Jane commanded, as she swung her heavy cloak from her shoulders and hung it on the peg beside the door. She leaned against the dark stone to catch her breath. The wind was fierce. She trembled from her exertion in fighting it.

Alfred glanced at Jane in surprise. "The dungeon, my lady?"

Jane nodded. "Yes, Alfred, the dungeon. I will tend his wounds there. I cannot afford to have a stranger wandering the castle. He must remain behind bars until I learn his intent."

Alfred nodded. His gaze was thoughtful.

Jane sank into a threadbare chair to rest her leg. "After you help Thomas take the stranger to the dungeon, bring my bag of medicine. I require clean cloth and warm water." Jane stopped. "And bring a knife to cut the shaft of the arrow."

"Of course, my lady." Alfred and Thomas disappeared with their burden.

Jane waited until her trembling ceased and the ache in her leg eased. Her mind returned to the stranger.

Give the man aid. He must heal.

The words danced through her mind. Jane grimaced.

Alfred reappeared with her supplies. "Do you need help, my lady?"

Jane shook her head. "I will be fine." She did not like the idea of a man in her castle.

Alfred nodded and disappeared down the long corridor.

With a sigh of resignation, Jane rose to her feet.

She did not like it, but what choice did she have? Her cane tapped on the wooden floor as she made her way to the dungeon. The sooner the stranger mended, the sooner he could be on his way.

The man is important to your future.

Jane stilled. Why?

There was no response. She shook her head. The voice could be so vague sometimes. It gave her enough to make her curious, and then was silent. Jane continued down the stone steps to the dungeon. Important could mean a hundred different things. It did not mean the stranger came to fulfill the deepest desires of her heart, that of having a husband and a child.

She entered the dark cell sometime later. Her twisted knee screamed with pain, but she ignored it. There was work to be done. The wounded man lay pale and still on the narrow cot at the back of the cell. Her bag of medicine and the knife lay beside him. Thomas stood guard. The flickering light of the candle danced over the scene creating an eerie atmosphere. Jane's shadow lengthened on the stone wall as she moved forward.

She waved Thomas aside and bent over the stranger. A touch would tell her everything. Jane closed her eyes and stretched her hand toward the man. She held her breath. The warmth of his skin sent tingles up her arm. She shivered and flattened her palm, increasing her contact with him. The dungeon disappeared, and she was in the forest surrounding Rathborne.

Jane stiffened in surprise. She never had a vision before.

She rode beside the stranger on a large black

stallion running through the trees. An arrow whistled through the air and hit him in the shoulder. The man teetered. He righted and nudged his mount with his knees, flattening his body against the horse's back. Suddenly the wolves were behind him. He said several colorful words and leaned closer to his stallion. A large male wolf appeared on the path in front of them, showing his teeth. The man's horse reared, and the rider flew backward into the shrubbery. The wolves leaped at his horse, and all Jane could see was blood. The stranger rose to his feet and turned toward the gates of Rathborne. He had a head wound, and his thigh bled from his catapult into the bushes. The arrow in his shoulder dripped red. The man ran with all his might. He lunged inside the gates of Rathborne and kicked them shut as the alpha wolf leaped to end his life.

Jane shook. Her vision was over. She brushed strands of hair from her face with trembling hands and wiped her eyes. Her heart pounded in her throat. The stranger barely made it to safety. The images still danced before her. Jane dabbed the perspiration from her forehead with one of the cloths. She sank onto the edge of the narrow cot beside the stranger, too weak to stand. Premonitions were a usual occurrence. Visions were not. Jane frowned. There must be a reason she had one now.

Your life and his are intertwined.

Jane froze. How could this be? Her life would never intertwine with any man. The words repeated themselves in her mind. Her hand trembled as she reached for another cloth.

Jane wished the future contained happiness. But how could it be any different than it was? She would never know the touch of a man, nor ever know what it was to be loved. She resigned her feelings to her fate the day she woke from her accident and realized she would never be normal again. Jane brushed wetness from her eyes and focused on cleaning the man's face.

The picture of the assassin danced before her, then disappeared. Jane had a quick impression of power and lethal determination. The man dressed in black, but she saw little else. Jane frowned. If only she spotted some identifying mark. Her instinct told her the assassin was the danger the voice warned her about.

The stranger beside her murmured, and Jane jumped. She would figure it out later. For now, there was work to do. She rolled up her sleeves and washed her hands. She probed the wound on the man's head. It was not deep, but it would require attention. She cleaned it thoroughly and bandaged it. She inspected the stranger's face as she worked. His dark hair was pulled back and bound with a thin strip of leather. The man had a straight nose, a square chin covered with dark stubble, and a high brow. He was extremely handsome. Jane frowned. The stranger unsettled her. He was dark and sensuous. The pit of her stomach tightened.

Your path lies beside his.

"Stop it!" Jane cried, putting her hands over her ears.

Thomas glanced at her in alarm. "My lady?"

Jane took a deep breath. "Never mind, Thomas. I was busy with my own thoughts."

Thomas nodded but kept his gaze on her.

Jane took the knife and slit the man's breeches to his thigh. Her eyes widened at the size of his muscled leg. He was well formed and tanned, his skin smooth and supple. Jane stretched out her hand, running her fingers the length of his thigh. Her breath hitched in her throat at the warmth of his skin. She caught the smell of sandalwood on his clothes. She had never seen a man such as this.

Alfred entered the cell.

Jane looked up. "Help me remove the arrow."

Alfred and Thomas took hold of the man's shoulders. Jane ripped his shirt open, revealing a muscled chest covered with crisp dark hair. She retrieved the knife and cut off the shaft of the arrow. The men lifted the stranger to a sitting position and held him while Jane pushed the arrow through, removing it. Blood ran down the stranger's chest and back. Jane reached for a cloth and water. When she cleaned it to her satisfaction, she applied an herbal salve and wrapped strips of linen around his large chest. When she finished, the men laid the stranger down.

Alfred dismissed Thomas. "Gertie wants you to gather some firewood."

Thomas nodded and left.

Jane washed the dried blood from the gash on the man's thigh.

"Is the wound deep?" Alfred leaned over to see what she was doing.

"No. It requires stitching, though. Hold the candle for me."

Alfred took the candle from the wall and held it up.

Jane took a needle and threaded it with her silk floss. She applied the needle to his skin, drawing the ragged edges together in tiny, neat stitches. Then she applied more salve and wrapped the wound with a clean cloth, tying the ends together. "Cover him with a blanket, so he does not catch a chill, and keep an eye on him. Let him have some broth when he regains consciousness. Inform me immediately once he is awake. I want to question him."

"Of course, my lady." Alfred placed the candle back on the wall and reached for a clean blanket. "There is something familiar about him, but I cannot decide what it is. Did you learn anything?"

"I know how he came to be here, but not who he is," Jane murmured. "It was the strangest thing, Alfred. When I touched him, I *saw* what happened. It was not a whisper in my mind." She gazed at the stranger.

He shall be your lover.

She jerked back as if burned. "He cannot stay. He is to leave as soon as he can travel." Jane rose and turned toward the door, easing her twisted leg before her.

"My lady, I thought you were urged to help him. What changed?"

Your lives are twisted together as your bodies shall—

Jane stopped in her tracks. "We have little enough to eat as it is. We do not need another mouth to feed."

She turned to Alfred. It was a feeble excuse, but it was all she had. She would not reveal the reason for her anxiousness. "Take Thomas with you to the gardens tomorrow, gather everything. Snow will come early this year. There was a chill earlier, and it smelled of frost."

"Yes, my lady." Alfred no longer questioned her. She saved his life on more than one occasion with her unnatural knowledge.

Chapter Two

Max opened his eyes. Flickering light danced across a low stone ceiling covered with mold. He frowned and glanced side to side, blinking rapidly. Everything was blurry. He put a hand against the pounding pain in his head and blinked again. He was in a small, dimly lit room. The air was moist and filled with the sour, musty odor of stale straw. It was cold and dark. Understanding flashed through his mind. He was in the dungeon. They caught him. His only chance was to kill them before they killed him. Max reached for his sword, but his hand came away empty. They relieved him of his weapon. Max frowned. No matter. He killed with his bare hands before, and he would do so again.

He rolled to his side carefully, and the narrow cot groaned in protest. The ropes holding the hay-filled mattress tightened as he moved. Pain shot through his shoulder and thigh. Max closed his eyes. He remembered the wolves and the arrow. An assassin followed him through the woods. He caught a glimpse of the villain before burning pain caught his shoulder on fire. The assassin was part of the group that ambushed him and Lord Darham in York. He was the one who got away. Max must find the traitor and end him before it was too late. But first, he must escape. There had to be a way out of this place.

Max opened his eyes and lifted his head to see

more of his surroundings. He groaned with pain. There were no guards. He was alone. Gingerly, he laid his head back. He could make out a battered wooden door with a tiny window. It had a rusty latch and bars across the window. He stared at the dark stone of the walls. A single candle flickered beside the door. Rodents crept from the shadows. Their tiny feet clicked on the stone as they scurried along the wall.

Dizziness washed over him. Max closed his eyes. The second he did, images of the wolves flashed through his mind. He would never forget the screams his horse, Brutus, made as the pack tore him to shreds. The stallion had been with him for some time and was as well-trained as it was possible to become. Brutus would be a loss not easily overcome. Standing toe to toe with his enemy on the field of battle was nothing compared to looking into the eyes of the wolves as they tore Brutus apart and then came after him.

How was he to escape without a horse?

Max wiped the sweat from his brow and opened his eyes once more. He remembered the wrought iron gates of Rathborne Castle. He remembered kicking them shut as the alpha wolf pounced. Max frowned. Why was the assassin in the forest outside Rathborne? Was the duchess involved? He must proceed with caution. If the traitor were here and knew of Max's mission, he would try to kill him. Max sat up slowly, his head swimming with the effort. He placed a hand against his forehead and felt the edges of a bandage. Someone tended his wounds, and his shoulder throbbed. He moved it carefully beneath the binding. It was stiff but intact. He frowned at the bandage wrapped around his thigh and the state of his breeches. Someone slit the inside of one leg to the groin, and his shirt was gone. He was naked to the waist except for the strips of linen binding him.

Max shivered in the cool air. Why would they tend his wounds if they planned to kill him?

He assessed his surroundings. There was nothing in the room except the narrow cot he sat on and a coarse woolen blanket covering his lower half. He ignored the stench of the dungeon and turned to look up at the window in the corner of the room. Stars glimmered through the narrow opening. No hope of escape there. The bars were too close together. He would never fit between them.

Footsteps approached. The metal latch lifted, and the door to his cell opened.

A red-headed man stepped inside. "You are awake," he observed. "I will fetch Lady Jane." The door swung shut, and the latch fell into place.

Max frowned. A million questions raced through his mind. Who was Lady Jane? Where was the duchess? Was Lady Jane responsible for the parchment? Did she send the assassins? Who tended his wounds? More importantly, who had the duke's signet ring? He was here to obtain answers and find the traitor. Max traveled alone and incognito for a reason. Disguised as a commoner, he could enter a tavern or lurk on a street corner without attracting attention. He learned a great deal in the shadows.

Shivers racked his body. Max reached for the blanket and drew it across his shoulders. Somehow, he must retrieve his satchel from what remained of Brutus. He carried extra clothing and a bag of gold to aid in his mission. He could not continue dressed as he was. The room blurred. Max closed his eyes and drew in a deep breath. He should rest and let his wounds heal. But if he did, the traitor would get away. Months of searching and watching lost.

He leaned back against the stone wall. Somehow, he must find the person who sold English secrets to the Spaniards. All he had to go on was a scrap of parchment containing information about the English fleet. It was addressed to Philip V of Spain and sealed with the Rathborne crest. Max grimaced. Several admirals had information on the English fleet. The traitor could be any of them or anyone connected to them.

He jerked awake when the door to his cell creaked and groaned as it swung open. Max gazed at his visitors. A bent, old woman hobbled toward him with a cane. A young footman and an elderly gray-haired man followed the woman into his cell. Max blinked. The old butler Alfred was still alive.

The woman stopped and folded her hands across the head of her cane. The hood of her black cape hid her face. The lady was silent for long minutes. The two men stopped behind her, blocking his path to freedom.

Max rose unsteadily to his feet. He opened his mouth to speak when the woman pushed the hood from her head. Max froze, as he gazed into the sweetest face he had ever seen. He realized with a start this was a young woman and incredibly beautiful. Auburn curls clung to the side of her heart-shaped face. Her brilliant blue eyes were alert and watchful.

He searched her face. She was so familiar. She looked like a younger copy of another woman he knew.

The woman flushed with color. "Who are you, and why are you here?" Her voice was soft but laced with suspicion and anger.

For the first time in his entire life, Max was speechless. This must be Lady Jane. A fleeting memory of a little girl holding her mother's hand flashed through his mind. Did he know her? He inspected her from head to toe. Was she the traitor he sought? Would she recognize him? He waited for her reaction with hooded eyes. Her face remained blank. Max nodded. His mission was to catch a traitor. Until he knew the person's identity, he trusted no one.

****

Jane gazed at the stranger. The man must leave as soon as he was well. She did not want him here. He must be feeling better for his color returned. Her gaze caught his. The stranger had the most amazing gray eyes. She stared, fascinated by the silver flashing there.

His gaze wandered slowly over her and returned to her face.

Heat rose in her cheeks at his lengthy inspection. She said nothing.

"This is Lady Jane Lenwood," Alfred announced.

The man's eyes changed color. They were liquid silver, alert and watchful. "My lady," the man said, bowing. "I am a traveler seeking shelter."

"By what name are you called? Why are you here?" Jane asked again.

The man's eyes flashed in the candlelight. "What import is a name?" He shrugged stiffly. "If I say I am the king or the high priest, it changes nothing. I would still seek shelter until my wounds heal."

Jane's eyes narrowed. "A name is of utmost import. If you were the king or the high priest, I would gladly give you anything you require. Were you the

Duke of Rathborne, I should let you rot in this cell for all eternity with nothing to keep you company but the rats and spiders. I should let you freeze to death, or better yet, turn you out to the wolves. He deserves an eternity in hell." Her gaze swept over him. "There is one example of a name making a difference."

The stranger's eyes chilled to a winter gray. "What has the poor chap done to deserve such devotion?"

Jane's chin came up a notch. "He is the reason my life and this castle are in ruins." She stared into his eyes. "Enough about him. I shall ask once more. What is your name, and why are you here?"

There was silence for several seconds. The man's silver eyes flashed. Then his lids dropped over them, hiding his thoughts. "My name is Max Radley, my lady. I am at your service." His voice was calm. "A pack of the largest wolves I have ever seen attacked me in the forest. This castle was the nearest place of safety. I just made it inside…your gates."

Jane waved her hand at his statement. "I know all this. Why were you in the forest?"

Mr. Radley was silent for a minute. "I come to Rathborne on business."

"Do you take me for a fool? No one comes to Rathborne." Jane looked Mr. Radley over with disdain. The voice warned her this man came with secrets.

"Rathborne Castle used to be one of the most luxurious castles in England," Mr. Radley went on. "Travelers stopped to avail themselves of the duke's hospitality. Everyone was welcomed. I wonder at how the times have changed. Instead of being welcomed, I am thrown in the dungeon."

Jane shrugged. "Be grateful this is all that

happened to you. I do not welcome travelers, nor do I entertain the curious. No one comes to Rathborne on business. This castle no longer welcomes visitors."

"So, I see. Surely a wounded man is no threat. Why not offer hospitality instead of hostility? What crime have I committed to be treated thus?" The stranger's eyes were mere slits as he studied her.

"You trespassed on private property. You are not welcome here," Jane answered. Then, she shrugged. "The only people who venture this far into the woods seek the Witch of Rathborne. They come fueled with superstition from the village below. Until you prove yourself different from the many who came before you, you will remain here. I require the true reason you visit a forest and a castle everyone else has forgotten. Then, and only then, will I release you." She waited for him to speak, to give a reason for his presence. When he did not, she turned to leave. "If you have nothing to impart, you will remain locked inside." She pulled the hood of her cloak back over her head.

"Then I seek an audience with the duchess. I will lay my case before her."

Jane stopped. "You wish to speak to my mother?" she whispered. She clutched the head of her cane and did not move. Her back was ramrod straight. Jane cleared her throat. "You cannot. She left in the night three years ago. I have not heard from her since." Her voice broke as she said the last of it.

Silence followed her statement. Jane turned to face him.

Mr. Radley's gaze was curious and watchful. "Who manages estate business if she is not here?"

Jane's chin rose. "I do. Such as there is. I do not

see where it concerns you."

His eyes gleamed in the candlelight. "I came here on business. I am to meet my partner in Rathborne village before traveling north. I do not know if I missed the man or not. I require a place to stay until I regain my health. I will pay for my keep, whatever price you decide. If times are as hard as you claim, a little coin would help. Will you allow me to stay until I am well enough to travel?"

Jane chewed her lip. Should she trust him?

He is not the danger you see. There is another.

"This castle is no longer luxurious. The village may be more suited to your taste. We have nothing to offer."

Mr. Radley gazed steadily back at her. "I am no stranger to hard work. I do not require pampering. Do we have an agreement?"

Jane sucked in a breath. "Who shot you? How do I know your presence will not bring us trouble?"

Mr. Radley shrugged. His eyes flashed silver and bored into hers. "I know not. I caught a glimpse of him through the trees before his arrow struck. I should like the chance to follow his tracks and find out. I cannot until I am well and purchase another mount."

Jane stared at him.

He must stay close.

Her stomach knotted with apprehension. "We do not have much to eat. Only a few vegetables from the garden and the fruit from the trees. Winter is on its way."

Mr. Radley nodded. "I will pay well for my stay. I must retrieve my satchel from what remains of my horse. My coins and extra clothing are there." He searched her face. "For the price I am willing to pay, I would like to convalesce in a chamber upstairs."

Jane hesitated for long seconds and then nodded her head. "I am a private person Mr. Radley. I do not enjoy company. I am reluctant to offer you hospitality without knowledge of who you are. However, we are facing starvation, and winter is upon us. I shall accept your offer in exchange for a roof over your head until you are well enough to travel." Her face hardened. "If you betray the kindness I offer, I shall see you in hell. You shall regret stepping foot in Rathborne."

Mr. Radley offered his hand.

Jane swallowed her nervousness and limped forward. Max Radley topped her by a head. His chest and arms rippled in the light of the candle, casting a golden glow over his near-naked body. Jane clamped her knees together to hide their trembling. Then, she lifted her gaze to his and shook his hand carefully. After the vision she had earlier, she was not sure she dared touch him. His warm hand engulfed hers. Jane felt the contact to the soles of her feet. Her breath hitched in her throat. He was so large, so warm, and so male. She stared at the black hair curling on his chest and blushed.

He is important to your future.

Jane dropped her gaze.

"You shall not regret your decision, Lady Jane. I shall see to it you have all you require." His deep voice rumbled by her ear.

Jane withdrew her hand quickly. If only such a statement were true. "You may come up to the salon where it is warm until a chamber is prepared." She took a step back and looked up at him. "Can you make it on your own?"

"I will help him, my lady," Alfred said. He stepped from his place beside the door where he stood through the whole exchange.

Jane nodded and turned away. She bit her lip. Was she doing the right thing? She slowly made her way back up the long stairs. It was risky to let the stranger out of the dungeon. Thomas and Alfred were no match for him should he turn out to be a villain.

He is not the threat.

If this were true, he could help them. Able-bodied men were scarce. Jane hobbled toward the small salon off the main entrance and took her seat beside the meager fire.

Another comes.

Jane shivered. If another came to do them harm, Mr. Radley would earn his keep.

Max Radley will solve riddles and answer long-asked questions. He will change everything.

Everything? She bit her lip. Everything covered a lot of ground. Jane's mind brought up an image of him. She saw the light flickering over his muscled chest and arms again. She remembered the feel of his skin as she ran her hands over his thigh. He was warm and hard. She wondered what it would be like to have such a man as her own. Jane shook her head. It could never be. She must keep him at a distance. Let him answer the riddles and questions. Disappointment and heartache were emotions familiar to her. Mr. Radley was dangerous and exciting. He might not hurt her physically, but a man like him could lay waste to her soul.

****

Max sat down on the edge of the cot when Lady

Jane walked away. His body trembled with the effort to stand. He put a palm to his head to steady it and stayed there for several minutes.

Alfred stood beside him, saying nothing.

The tapping of Lady Jane's cane and the slide of her foot on the stone floor disappeared in the distance. Silence filled the cell.

"Are you all right, my lord?" Alfred peered down at him.

Max dropped his hand and gazed into Alfred's weathered old face. "You recognized me." His heartbeat accelerated.

Alfred nodded. "It took me a few minutes, but I remember. It came to me while Lady Jane stitched your leg. I remember the time you fell out of the apple tree and Nurse stitched you up."

Max gazed into his old eyes. His chest tightened when he thought of all he would lose if he were found out. "Do you plan to tell Lady Jane?"

Alfred shook his head. "I figured if you did not tell her who you are, you must have a reason." He cleared his throat. "We thought you were dead. I am relieved you are not. Do you plan to stay?"

Max put his head in his hands. The dizziness was hard to bear. "I am looking for someone. He took something of mine. I will tell you the details another time. The important thing is, I must stay in Rathborne until I find him. No one can know who I am or why I am here."

Alfred nodded. "I will keep your secret, my lord."

"Will the other servants recognize me?"

"There aren't any other than Thomas, Gertie, and I. Gertie came to tend his lordship before he passed on.

She knows nothing."

Max nodded his head. "Good."

"Let me help you upstairs, my lord. Once you are settled beside the fire, I will tend to your chamber."

"You must treat me no different than any other visitor. Lives depend on my mission being a success. You must address me as Mr. Radley until I tell you otherwise."

"Of course, sir."

Max stood and allowed Alfred to help him up the stairs and toward the small salon. Max's mind whirled as they walked along the dark, empty corridors. This was not the castle he remembered. It used to be warm, with tantalizing smells wafting from the kitchens. The corridors filled with liveried servants hurrying about their duties. The floors shone from recent scrubbing. There used to be mahogany tables topped with crystal and fresh-cut flowers. Portraits, paintings, and tapestries hung high on the walls. There were thick carpets on the floor and heavy gilded furniture. It was all gone. The halls were dark or dimly lit. It was cold, covered in dust, and empty.

"What happened to the tapestries and the portraits? Where are the candlesticks and snuff boxes? My God! What happened?" Max asked furiously.

Alfred shook his head. "The late duke burned it all except a bit of furniture a few months before his death."

Astonishment widened his eyes. "Why would he do such a thing? The portraits and tapestries chronicled the history of Rathborne. The honor of the Rathborne name meant everything. He gave up his only son and heir for the glory of it all."

They turned the corner next to the salon.

Alfred sighed. “His grace no longer cared for any of those things. He died a lonely, broken man.”

Max stared at Alfred in disbelief. “Why?”

They stood in the doorway to the salon.

“He grieved for the loss of his son, Mr. Radley,” Lady Jane said from her seat beside the fire.

“He never wanted him to come back,” Max whispered beneath his breath. He could not believe the empty, cold, broken rooms before him. The parchment was a nudge from the gods. Without it, he never would have ridden toward Rathborne.

Chapter Three

The nightmares started again. As before, Jane hurried to her mother's room with a tray of breakfast. She stopped outside the closed chamber door and stared at it. She knew what she would find within. The nightmare urged her forward. With trembling hands, Jane pulled the latch and walked inside. The pain hit her anew. She choked back the sob and doubled over. Her mother was gone! Everything was gone! Shock made her trip. She set the tray on the table beside the bed and hurried to the wardrobe. It was empty except for one of her mother's old cloaks hanging in the back. As Jane touched the garment, it happened. She knew where her mother was, and she was not alone. A gentleman was with her. They rode in a carriage along the cliffs headed east.

Jane fell to the floor.

She will never return.

Panic roared through her system. Never was a long time. Why would Mama leave her?

She loves another.

Jane sat up. Who? There was no answer. Why not her? She did everything Mama asked. What had she done to deserve this?

Tears flowed down her cheeks. Loneliness filled her bosom. The ache of betrayal broke her heart. Jane wept until she had nothing left. When her weeping ceased, numbness stole over her. Jane analyzed the situation. What if she promised to do more? Determination straightened her spine. If she could find her mother, she might convince her to stay. Surely the love of a daughter meant more than the love of a man. The thread of hope was enough to help her to her feet. She ran to the stables and saddled her mare. Jane galloped away, rehearsing her argument. She took the east road along the cliffs. A giant storm crashed through the air. Lightning struck the ground in front of her. Her mare reared, throwing Jane from the saddle. She fell over the side of the steep mountain road and into the ravine below. Her horse crashed down after her, landing on her leg and breaking her knee. Jane had not been the same since.

Jane woke with a start. Every time she had the nightmare, she relived the scene feeling every nuance of torment. Perspiration drenched her. Her night rail stuck to her and her pillow was damp. She shivered in the dark, remembering what happened. When she did not return, Alfred and Thomas went searching for her. They found her several hours later and brought her home. It took weeks for her knee to heal and even longer to put any weight on it. Alfred made a cane for her, and slowly Jane learned to walk again. Her mother never returned, but Jane knew she lived. The voice told her so.

A knock sounded on her chamber door. Jane jumped in alarm.

"My lady, are you all right?" Max Radley's deep voice penetrated the silence.

Jane sat up. Her nightmare disappeared, and her torment vanished. She shivered in the dark, staring at the door. "I am fine," she called. Her voice shook. She must have cried out in her sleep.

The latch lifted, and the door opened. Mr. Radley held a candlestick and limped into the room. He wore an old pair of breeches from the late duke and a flowing white shirt.

"You screamed. What happened?" His silver gaze sought her face. The shadows retreated as Mr. Radley walked closer with his candle. They promised to return as soon as he left.

Jane tugged her nightclothes to her chin. "Nothing." She trembled with nervousness. Why was he here? No man came to her chamber.

He will not harm you. He comes to aid you.

Jane swallowed as she looked up. Their gazes met and held. Her fear melted away.

Mr. Radley stopped beside her bed. He smelled of sandalwood and security. His expression was quiet and thoughtful. He made no move to touch her. The room was silent except for the crackle of the fire on the hearth.

Jane's shivering ceased. Mr. Radley's presence filled the room. The evil retreated.

Mr. Radley limped to the window and checked the latch. It was locked. "What frightened you?"

Jane flushed. "I do not know." She dipped her head as she told the lie.

Mr. Radley's gaze swung back to her and settled on her face.

Warmth flooded her body. Her thoughts jumped from the terror of her dream to the vivid reality of Mr. Radley. Jane licked her lips nervously, holding her nightclothes tight against her chest. It was surreal to be in bed with a man inside her chamber. Mr. Radley was so handsome she forgot to breathe. What if he tried to kiss her? The air was suddenly too warm. Jane fanned her face with her hand. Perspiration beaded her brow. Her body quivered beneath her bedclothes.

"Something made you call for help." Mr. Radley frowned as he checked every corner of her chamber and came up empty-handed. Limping, he made his way back to her bed and checked underneath.

Jane stared at her hands trembling in her lap. Whether from aftereffects of the nightmare or Mr. Radley's presence, she did not know. No one had ever come to her defense before. It was unbelievable, and so was he. She stared with fascination at the ripple of muscle as he moved. She remembered how he felt when she touched him, so warm and so male. All she could think about was him and the fact they were alone in the middle of the night in her bedchamber. She felt every breath he took. Jane lifted her gaze to his. She never thought to be this close to a man, especially one of Mr. Radley's caliber.

"You should not be here," she managed to say and blushed at the breathlessness in her voice. Did he know she trembled? Jane tightened her grip on her blankets to keep her hands from reaching out to touch him. Her gaze followed him as he moved around her chamber.

"Tell me why you cried out. There is no one here and no evidence of danger." Mr. Radley's silver eyes flashed in the firelight as he glanced in her direction.

She blushed beneath his steady regard. How could she explain?

Trust him.

Jane hesitated for a moment. "I have nightmares,"

she confessed, twisting her hands together. "But they are gone now." Shyness stained her cheeks. She never talked about her injury or the night it happened. "I am all right. Thank you for coming to my aid. As you say, I am not in danger. You should leave. It is not proper for you to be here."

Mr. Radley's eyes turned metallic. He stepped closer to the bed.

Jane's heartrate accelerated. Her body trembled, and her lips parted. Time stood still. She gazed into the liquid silver of his eyes and thought a million improper thoughts. When he picked her hand up in his, Jane stopped breathing. He gazed deep into her soul as he bent and placed a kiss on her knuckles. She went limp. His lips were warm and firm. Just the way lips should be. She gazed at his dark head and struggled for breath.

He searches for something.

Jane pulled her hand away.

Mr. Radley straightened. "Do not be frightened. I am here to render aid, nothing more. Have a good night, Lady Jane." He turned and left, closing her door behind him.

Jane quivered in the dark. If there were a villain in her chamber, she did not doubt he would be dead. Mr. Radley looked like the kind of man who could hold his own in battle. How was it her mother left in the night with no thought of Jane or her welfare, and a stranger made his way down the long corridors in the dark to rescue her?

Jane slid down into the bed. Perhaps she was wrong about Mr. Radley. Perhaps the danger he brought was for someone other than her. For the first time in her life, Jane was safe. When she fell to sleep, her nightmares did not return. She dreamed she held a red-haired baby girl and swung her up in her arms. Jane reveled in the joy, for she knew such a thing would never be possible.

****

Max returned to his chamber, deep in thought. When Lady Jane called out, he dashed to her chamber, hoping he would find some answers. He wondered if the traitor attacked in the night, but came away disappointed. Lady Jane's fear came from her dreams, nothing more. What caused her terror? Did she know the traitor? Did she know about the parchment? He had so many questions. Was there more to Lady Jane and Rathborne than the obvious? He planned to search until he found the answers. Someone had the duke's signet ring. The old duke wore it on his third finger until the day of his death. He had to find out who took it. Whoever held it was the traitor or knew who was.

Thomas and Alfred went into the forest and retrieved Max's satchel the morning after his arrival. Max gave Lady Jane one gold coin for every week he stayed. With their newfound wealth, Thomas went to the village and purchased meat, cheese, and bread which Gertie used to prepare a thick, hearty stew for dinner. The aroma drifted through the castle, causing Max's stomach to grumble.

The second week he was at Rathborne, Max's strength returned. He no longer had dizzy spells, and his wounds were healing nicely. He was ready to resume his search.

One afternoon, Max rose from his place beside the fire in the small salon and listened to the castle noise. Lady Jane walked in the courtyard. Gertie was in the kitchen, and the men were out chopping wood.

Now was his chance. Max slipped out of the antechamber and down the corridor toward the family apartments. He pulled the latch on the duke's chamber and opened the door. The hinges squeaked in protest. Max glanced up and down the corridor. Satisfied he was alone, Max stepped inside.

The room was dark and musty. Cobwebs hung from the corners. The giant master bed stood in its place in the center of the room, covered in dust cloths. Either the old duke wanted the comfort of his own bed after burning the rest of the castle furnishings, or it was too heavy for him to move. The giant four-poster bed with carved headboard was massive. The workmen assembled it in the duke's chamber for his great, great grandfather, one hundred and twenty-five years previous. No one moved it since. An elaborate wooden chest stood beside the bed bearing the Rathborne Crest.

Max limped toward it and lifted the lid. The chest contained a few old garments left behind by his father. Max sifted through them, searching for papers or anything to help him in his mission. His hand closed around a leather jewel case. Max pulled it from the chest and released the catch. A brilliant diamond necklace lay on a bed of satin. Matching earrings and a bracelet nestled beside it. His mother's jewels. He remembered her wearing them. Max stroked the large diamond in the front of the necklace. The jeweler was good at his craft, but better cuts were now being made.

A noise in the courtyard drew his attention. Hastily, Max closed the case and returned it to its former place inside the chest. He put the clothing back where he found them and closed the lid. On silent feet, he slipped out of the duke's chamber and hurried toward the antechamber.

He met Lady Jane in the corridor.

She stopped short. She gazed at him and then looked behind him. "What are you doing here?"

"I am stretching my leg," Max answered. "It stiffens when I do not move it."

Lady Jane stared at him for long seconds. "If this is truly the reason you are in the corridor outside the family apartments, perhaps you would join me in the courtyard tomorrow when I exercise my knee?"

It was a challenge, and Max accepted it with a brilliant smile. "I would be delighted to accompany you, Lady Jane." He bowed and walked toward his chamber, deep in thought.

****

Why was Mr. Radley in the corridor? Had he been searching the family chambers? Her instinct told her he was. Jane opened the door and looked inside. Everything was in place. She walked to the chest and lifted the lid. She found the jewel case and flipped open the catch. The diamonds were all there. Jane put the case back in the chest and closed the lid. She gazed around the empty chamber. What could Mr. Radley possibly want in the duke's chamber?

He searches for answers.

Jane bit her lip. She should have left him in the dungeon.

Trust him.

Jane sighed. "All right, but you better be correct about him."

Chapter Four

"Lady Jane!" Gertie called.

Jane closed the door to her chamber and turned to Gertie.

"My lady, your uncle's carriage stopped outside. He has Lady Melissa and Lady Emily with him."

"What?" Jane leaned against the plaster wall of the corridor and closed her eyes. She did not sleep well last night. Images of the assassin and Lady Margret's diamond necklace kept her awake until dawn. Voices spoke in her head, but she could not decipher what they said. Her mind kept taking her to the duke's chamber, where she stared at the empty walls. Jane had no idea what any of it meant.

Gertie put her hands on her hips. "I ain't waitin' on 'em," she warned. "They ran me ragged the last time they were here. Ain't nothin' we have or nothin' I do is good enough for 'em."

"I know, Gertie. I am not happy about their arrival either." What a time for Uncle Harold to call. Jane had enough on her mind with the arrival of Mr. Radley and the wolves.

Jane looked up at the cream plaster ceiling. "Why, God? What did I do to deserve this? After years of solitude, Rathborne is suddenly the destination of choice."

Gertie gasped. "Miss Jane! Do not blaspheme God!

He had nothing to do with it. Sir Harold and their ladyships cause the trouble. The good Lord is sure to be as put out as the rest of us."

Jane rolled her eyes. Her cane tapped on the wooden floor as she made her way to the great hall.

Sir Harold Roswell was her mother's younger brother. He was in his thirties with brown hair and narrow, squirrelly eyes. He was several inches taller than Jane and portly from excessive drinking. He had a nervous energy that set Jane's teeth on edge. She did not trust him. The voice told her he was an evil man, and her gut confirmed it.

His older daughter, Melissa, was not any better. She had a disagreeable personality and complained about everything. Nothing ever satisfied her. Melissa believed the world owed her homage, and it was Jane's duty to see she got it. Melissa was tall and thin with sleek red hair. Her narrow green eyes stared holes through those she deemed inferior. Jane was one of those individuals. Melissa put on a pleasant, chatty air when she wanted to impress someone. Mr. Radley fell into this category.

Uncle Harold's younger daughter, Emily, was petite and quiet. She had red curly hair and enormous blue eyes. She sat in the corner playing with the strings of her reticule. Emily avoided drawing anyone's attention and never joined the conversation.

Jane entered the great hall in time to see Alfred take her visitors' cloaks.

"Jane. Why do you make us wait on the doorstep? I am cold, tired, and hungry. I require a hot bath and a decent meal. See to it immediately—" Melissa's tirade stopped short.

Mr. Radley stepped to Jane's side.

Melissa's transformation was astonishing. Her scowl changed to a calculating look as she assessed Mr. Radley from the top of his dark head to the soles of his leather boots. A wide smile split her face. She came toward Jane with arms outstretched. "My goodness! I did not know you had company! Who is this, dear cousin?"

Jane glanced heavenward. Melissa's blatant play-acting fooled no one.

Mr. Radley's face was expressionless.

"Lady Melissa Roswell, may I introduce Mr. Max Radley. Mr. Radley, this is my cousin, Lady Melissa Roswell," Jane intoned with no emotion. This week got better and better.

Be cautious.

Caution was her top priority when the relatives came to call.

Melissa sank into a deep curtsy and held out her gloved hand for his kiss.

Mr. Radley complied.

"Jane? Where are your manners, girl?" Uncle Harold's voice boomed across the great hall. He stalked toward them, his greedy gaze darting here and there.

Do not trust him.

Jane did not. She turned to her uncle and gave him a quick bob. It was awkward with her stiff knee and came off as more of a tilt than a curtsy. "Uncle Harold. How nice to see you again." Jane choked on the lie and coughed into her hand to cover the sound.

Uncle Harold's eye twitched when Jane introduced Mr. Radley. He stared without blinking.

Mr. Radley held his hand out. The men gazed at

each other for several long seconds. After a moment, Uncle Harold shook it.

Did they know each other? Jane studied both men before turning to Emily.

Emily shook her head and stepped behind her father to avoid an introduction.

Jane sighed. Poor Emily was so shy it hurt to watch.

Lady Emily hides her true self.

Jane limped toward Emily and caught her hand. She pulled Emily around Sir Harold and tucked her arm in hers. "Mr. Radley, this is my cousin Lady Emily Roswell. Emily, this is Mr. Radley."

Mr. Radley stepped forward and kissed Emily's hand. His gaze lingered on her face.

Emily blushed as red as her hair. She dipped a curtsy, refusing to meet his eyes.

It was too much for Melissa. She pushed between them and caught Mr. Radley's arm. "I would enjoy your escort to the salon."

Jane rolled her eyes. She turned to Uncle Harold. "If you will come with me?" She held her arm out in invitation.

"I know my way around Rathborne," he bellowed and elbowed Jane aside.

Uncle Harold did not like it when Jane stepped out of line. Men were important members of society. Women were not. Their duty was to see to the needs of the men, their lords, and masters. Women were not allowed to have an opinion nor speak out of turn. They should be seen and not heard. His rules applied only to Jane. Melissa could do and say anything she pleased. Jane learned her lesson the hard way as a young girl.

Uncle Harold took Jane aside and beat her when she did not adhere to his rules. He never raised a hand to his own daughters.

Mama never said a word about the black eyes or the bruises on Jane. She would look and then pretend they were not there. Jane was left to suffer alone. It was Nurse who bandaged her ribs and applied salve to her bruises. It was Nurse who held her when she cried because of the pain. And it was Nurse who helped her realize it was her uncle who was bad, and not her.

They entered the salon and took their seats. Jane sat beside Emily on the threadbare settee. They faced Uncle Harold and Melissa. Mr. Radley opted for the large leather armchair. Alfred left with the excuse he would tell Gertie there would be three more for luncheon. Gertie already knew.

Jane smiled. Alfred wanted to get away from Uncle Harold.

Uncle Harold stiffened when he faced Mr. Radley.

Sir Harold has secrets. He speaks lies and deceit.

Jane grimaced. She knew as much on her own.

Mr. Radley's face was expressionless.

An awkward silence followed. Then the men began the dance of polite conversation, asking about the weather, talking about horses, and discussing the travel times between London and Rathborne.

Uncle Harold disagreed with everything Mr. Radley said and shifted side to side in his seat as though he had an unbearable rash on his backside.

Jane frowned. What was wrong with Uncle Harold? Usually, he dominated the conversation. He liked to wear his listeners down with his superior knowledge. Today he joined the conversation absentmindedly. He paid enough attention to say, "did not" if Mr. Radley said, "did." His mind was elsewhere.

Melissa did not say anything for some time, which was unusual. She stared at Mr. Radley as if he were a five-course meal, and she had not eaten in a week. She bent over repeatedly with some excuse after another. The square neckline of her gown dipped low and her bosom came dangerously close to spilling over.

Mr. Radley smiled thinly over Melissa's blatant bid for his attention and turned back to Sir Harold to continue their one-sided conversation.

Emily sat as still as a mouse beside Jane, gazing down at the floor. Emily's hands were folded in her lap as if she were at ease.

Jane knew otherwise.

Emily gripped her hands together so hard they turned white, each time Melissa leaned forward or baited Mr. Radley.

Jane patted Emily's hands. She felt the same way when Melissa put on a display.

After an hour of the nonsensical small talk, Melissa rose and excused herself.

When Alfred announced luncheon in the dining hall, Jane turned to Uncle Harold. "Will you be staying the night?" she asked sweetly. Her stomach twisted with apprehension as she waited for his answer.

Uncle Harold was a regular visitor since the duke died. He came once a month unless the roads were too bad to travel. He used the excuse he must check on her to keep her safe. Jane knew it was a ruse. He never visited Rathborne without staying for at least a week. Jane caught him on several occasions in different rooms of the castle, looking through what remained. He never explained his presence . When she asked him what he searched for, he stalked past her and warned her to remember her place. He strutted through the castle as if he owned it. Something which grated on Jane's nerves.

"No. No." Uncle Harold looked side to side. His backside shifted. He clutched his jacket pocket and mumbled, glancing at Mr. Radley. "I planned to stay, but I remembered I have an important meeting I must attend." He rose to his feet. "I wonder if I have time to eat. I think we should go. Yes, this is what we should do. I must go to my meeting. It is a matter of urgency, you understand." He gazed down at Jane. "Go find Melissa, girl, and tell her to come right away. We must leave."

Jane gaped but rose to her feet and hurried from the room before he changed his mind.

She found Melissa exiting the duke's chamber. "What are you doing?" she asked. "Why were you in there?"

Melissa looked down her thin nose at Jane. "I got lost."

Jane snorted. "You did no such thing. Stay out of this part of the castle. I do not know what you were looking for, but do not enter the duke's chamber again." Jane gripped the head of her cane rather than Melissa's neck.

"Or what?" Melissa asked. "You can do nothing to stop me. I can go where I like."

Jane swallowed. They both knew Jane was no match for Uncle Harold. "Your father wants to leave. He sent me to tell you to come."

Melissa put her nose in the air and stalked away.

Jane hobbled along behind. She wanted to search

the master chamber and see what Melissa had done in there, but it would have to wait. Uncle Harold would be angry if she did not appear to see them off. She frowned as a thought danced across her mind. She caught Mr. Radley in the corridor outside the duke's chamber too. Why was everyone searching it? Jane was not happy, and where was the voice in her head? Why was it suddenly silent?

Jane entered the great hall and walked toward the entrance where Mr. Radley, Uncle Harold, and her cousins waited.

"There you are." Uncle Harold turned to take his cloak from Alfred. As he reached, his sleeve rode up, revealing the number three tattooed on his wrist

Jane frowned. Did he have the mark before? She did not know, for she avoided Uncle Harold as much as possible.

Mr. Radley turned to Uncle Harold with his hand out. Uncle Harold took it. The men stared at each other.

Then Mr. Radley stepped back. "Have a pleasant journey. I hope your meeting is successful."

Uncle Harold slapped his hat on his head and stomped away without answering. The cousins followed suit. The castle door slammed shut behind them.

Jane stared at the door and then at Mr. Radley. "What happened? Why is he upset?"

Mr. Radley smiled thinly. "He realized his last meeting had not gone as planned."

Jane frowned. There was an undercurrent between the men, and the voice in her head was silent. Something important happened, but she could not say what it was.

Chapter Five

The earl poured a splash of whiskey in his glass and set the decanter back on the trolley. “So, you failed.” He walked around behind the large oak desk and sat down.

Mauldrin Kane ran his finger down the blade of his razor-sharp knife. “I never fail.” His gruff voice vibrated in the silent room. “I shot him before he reached the gates.” He shifted his weight from one foot to the other.

The earl expected Mr. Kane to stand when in his presence. “What if you missed?” He swirled the amber liquid in his crystal glass.

Anger darkened the assassin’s eyes. “I never miss.” He leaned against the marble column behind him and glared.

The earl assessed the man. Mauldrin Kane was a well-known name. He was an assassin for hire and the best in his line of work. He stood over six feet and was built like a bull with thick meaty shoulders and thighs. He had dark hair and cold brown eyes. He could shoot a bow with deadly accuracy and snap a man’s neck with his bare hands. He was expensive but well worth the coin.

When the earl learned Thaddeus Rathborne was in London, he went in search of the killer. Rathborne must die. He hoped Thaddeus would fall in battle or die of jungle fever. Neither happened. Years went by with no word of Thaddeus's whereabouts despite the army of spies the earl employed to find him. When the earl decided Thaddeus must be dead, he appeared in London at the royal palace. Sir Harold Roswell brought the news. He was in court when the Duke of Rathborne was announced. King George welcomed him with open arms and retired to a private chamber to converse with him.

The earl swallowed the bile rising in his throat. Soon after, the earl learned Thaddeus Rathborne and his closest friend Lord Darham had diamonds to fund Spain's war against England. They sought the man responsible, and the earl saw his opportunity. So, he arranged a 'meeting.' He hired Mr. Kane to kill Rathborne at the meeting. Somehow, Thaddeus escaped. Mr. Kane tracked him north and shot Thaddeus before he reached the safety of Rathborne Castle.

"He is not dead." Sir Harold Roswell entered the elegant study and sank onto one of the thick leather settees.

"Do come in and make yourself comfortable," the earl drawled sarcastically.

Sir Harold's face was red from exertion. "I went to Rathborne, and the duke sauntered in behind my crippled niece as if he owned the place."

Mr. Kane looked up. "He does."

"Not for long," the earl replied. He stared at Mr. Kane. "Show me I have not wasted good coin hiring you. Bring Rathborne's body to me. I want to see him dead before I pay you another ounce of gold."

Mauldrin Kane nodded and left, walking as silently

as a predator.

The earl shivered. One did not trifle with Mr. Kane. If he did not accomplish his task this time, the earl would think of a way to dispose of him.

He turned to Sir Harold. "I hope you do not disappoint me too. Did you obtain the item I sent you for?"

Sir Harold shifted in his seat. "I did not have the chance. As soon as I saw Thaddeus was alive, I made up an excuse and hurried here. I figured you would like to know Mr. Kane failed once more." He licked his thick lips. "Thaddeus Rathborne goes by Max Radley. My niece introduced him to me as such."

The earl shrugged. "Radley is his name. What difference does it make what he goes by? He will be dead soon enough." He took several gold coins from his pocket. "Here." He tossed Sir Harold his pay. "Next time I send you after something, do not disappoint me, or I shall find a new informant."

****

Sir Harold paled. He understood. The earl would kill him next time. He sulked for the next hour and a half. The earl was an arrogant, rich, old bastard. If he had half the money the earl did, he would rule the world. Sir Harold earned a few coins here and there. He disliked being at someone else's beck and call. He wanted to be the one in charge, to snap his fingers and have the world at his feet.

He made small talk with the earl for a reasonable amount of time. The last thing he wanted was to draw the earl's suspicion. The earl obsessed about killing Rathborne. His plan was not bad, but Sir Harold had other ideas. The earl did not see the true potential of the situation. Sir Harold planned to take Rathborne Castle and the duke's diamond mine in Brazil. He had a plan in motion to convince the king to give it to him. The earl knew nothing about the plan. The only concern he had at present was Thaddeus Maximillian Rathborne. Did he recognize Sir Harold from the ambush at the tavern in York? It was difficult to tell. He caught Maximillian's gaze on his tattoo when he left Rathborne.

The situation in the tavern went from good to catastrophic in a heartbeat. Sir Harold had no idea Maximillian and Andrew Darham were so good with a sword. One minute the earl's paid fighters attacked; the next, they were dead. Only Mauldrin escaped.

Sir Harold was the earl's go-between in the war between England and Spain. The earl sent Sir Harold to steal the location of the English fleet and then sold the information to the Spaniards. The plan worked well. Pleased with his success, the earl paid Sir Harold in gold. Then Maximillian and Lord Darham wanted in on the venture. They contacted one of Sir Harold's runners to set up a meeting. Neither one knew who was in charge. Their message said they wanted to aid the cause of Spain. They had a bag of diamonds as proof of their loyalty. Sir Harold saw the perfect opportunity. Instead of tracking Maximillian down, he came to them.

When Sir Harold told the earl, the earl was delirious with excitement.

"Well done, Sir Harold. At last, I kill the remnant of my enemy, and my revenge is complete. I have waited years for this day. Now it has come, I hardly know how to contain my excitement." The earl sent Mauldrin and his band of assassins to end

Maximillian's life.

While Sir Harold was in York setting up the meeting, he paid Sir Matthews a visit.

Sir Edward Matthews was an admiral in the royal navy, who kept the latest information on the fleet's movements. He was a crafty devil, who would sell his own mother if he thought he could make a coin. The admiral had a penchant for pretty girls. His wife was old and did not accommodate him as much as he wished. So, he took his pleasure wherever he could.

Sir Harold sent his daughter into Sir Matthew's office while he kept guard in the corridor. She stole the information off Sir Edward's desk while the old devil was busy lifting her skirts. Instead of giving the vital information to the earl, however, Sir Harold kept it. He needed the document more than the earl did. With it, he planned to secure his future and make his dreams a reality.

Afterward, Sir Harold threw on a disguise before going to the meeting in the tavern. He went because he wanted to watch Maximillian die. He wore a long, black cape to avoid detection. When the assassins jumped Maximillian and Lord Darham, Sir Harold smiled with satisfaction. But his moment of triumph was short-lived. Maximillian and Lord Darham drew their swords and fought like devils. The bandits fell one after another.

In the fray, Sir Harold turned his head. The diamonds Maximillian brought sat on the table alone. No one paid any attention to them. They were too busy fighting. Sir Harold worked his way around to the table in the corner. He thought he was undetected until fire burned his side. Someone struck him with a sword. Sir

Harold grabbed the diamonds and hit the floor, rolling beneath the table. He moved to the back wall and turned toward the front of the table. He recognized Maximillian's boots. The table tilted as if Maximillian thought to roll it away. Bile rose in his throat. Sir Harold swallowed and curled into a ball. Another pair of boots approached. Metal struck metal. When Maximillian's boots danced away, Sir Harold crawled to safety.

Once he reached the back door of the tavern, he jumped to his feet, and raced for home as if the very devil nipped at his heels. He did not draw a full breath until he stood beside the hearth in his chamber. Then, he discovered the sword which sliced his middle, cut through his cloak and jacket, severing his pocket. The precious parchment with the details of the British Fleet was gone! He dared not go back to the tavern to search for it. He could not risk running into Maximillian. Sir Harold was furious. He had to get the parchment back. His plan to take Rathborne and Maximillian's diamond mine would not be realized without it.

****

Jane woke with a start.

Danger approaches. Hurry…Hurry.

She threw back her bedclothes and slid to the floor. Her knee buckled in the cool room. Jane grabbed her bed until her leg adjusted to the sudden weight. Plucking her dressing gown from the chest at the foot of her bed, she threw it on. Then she pulled woolen stockings over her cold toes. Jane grabbed her cane and limped toward the door. Quietly, she slipped from her bedchamber and listened. The dimly lit corridor flickered from the light of the single candle burning on the wall. There was silence except the pounding of her heart. Jane focused her thoughts inward.

A man enters the kitchens.

The smell of death wafted toward her. Jane turned toward the kitchen. A sound in the corridor echoed through the empty castle. She limped to the wall and waited, her breath coming fast.

She saw this night in a vision two nights ago at dinner. Jane reached for a slice of bread the same time Mr. Radley did. As her hand brushed his, the vision filled her mind. She was in the woods on the east end of Rathborne with a large, roughly dressed man. He carried a broadsword and darted from tree to tree to avoid detection.

Jane sucked in a breath.

The man had a rope with a hook attached to one end. He threw the hook and scaled the castle wall. When he dropped into the lower courtyard, he stayed in the shadows. The invader slunk toward the kitchens and slipped inside. As he turned his head, Jane got a look into his soul. He came to kill Mr. Radley. He was the same assassin who shot Mr. Radley the night he arrived at Rathborne. She recognized the assassin's bulky body and the flat dead look in his eyes. He was the danger she sensed the night Mr. Radley appeared.

The scent of evil permeated the air. Jane shook her head to rid her nose of its stench. She considered waking Thomas and Alfred and changed her mind. The only person capable of defeating the villain was Mr. Radley. She turned toward the guest chambers. Her mind relived the vision.

Suddenly, a strong arm caught her and pulled her into an empty chamber. Jane opened her mouth to scream.

A large male hand clamped over her lips. “Do not make a sound. An intruder is nearby. I do not want him to know of our presence.”

It was Mr. Radley. Jane slumped in relief, the fight going out of her. “He came over the east wall. He hides in the kitchens. He is here to kill you.”

“I know,” Mr. Radley answered. He took Jane by the hand and led her toward the wardrobe in the corner. “Climb in. You will be safe here.”

Jane could not see his face, but she heard the concern in his voice. “I will go back to my chamber.”

“No,” Mr. Radley said. “If the villain seeks to kill more than me, your chamber is the first place he will search.”

Jane swallowed. Mr. Radley was right. “Beware. He will fight with his right hand and switch to his left hand. He is good with both.”

Mr. Radley stilled. “How do you know this?”

“I just do.” She clutched his sleeve. “He carries a knife in his boot. He will use it as a last resort.”

Mr. Radley did not answer. He helped her into the wardrobe. “Do not come out, no matter what you hear,” he said. “I will come for you when it is safe.”

Jane nodded, although she knew he could not see her. The door shut, and Mr. Radley slipped away. Jane leaned back in the corner and closed her eyes. For the first time since her mother left, she prayed.

****

Max slipped from door to door as he made his way down the corridor toward the kitchens. Once he entered the great hall, he stayed close to the whitewashed wall. He considered what Lady Jane said. She spoke with certainty about the intruder. Did she know him? Or was she a witch, as the villagers said? An incident that occurred two nights ago came to mind. Lady Jane reached for bread the same time he did. She stiffened when their hands touched, and her face froze. At first, he thought it was him. He thought his touch terrified her. Then he realized she was somewhere else. Her eyes were blank, as she stared in front of her. Emotions raced across her face. Wherever she was, it was not a pleasant place. Then Lady Jane went limp and slumped in her chair.

Max jumped to his feet and caught her before she slipped to the ground. Scooping her up in his arms, he carried her out of the dining hall.

It took her several minutes before she woke. When he asked after her strange behavior, she did not answer. She excused herself and left the room.

When he came to her chamber the night of her nightmare, she was nervous. She was such a little thing, lost amid the blankets with her wide blue eyes. The urge to protect her and chase away her fear overwhelmed him. When Max bent to kiss Lady Jane's hand, desire lit her brilliant blue eyes, and then it was gone. He was used to women looking at him in a predatory way. The gleam in Lady Jane's eyes was different. She was like a little girl looking at sweetmeats just out of reach, knowing she could never have any.

Life had not been kind to Lady Jane. She was left alone in the dark empty castle, deserted by her mother and everyone else in her life.

Max's anger rose. Where the hell was the duchess, and why did she leave? Lady Jane should not be left unprotected. With her limp, she was extremely vulnerable. He wanted to find the duchess and shake some sense into her. What mother left in the night and never returned?

He frowned. He did not know who the traitor was. Until he did, Lady Jane was a suspect. He must not let her beautiful blue eyes tempt him to think otherwise.

A shadow emerged from the kitchen and entered the great hall.

Max held his place and waited.

The shadow passed him, slinking toward the corridor beyond.

"Only a coward shoots a man in the back." Max lit the candle on the wall. "Real men face their enemies."

The man swiveled to face him, sword in hand. *Mauldrin Kane*. Max knew of him. He recognized the diagonal scar across the man's face.

Rage shot from Mauldrin's eyes. "I am no coward." He rushed at Max, swinging his massive sword.

Max parried the blows and danced beyond the reach of his sword. "That remains to be seen," he taunted. "Can you look your victims in the eye and give them a chance to defend themselves, or do you scurry like a rat looking for opportunities to kill them when they least expect it?"

Mauldrin rushed again.

Max noted he used his left hand and parried accordingly. The force of the assassin's blows knocked Max backward. "Men face their enemies. Women use poison. Cowards slink in the shadows with no honor. Assassins are the worst. They slit anyone's throat for the right amount of coin, be it women, children, drunkards, old men, goats, or pigs. Nothing is safe from their greed. They are miscreants." He struck Mauldrin across the face, slicing his other cheek.

The assassin slipped and fell. He shook his head in pain and rose unsteadily to his feet, bringing his sword up. A slow grin crossed his face. "Prepare to die, Rathborne. I have played with you thus far. I tire of your taunts." He charged with his sword high in the air.

Max stepped out of his way. He swiveled at the last second, but he was not fast enough. Mauldrin's sword sliced his upper arm. Blood dripped to the stone floor.

Mauldrin laughed. "After I kill you and cut you in tiny pieces for my employer, I am going to find the cripple. I am thinking she is a virgin. Alone in this castle, looking like she does, what man would want her?" He scratched his groin. "I am going to rip her clothes off and bury myself in her until I cannot walk. I hope she screams." He chuckled. "It is more enjoyable when they do."

Rage fired Max's blood. He charged Mauldrin and knocked the smile from his face.

They struck steel to steel time and again. They both caught the other one unprepared, and blood ran freely.

Max broke away and took a deep breath. This was no good. He let Mauldrin goad him into losing his temper, and he had the wounds to prove it. "Who is your employer? Why does he want me dead?"

Mauldrin rested his hands on his knees dragging in deep breaths. He laughed. "Why should I tell you?"

Max lifted his sword. "I want to know where to send your body when I am done with it."

Mauldrin stared at him. Then he shook his head. "It does not matter because you are not going to win. I am.

I tire of this game." He lunged at Max, swinging his sword with one hand and then the other.

Max parried and thrust, using every ounce of the experience he gained over the years in battle. If Lady Jane had not warned him of the devil's ability to use both hands equally well, he would have fallen. Max dodged a blow and changed hands with his sword. He caught Mauldrin unprepared and knocked the sword from his hand. It landed with a clank and slid across the stone floor. Max hit Mauldrin in the face and knocked him off his feet. Then, he gripped the hilt of his sword and moved over Mauldrin. Lifting his sword high, he planned to kill the bastard when he saw the blade flash in the candlelight.

Max jumped to the side and brought his sword down hard. Mauldrin died with a look of surprise on his face. Lady Jane warned him of the blade. Had she not, he would have died. Max nudged the assassin with his toe to make sure the bastard was gone. Satisfied, Max rested his forearms on his knees and sucked in huge breaths of air.

Suddenly, Lady Jane was beside him.

He caught the scent of roses before he felt her presence.

She murmured over his wounds, fluttering around him like a butterfly.

"Why did you come out? I told you to stay until I came for you." He gasped.

Lady Jane nodded. "I knew the battle was over and came to tend to your wounds."

He stared at her in surprise. "How do you know these things?" He passed out before she had a chance to answer.

Chapter Six

The weather took a turn for the worst. The temperature dipped to unprecedented levels. It was the coldest winter in years.

Jane bent over Mr. Radley, checking his wounds for signs of infection. The deep cut on his side caused her the most anxiety. She had not seen rib bone before. Now, she had. The wound required a great deal of stitching. Thankfully, it remained cool to the touch.

Jane mixed a draught of poppy and held it to Mr. Radley's lips. He had been asleep for several days. The slumber was a mixture of blood loss and poppy. She had no qualms about sedating him. It was for his own good.

On the fifth day, she allowed him to wake. His wounds were healing nicely, and there would be no infection.

She stood inside Mr. Radley's chamber, looking out at the frost. Her uncle paid her a surprise visit the day before. He brought his condolences for Mr. Radley.

Jane studied her uncle's face. "How did you hear of Mr. Radley's demise?" she asked curiously.

Sir Harold drew up to his full height. "I am a man, niece. I know many important things a woman could not understand."

Jane's mouth twitched. "Your source is misinformed, Uncle. Mr. Radley is very much alive."

Uncle Harold's gaze narrowed on her face. "Do you challenge my superior knowledge?"

Jane contemplated her options. In the end, she said, "Please come with me," and led him to Mr. Radley's chamber door. "As you can see, Uncle, he is alive and resting from his injuries."

Her uncle left soon after, making some excuse about another meeting. Jane waited at the door until his carriage disappeared down the overgrown forest road. Only then did she realize her uncle did not ask how Mr. Radley got injured.

****

Max opened his eyes slowly. Every part of him ached. He groaned and closed them again. He moved his arms and legs and discovered new bandages around his upper arms and chest. His thigh hurt like the devil, and his side was on fire. A smooth hand brushed his cheek. Max's eyes flew open.

Lady Jane's sweet face appeared above him. "How are you feeling?"

"Like hell," he answered.

She smiled. "I imagine so." She brought a cool cloth to his face and dabbed at his brow. It felt good.

"How long have I been asleep?" He looked at the window. The sun shone through the panes highlighting the dust particles in the air.

"Five days."

Max groaned. He'd never slept so long in his life, not even as a babe. "How? I did not think I was hurt that bad."

"I gave you poppy to help you rest. You heal faster when you are asleep," she explained.

He'd lost nearly a week when he could have been

solving the mystery. He wanted to be irritated but found he could not. Her innocent expression stopped the words in his throat. She meant to help, nothing more. If she were the traitor, she would not be tending his wounds.

He studied her face as she checked his bandages. She had dark circles beneath her eyes. She was pale from lack of sleep, and he was the cause. Lady Jane stayed beside him day and night. He knew for he woke on several occasions, and she was always present. His urge to protect her grew stronger. Never had he known a woman like her. She gave with no thought of herself. His previous relationships with women were quite different. It was an even exchange, their bodies for his money. Whether in the form of jewels, furs, or coins, it amounted to the same thing. No one gave him something for nothing, not even his mother. "How do you know so much?"

Pain crossed her face and clouded her beautiful blue eyes. "I took care of my stepfather before his death. I learned to use poppy to help him deal with his pain."

Max stilled. "He was ill?"

Lady Jane sighed. "Not ill, exactly. His was emotional pain. He lost everything and everyone. He would go days without eating or sleeping. He would stare at the wall or into the fire. It was as if he were a statue, frozen in position. He gave up the will to live. Mangus died of a broken heart."

Max studied her face intently. "Why so? If what I have been told is true, he tossed his son out and burned the furnishings in the castle."

Lady Jane smoothed the hair from his brow. She

dabbed the cloth at his temple again. "His son, Thaddeus, wanted to marry a woman older than him. Someone unsuitable. When Mangus refused to give his blessing to their union, they had a terrible row." Lady Jane placed the cloth in the bowl of water beside the bed. "He forced Thaddeus to make a choice, the woman or Rathborne. Thaddeus chose the woman," Lady Jane said softly. "It broke the old man's heart."

She stopped, lost in her thoughts.

"Please continue," Max urged. He wanted to hear this story. "The duke told his son never to come back and washed his hands of him."

"Thaddeus discovered the woman was everything his father warned him about. He was prideful and guilty. He did not want to face Mangus and admit he was wrong. So, Thaddeus ran away and joined the fighting. For years, my stepfather wrote letters and searched for his son, begging him to come home so they could be reconciled." Lady Jane twisted her hands together in her lap. "But there was no reply, and Thaddeus never returned home."

He swallowed the need to refute her story. How could she know what he thought or did? "What happened?" Max asked at last.

Lady Jane smiled sadly. "One night, Mangus snapped. He went crazy. He ordered the servants to strip the castle and pile it in the courtyard. Then he lit it all on fire. It was a tremendous blaze. The servants were afraid the castle would catch fire, but it did not. I remember the flames and the smell. The yellow and orange inferno reached the sky. It terrified me. The fire blazed for days. Ashes darkened the sky. They fell and covered the ground like snow. After the flames disintegrated everything he owned, Mangus went to his chamber and climbed into his bed." Lady Jane choked at the memory. "My mother would not come near him. She hated him for what he did. She blamed Mangus. I blame Thaddeus."

"So, you were the one who took care of the duke? I thought Gertie came to look after him," Max commented. Alfred told him so the night in the dungeon.

"She did. Gertie is Alfred's cousin by marriage. She knows a great deal about herbs and their uses. Alfred thought she might be able to help the duke rise from his melancholy. Mangus disliked anyone near him but me. He threw a fit whenever Gertie entered his chamber. He quieted when I sat beside him. So, Gertie taught me what she knew, and I tended my stepfather." After a long silence, she continued. "I begged him to eat, to get up, to come outside. He refused. For weeks he spoke of nothing but Thaddeus and how much he regretted their fight. It broke my heart. I could not do anything to ease his pain but hold his hand and listen. He loved his son, and wished to be reconciled before he passed on." She glanced at Max. "When Mangus got too upset, I gave him poppy to calm him down and help him sleep." Her voice hardened. "The least Thaddeus could have done was come to his father's funeral. He did not. My stepfather died alone and broken-hearted. After his death, my mother stayed for a few days and then disappeared in the middle of the night." She related the story of her accident and how her knee came to be the way it was. When she finished, she glanced at him. "This is why I hate Thaddeus Rathborne with every ounce of my soul. He could have made the old man happy, but he did not." Her eyes turned to blue ice. "If he returned home and took his place, my mother would be here still, and my knee would not be twisted. I learned how to care for the brokenhearted all those months sitting beside Mangus while he poured out his grief and pain. It all could have been avoided."

Max stared at her. "What if Thaddeus did not know of his father's wish to be reconciled?" If he had, nothing would have kept him away.

Lady Jane stared back. "He knew. Mangus wrote him every day for months. I wrote some of those letters while Mangus dictated. Thaddeus Rathborne is detestable. I have spent a great deal of time thinking of ways to make him suffer. It would please me to see him hang. My knee reminds me of his transgressions every time I take a step."

Anger tightened his mouth. "You say Mangus wrote letters. How do you know Thaddeus received them? You act as though he read them and created the circumstances which led to your injury. He may not have known any of this."

Lady Jane flushed. "Mangus gave the letters to my mother. She promised Mangus they would get to Thaddeus."

"This is the same mother who left you in the middle of the night with no thought as to your safety or welfare? You believe she sent the letters to Thaddeus because she is so…trustworthy?"

Lady Jane jumped to her feet. "Do not dare defend Thaddeus Rathborne to me!" Her hands fisted at her side. Her eyes shot blue flames. "Just when I decide I like you, Max Radley, you do something despicable! I will not change my mind about Thaddeus Rathborne!

Nothing you can say will alter how I feel. I held Mangus' hand while he died of a broken heart!" She stomped over to the door. "I will return when I no longer want to strangle you with my bare hands."

Max stared at the door when it slammed behind her. He had much to think on. He could see young Jane in his mind, sitting beside the old man and weeping. He could see her brushing the hair back from Mangus' face and spooning broth into his mouth. He knew her pain. It was his as well. She did for the old man what neither the wife nor the son had. She loved him and listened to him when he needed someone the most. Max's heart ached for her. He ached for his father, and he ached for himself. He wished he had known. He hurt when he thought of Lady Jane's loneliness and fear the night her mother left her. If only he could have been here to comfort her. Max marveled at her strength. Shaking his head, he rolled to his side. After all she suffered, life was not through with her. Shortly after her mother's desertion, she injured her knee, and still, she carried on. Max did not know how a young woman could survive such tragedy. He thought of her accusations against Thaddeus. If she believed the things she said, he could see why she would hate him.

Max rubbed his forehead wearily. He must convince her of the truth and prove he was not the monster she believed him to be. Wishing did not change the past. But he was here now, and he could improve the present.

The next day, when Lady Jane came to his chamber to check his bandages, he informed her he wanted to get up. He had rested long enough. He had business to attend to.

Lady Jane nodded, eyeing him cautiously. "I have no objection." She touched his hand and froze. For several seconds she said nothing. Her eyes glazed over, and her body stiffened. Then she came back. "Your battle is just beginning."

Max glanced at her. He recognized the look. She saw something. "I defeated the assassin. Who is there to fight?"

"The one who sent him is full of hatred. He will try other ways to get rid of you." Jane rose to her feet.

Max studied her face. "How do you know these things? And while we are on this subject, how did you know the assassin's fighting style? Without your warning, I might have died. Did you witness it before? Do you know him?"

Lady Jane flushed. "Why would I know him?"

Max picked her small hand up with his. "I am curious about your premonitions, nothing more. You have nothing to fear from me."

****

Trust him. He will not betray you.

She lifted her chin and gazed into Mr. Radley's eyes. "There is a voice in my head telling me things. It has never been wrong—" She remembered what it revealed about Mr. Radley and her. They came from different worlds. It would never work.

"Until recently," she added softly.

"Do you have any other…gifts…besides knowing things before they happen?" He stared into the fire.

"I am not a witch if this is what you are asking. I do not cast spells nor practice magic." Her voice was defensive and angry.

Mr. Radley turned toward her. "I do not suppose

you do. Such things are nonsense." He gazed into the fire once more. "I am curious as to how you acquire the knowledge. Does it simply pop into your head?"

"Sometimes. Other times, a voice warns me of things to come. I have had three visions so far. They involved you. I know not why it works, and other times it does not."

"The people in the village know of your gift?"

Jane gazed at him and nodded. "I went to the village often after my mother left. The children there cheered me with their chatter. One boy was my special friend. He followed me everywhere. I was near the shops when I discovered the lad was gone. His little cap lay beside me on the ground. As I picked it up, the dizziness hit me. The voice in my head told me the boy was in danger and where to find him. I dropped the hat and hurried to the spot. The boy was there. I made it in time to catch his hand before he dashed into the road. His mother stood across the street calling him. The boy and his mother both scolded me for not letting him go. Then the carriage came, exactly as I was told. Had I let the boy go, he would have been killed. The boy's mother should have been happy I saved his life. Instead, the whole village spurned me, saying I must be evil if I had the sight. I have been the Witch of Rathborne ever since."

Mr. Radley nodded his head. "Have they threatened you?"

"They avoid me. I hear whisperings they want to try me for witchcraft, but a few of the tradesmen keep them from doing it. Trials for witchcraft have been abolished." She was silent for long moments. "Are you frightened of me?" Jane asked. She gazed steadily into his eyes.

Mr. Radley looked up in surprise. “No. Why do you ask?”

Jane shrugged. “Most people are frightened of things they cannot explain.”

“I am not so foolish.”

Jane stared at him. She believed what he said. Mr. Radley was full of surprises.

****

Emotions chased across Lady Jane’s face as she told her story. At one point, she straightened her spine, and it occurred to him Lady Jane was not bent over, as he supposed. Her cane was too short, and she stooped as she walked. Stooping must make her extremely tired and irritable. Max nodded when Lady Jane finished speaking. She required a taller cane. Perhaps if she had one, her limp would not be so pronounced. He would start with her cane.

He borrowed their only horse three days later to go to the village. He took his gold to purchase a horse. The only one available turned out to be a large draft horse eighteen hands high. The horse was not fast, but he had stamina. Max bought more food and candles. Then he paid a visit to the local carpenter, after which he had several more errands to run. When he finished, he loaded his purchases on the horse and swung into the saddle. The sky darkened. Max looked at Thomas, who came along to ride the mare back to the castle, and shrugged. They both knew they would not outrun the storm. The wind picked up and tugged at their caps. Rain quickly turned to hail. Max clucked his tongue, and they were off, hurrying for the safety of Rathborne.

****

The wind howled and whistled through the halls of Rathborne Castle. The temperature dipped. Freezing hail battered the castle and surrounding countryside. The small salon blazed with a hearty fire. Mr. Radley and Jane retired there after dinner.

Jane sat on a threadbare settee and thought on her earlier conversation with Mr. Radley. As much as it hurt her to admit it, he had a point. She did not know of a surety Thaddeus Rathborne received the letters Mangus sent. He was also correct about her mother. Trustworthy she was not. Jane gazed at Mr. Radley. He leaned against the side of a floor-to-ceiling oak bookshelf which should have been filled with expensive leather volumes but was dusty and barren instead. He stared into the flames, lost in thought.

He will change your future.

Jane swallowed and tucked her trembling hand into the pocket of her gown. Mr. Radley was tall, lean, and extremely well built. Naked, he was all muscle and sinew, golden and sleek. Her gaze dropped to his thighs. When she stitched him together, his skin rippled and bulged beneath her fingers. The memory burned itself into her mind. A picture of the two of them naked danced before her eyes. Red color burned its way up her cheeks as she realized where her thoughts took her. She was no better than Melissa. Jane hoped to God Mr. Radley was not a mind reader. She glanced at him beneath her lashes. He studied her face with interest. Her breath caught at the gleam in his eye. This was awkward. She had no intention of staying in the same room with him for another second until she got her wayward mind under control. What if he guessed the nature of her embarrassment? Hastily she rose to her feet.

"My lady?" Mr. Radley rose also.

Jane rose too hastily, it turned out, for she gave a cry of pain and fell. Her hands grasped wildly for her cane as it fell to the floor with a crash. Mr. Radley was there in an instant, catching her before she hit the cold wooden floor. His arms slid around her, holding her tight against him. She looked up at him in surprise and found him staring down at her, a strange expression on his face. He cupped her chin with his hand. The last thing Jane saw before closing her eyes was his well-formed mouth descending toward hers. His kiss was warm, gentle, and searching. Jane trembled in his arms. She wondered what it would be like to have a man kiss her, to feel his arms around her but knew it would never happen. No man would find her attractive. The fact Mr. Radley held her now, in his muscular arms, pressed so intimately against him, was a miracle. Jane shivered against the warmth of his broad chest and wrapped her arms around him.

He licked her lips. Jane gasped in surprise. Mr. Radley was quick to take advantage and slid his tongue into the recesses of her mouth. Jane's eyes flew open in surprise at the first languid stroke of his tongue along hers. Tentatively she stroked him back. Her knees buckled when he groaned and angled her head to deepen the penetration of his tongue. Jane was overcome. She clung to Mr. Radley's neck for dear life, mimicking his every move. When he licked, she licked back. When he stroked, daringly, she stroked back. Their tongues mated with each other, each learning the other's taste, texture, and touch. Jane shook against him whimpering, her breath coming fast. Liquid heat in her stomach poured into the juncture between her legs, and she squirmed. Mr. Radley clamped her hips to his with one large hand, holding her still. He groaned into her mouth. Jane pressed herself into the hardness against her belly. The heat increased. She thought she might faint for lack of air.

****

He stilled when her soft, full bosom pressed against his chest. His hands grasped her by the waist. Surprised to find her so tiny and delicate, his gaze darkened as his body told him Lady Jane had more beneath the voluminous clothing than he supposed. In fact, from what he could feel through her gown, she was well developed and quite voluptuous. He stared at her mouth. Then he kissed her, and damn if she did not kiss him back. He drank from her mouth repeatedly. She whimpered, begging him for more. Max lifted his head, his breathing erratic. He had to stop this now, or he would lose all control and take Lady Jane right here. He pressed her flushed face into his chest and concentrated on taking deep breaths. He fought to regain his composure. Lady Jane had a death grip around his waist. Max leaned his head against her and held her gently. This woman was a surprise in so many ways. Who would have thought she would respond with such passion and abandon? He stroked her back with his hand. He inhaled the delicate rose scent of her skin and forced himself to relax. He wanted nothing more than to lift Lady Jane into his arms and carry her back to his chamber where he could explore her in every way possible. But he could not. She was a lady and deserved to be treated as one.

****

Jane's face was against his chest. She inhaled his masculine scent mingled with the smell of his sandalwood soap. He smelled so good. He felt so good. She wanted to keep on kissing him, to beg him to take her to his bed. She wanted to know what it was like to mate with Mr. Radley. This might be the only chance she would ever have to discover what happened between a man and a woman. Mr. Radley kissed with such knowledge. One night in his bed would be an unforgettable experience. He would show her all the things she would never experience again. Without him, she would die a virgin, unwanted, un-awakened, and inexperienced. Jane slipped her hands beneath his jacket and stroked his back. She closed her eyes and prayed Mr. Radley would do the unthinkable and take her to his bed.

He lifted her face up to his. She opened her eyes and met the heat of his gaze. Mr. Radley wanted her! Jane smiled shyly and pressed her body against him. She leaned forward to put her lips against his, but he stopped her.

His lids dropped over his eyes. "I apologize, my lady. I should not have taken liberties with you. It will not happen again."

She stilled. Never? Confused, Jane pushed from his arms. The voice told her differently. Her timing must be off. "Thank you for catching me." Embarrassment heated her face. She dipped her head, fixing her gaze firmly on the fire.

"My pleasure." Mr. Radley cleared his throat. "I want to thank you for allowing me to stay at Rathborne these past weeks and for caring for my injuries. You have been exceedingly kind. It was reprehensible of me to repay your kindness by making free with you."

Jane's gaze rose to his. "You are leaving?" Her heart pounded in her chest. He could not walk away, not now. How could they intertwine if he left?

A wry smile tugged at the corners of his mouth. "No, not yet. It is too cold. I do not consider hail and ice enjoyable traveling companions. I would like to stay a bit longer." He strolled over to the opposite settee and took his seat. "I have to find my business partner. Now I am well enough to ride, I must begin my search."

Jane was quiet for a minute or two. She studied his face. Every trace of passion was gone. If he could pretend the last fifteen minutes never happened, so could she. "Come now, Mr. Radley. I do not mean to be contrary, but I know there is no business acquaintance. I have known from the beginning you are here to search for something. And I did discover you outside the master chamber. I do not know what you seek. The voice has not told me." Jane gazed deep into his eyes. "I trusted you enough to discuss my…gift…with you. Perhaps you would return the favor. Tell me your true purpose here. I may be able to help."

****

Max sat silent. Lady Jane's gaze was sincere. His gut told him she could be trusted. "Should we start anew? Since we are no longer strangers, please call me Max."

Lady Jane smiled. "You may call me Jane. Now what?"

Max rose and stood beside the fire staring into the flames. He rested his forearm on the marble hearth. "The object I search for is the Rathborne signet ring. The last time it was seen, Mangus Rathborne wore it on his third finger." Max turned to face Jane. "I must find it. The Rathborne insignia has recently appeared on some disturbing documents."

Jane's eyes widened. "After my stepfather's death, I put it inside the chest in the master chamber. It was there last time I looked." She stopped. "Is this why the duke's chamber is suddenly so popular? Everyone is searching for the signet ring?"

"Who else was in there?" Max questioned.

Jane rose to her feet. "I caught Melissa coming out of it the last time she was here."

Max was silent. He had his suspicions about Sir Harold Roswell. Max offered his arm to Jane. "Shall we investigate?"

Jane nodded. "If the ring sealed some documents recently, it means someone took it, and it is no longer in the chest."

Max nodded. "Precisely."

Chapter Seven

The ring was in the chest.

Jane pulled it from the heavy bag protecting it and held it up. "I told you it was in there. Whatever document you have with the seal must be forged. The ring is where it should be."

Max sat back on his heels. He had not expected this outcome. He rubbed his chin. "The document is not forged. I examined it." Whoever took the ring had access to the chest. That document sealed his fate. He was here, at Rathborne, and so was the ring. He would never be able to prove his innocence if the parchment reached the king. He must destroy it as soon as he could. Could he trust Jane? He looked at her where she stood beside the chest. The sun coming through the window lit her hair on fire. His instinct said to trust her, and yet she wished death on Thaddeus. Was she capable of such treachery?

Jane rubbed a hand over her face. "Someone took the ring and put it back. Whoever it is seeks to destroy Rathborne."

Max watched her with hooded eyes. "Who would do such a thing?"

Jane turned to him flashing blue fire. "How do I know? If you are suggesting it is me, you are wrong. No one in this castle has reason to destroy Rathborne."

"Except you. If the document I spoke of reached

the king, Thaddeus Rathborne will hang for treason."

Lady Jane's expression changed from outrage to satisfaction, then back to outrage. "I may have reason to hate Thaddeus Rathborne, but I would never accuse someone of something they did not do."

"Would you not?" Max asked. "Your exact words were it would please you to see him hang."

Jane was still. Her face suffused with color. "I may wish a lot of things, but that does not mean I get them. I did say I wished Thaddeus Rathborne hung." She drew her body up to her full height, surprising him once more with her beauty. Outrage flashed from her brilliant blue eyes. "Just because I said it, does not mean I created a situation to bring it to reality. If Thaddeus Rathborne hangs, it will be his doing, not mine." Her hair was on fire. Her thin body silhouetted by the afternoon sun shining through the window. Lady Jane Lenwood was an incredibly beautiful woman.

He stood transfixed for several moments. Then he turned around and walked away. Jane had every opportunity and every reason to hate him. He hoped to track the ring to the traitor. All his theories plunged to their deaths the second they found the ring in the chest. He walked outside for some fresh air. Was Jane capable of framing him as a traitor? He paced in the castle courtyard while he thought. There were only five people in the castle who had access to the chest, other than any visitors. He suspected Sir Harold. Jane found Lady Melissa outside the duke's chamber. Was she putting the ring back or taking something else? Jane's outrage over her innocence seemed real enough, but then, so was her hatred. Max stood in the center of the courtyard with his hands on his hips. The sky darkened, and snow swirled around him. It was a fitting backdrop for his mood. He was no closer to solving the puzzle than the day he arrived. The best thing to do now would be to destroy the document. He should have done it the second Andrew showed it to him in York.

Max returned to the great hall and hurried to his chamber. He searched his saddlebags. *The document with the location of the English fleet was gone!* He searched every corner, every pocket, every possible place the parchment could be. It was not there. Max shook his head. Who would know about it? Who took it from his chamber? The only person he told was Jane, just now in the duke's chamber. Since Jane was with him, one of the servants must have taken it. Max hit the wall in frustration. He put the damning parchment in the bottom of his saddlebag the night he rode for Rathborne. He had not pulled it out since. Sir Harold had come to the castle twice since his arrival.

Max paced back and forth. Lord Andrew Darham was his only chance now. Andrew found the parchment on the floor inside the tavern after the fighting and showed it to Max. They both knew it falsely presented Max as the traitor. Andrew was the one person alive who could vouch for Max's innocence. He had been undercover with Max since their return to England. He alone knew Max had not the time, nor the opportunity, to create such a document.

Max stopped beside the hearth and rested his forearm on the edge. He stared into the flames. Lord Darham would testify for him. He must find the person who took the parchment and destroy it before it reached the court. The first thing to do was investigate the servants. After that, he would pay Sir Harold a visit.

****

It snowed for several days. The temperature in the castle dipped well below freezing. The wind brought arctic temperatures from the north. It was the coldest winter since 1715. The firewood depleted faster than expected. Soon, the only room they could keep warm was the small salon. The rest of the firewood must be kept for the ovens in the kitchens.

Jane found a heavy woolen blanket and huddled beneath it on one of the threadbare settees. Still, she shivered with cold.

When Max entered the room later the same day, her blanket moved. There was a rush of frigid air, and then Max was beside her.

"This is not proper," she chattered. Moving closer to his warmth despite her words. She was not close enough to touch, just close enough to feel the heat of his body.

Max chuckled. "Either we are not proper, or we freeze. This is the choice we must make."

Jane nodded. "It is not much of a choice. But since it is forced upon me, I prefer to be warm." She inched as close as she dared and turned her back. Soon after, the heat of his body lulled her to sleep. The storm lasted for several days. They ate beside the fire in the small salon. They only left when it was necessary. Alfred, Gertie, and Thomas huddled together on a pile of furs beside the fire. When the storm moved on, a thick blanket of snow covered the ground.

Jane stared out the window at the icy scenery. Max sat beside the fire warming his hands.

"What are you going to do now the ring is here? Are you leaving?" she asked quietly. She did not want him to go. It was nice to have a fit man close at hand. She was safe, and her nightmares stopped altogether.

Max rose to his feet and approached the window. "It appears I will not be going for some time. Look at the snow."

Jane nodded.

He searches for someone who betrayed him. Help him.

Jane cleared her throat. "You said you were searching for the Rathborne signet ring. It is here, and you have not mentioned leaving. Is there something else you seek?" She waited to see what he would say.

Max glanced sideways at her. "I search for a traitor. He sides with Spain against England. It is he who had the signet ring."

Jane let out her breath and smiled. "At last, you tell me the truth." She stared out at the whiteness. "I shall help you with this cause."

Max said nothing.

"Do you have someone in mind?" she asked.

Max turned and regarded her with a closed expression. "What do you know of Sir Harold?"

Jane shook her head. "He comes every month since my mother left. Sometimes he stays for a week. I do not trust him. He has a nervous energy I do not like."

Max nodded. "I agree. Have you seen him searching through things here?"

Jane shrugged. "I would not know if he did. He walks faster than I do. When he comes, he stays up late or rises early. He wanders the corridors of this castle freely. I could never hope to catch him." She shrugged again. "Even if I did, he would remind me I am female and tell me to mind my business."

Max nodded. "I would like to pay Sir Harold a visit once the snow clears." He searched her face. "What do the voices in your head say about him?"

"They tell me to stay away from him. So, I do."

"What about your cousins? Do you think they would take the Rathborne ring and put it back?"

Jane shook her head. "Whoever took it would have to know where it was to put it back."

"This is true," Max said. "Unless they came upon it by accident, used it, and then returned it."

Jane nodded. "Melissa is capable of such a thing. So is Uncle Harold. Emily never leaves my side when she is here."

"What about the servants?"

Jane considered his question. "Alfred has been here too long to do something to endanger Rathborne in any way. Gertie is Alfred's cousin by marriage. He vouched for her character before my mother hired her. And Thomas grew up in the village. They all stayed on when things got bad. Every other servant left. I cannot imagine any of them being involved." She said the words, but apprehension rose in her chest. What if one of her servants was a traitor? If Thaddeus Rathborne hanged for whatever the documents contained, Rathborne Castle and all her tenants, property, and possessions would become forfeit to the crown. Jane searched her feelings. The voice was still. She stared out at the bleak landscape. Who else could it be but one of them? Jane frowned. Why had the voice not warned her of this treachery?

****

"It shall be several days before the snow melts enough to travel," Max commented.

Jane merely nodded.

"What shall we do to pass the time?" He knew what he wanted to do, but he had to draw Jane along gently.

She shrugged. "Do you want to search more of the castle?"

Max gazed at her. "Yes. I lost a piece of paper I would like very much to find. Would you help me search?"

Jane nodded. "I told you I would. Where should we begin?"

"How about the duke's chamber?" he asked. At her questioning look, he said, "I would like to make a list of things the duke burned as we search each room. Perhaps there is a clue I may have missed."

"Why would there be?"

"Whoever took the ring wants to destroy Rathborne and her master. Perhaps if we have an accurate picture of Rathborne as it was, we can determine who this person is and why they wish to destroy it," Max said. He had enemies. He knew several who would like to see him dead. But his enemies were men of action. The kind who took their revenge with their swords, not the kind who used lies, forged documents, and hired assassins.

Jane was silent. "Your theory makes sense. There must be a reason this person took the ring now and not three years ago when Mangus died."

"Exactly. Sometimes you have to step back to find the answer you seek." He called for Thomas as they walked toward the master chamber.

Thomas appeared in the corridor.

"Fetch us a sheet of parchment and some ink,"

Max commanded.

They made a list of all the items missing from the duke's chamber. The portraits could never be replaced.

Jane sighed as she mentioned the fact. "A large one of the Duke's first wife, Margret, hung next to the hearth. She wore a magnificent diamond necklace and a red silk dress."

"I remember," Max murmured.

Jane swiveled toward him. "What?"

"I remember the duchess," he said and cleared his throat. "The portraits are a tragedy for sure. Shall we continue to the duchess' chamber?"

Jane was silent for several seconds. "My mother hated that portrait. Mangus took it from the wall the week before he burned everything." Her expression was thoughtful. "Yes, we should search the duchess' chambers."

Max's gaze followed her as she made her way to the communicating door. Her new cane should arrive any day now. He could not wait to see if it improved her gait.

Jane glanced at him. "Are you coming?"

Max strode toward the door and followed her through. The large four-poster bed in the duchess' chamber remained as well. It was made by the same craftsman as his grandfather's bed. Max ran his hand over one of the corner pillars, elaborately carved with vines and flowers. It was the most intricate bed in the castle. The only articles within the chamber were the bed and the wardrobe. Jane's mother took everything else.

Jane walked to the wardrobe. She stared at the doors without touching them.

Max stopped beside her. “What is wrong?”

“This piece of furniture features in all my nightmares. I opened the doors the morning after my mother left to find it empty, except her old cloak in the back.”

Max opened the doors. The cloak was there. He glanced at Jane. Her face was frozen, her hands fisted at her sides. The last thing he wanted was to upset her. “I see no reason to search further. Do you?”

Jane shook her head.

Max placed the parchment and ink on the edge of the hearth. “Tell me what you remember about this chamber.” He dipped his pen into the inkwell and began to write.

Jane’s soft voice floated toward him. She had an excellent memory. He had been in this room only half a dozen times. Jane knew every inch of it by heart. When they finished, he ushered her out into the corridor. “Is this too much for you?” he asked.

****

Jane looked up at his question. What had her face given away? She shook her head. “The duchess’ chamber speaks to me in a language I do not recognize.”

She heard whisperings in her mind while she stood beside the wardrobe, but nothing made sense. It was like she listened to several people’s thoughts all at once. Jane shivered. The aura of the duchess’ chamber chilled her. There was something there demanding her attention. Something she could not understand.

Max did not question her. He urged her down the corridor toward the next chamber as if he, too, were anxious to be away from there.

They spent the next few days searching chambers and making lists of all the missing items. They talked as they worked. A companionable friendship grew between them. Max hinted once or twice that he should be on his way, but the temperature dipped every time he did. Gales from the north kept the land covered with ice and frost. Frequent snowstorms blew down from Scotland. They would shrug and continue making their lists. Neither one wanted their time together to end.

Jane was reluctant to reveal anything about her life. But as the days flew by, she opened up. She found Max to be an entertaining companion and a sympathetic listener. He never criticized her or questioned her motives. He offered his shoulder to cry on and let her say as much or as little as she chose. He was intelligent and had a quick wit. She laughed more when they were together than she had her whole life. Max was nothing like the other men she knew. He did not assume because he was male, he was her superior, like Uncle Harold. Nor did he order her around like Mangus. He was kind, thoughtful, and considerate of her feelings. Jane went to bed each night, thinking of Max and the stories he told her.

Your life and his are intertwined.

What did it mean? Jane stared at him during the day and thought of her premonition.

Could a man of Max's caliber come to see her as someone other than she was? She wondered what being his wife would be like. She imagined him sweeping her into his arms and kissing her as he did before. She trembled at the thought, her breath coming fast. She remembered the feel of his skin and the bronzed beauty of his naked chest. She wanted to run her hands over his body and touch every inch of his muscled form. Jane licked her lips. He was hard, warm, and lean. He would hold her tight and protect her from harm. He would defend her honor and challenge anyone who mistreated her to a duel. Max would hold her arm with pride as he introduced her to his circle of friends. "This is my wife, Lady Jane Radley," he would say.

Jane caught sight of her twisted reflection in the long paned windows and sighed. It was a dream, nothing more. What she would give to be whole, to walk without a limp, to dance, to run, but most of all, to be normal. Who could want such as her? No one was the answer. She put thoughts of Max out of her mind and banished them to the far corner of forgetfulness. Just because her premonition said their lives were intertwined did not mean their hearts would be. She resolved to help him as much as she could but nothing more. Her heart wanted a future with him too much to allow him any closer. He should leave Rathborne before it was too late.

****

Max marveled at her beauty. Every day he spent with Jane, she impressed him more. She was not silly like most girls her age. She did not giggle and make nonsensical phrases to fill up silences in the conversation. She had a giving heart and a loving nature. Her features softened as she spoke of her childhood and her mother. Jane loved the woman, despite her betrayal. He discovered Jane did not realize her gift of sight until the morning after her mother left. He wondered at the situation. Did the trauma cause the voices in her head? Or had she had them all along but never paid any attention to them?

Max found he enjoyed her company more than he thought possible. She had wit and charm plus the added benefit of a working mind, something lacking in most society girls. She fascinated him and he found himself hurrying with his other tasks to be with her. She was on his mind constantly. The urge to put his arms around her and protect her overwhelmed him. He caught himself remembering little things to tell Jane later, because he knew it would amuse her. The more he was around her, the more he wanted to be with her. As they talked, he realized she dealt with the trauma of her mother's leaving, Mangus' death, and her accident, by blaming it on Thaddeus. Whenever he tried to defend himself, she got angry. It was the only cloud in an otherwise enjoyable situation. He wondered what she would do when she found out the truth.

Max spent the time he was not with Jane by keeping an eye on Thomas and Gertie. He could not fathom Alfred being involved. He had been with the family too long and was loyal to a fault. But Max could not rule it out entirely. His main lead was Sir Harold. No one in the castle would have access to sensitive information about the English Fleet. Someone had to have connections in London.

Thomas was the only one who left the castle. Friday was his day off, and he spent it in the village. Max followed him. There was nothing out of the ordinary. Thomas was sweet on the baker's daughter and spent his time mooning around the ovens on his day off. He sent letters to his mother, who lived in York. Max wondered at the contents. Those letters were a possible source of information. He slipped into Thomas' room one day when Thomas was gone and searched until he found a stack of letters. Nothing suspicious there, just the normal platitudes on health, and weather, and a few odd comments about relatives.

Gertie spent her time in the kitchens or the gardens. She never ventured far from either. Max found no evidence she was involved in anything other than her duties as cook.

Alfred proved to be the same. After a thorough investigation of the old man's rooms, Max wrote him off the list of possible suspects. Only Sir Harold Roswell and his two daughters remained.

Having reached this conclusion, Max was reluctant to leave Rathborne. He could not leave Jane alone. She was crippled and dependent upon her cane to move. It was a wonder someone had not taken advantage of her by now. She was beautiful and had no defenses. Alfred and Thomas would be no help in defending her honor. Irritation burned through Max when he realized he could be considered dangerous, as well. He could take her virtue with little effort. The thought angered him. Dammit, it was not right she was all alone here. He would make inquiries and see if he could find any family for her. Jane should be living somewhere safe, with relatives and servants to protect her. In the meantime, he would hire soldiers to guard her. He could not leave Jane in such a vulnerable condition. His honor would not allow it.

****

Christmas arrived with a flurry of snow. The drifts piled high along the castle walls.

Max left for the village early in the morning. He returned with a long, skinny package wrapped in paper. He waited until they were seated in the antechamber before handing it to Jane.

She glanced at him in surprise. "I do not have a gift for you," she said in consternation. She blushed as she looked from him to the gaily-wrapped package.

"Your smile is gift enough. Now open it."

At Max's insistence, she unwrapped the package carefully, a gasp coming to her lips. The package contained a beautiful, polished cane with an elegantly carved handle. It fit her hand exactly. Jane gazed at him in surprise. "I do not need a new cane. My old one is fine."

"No, it is not," Max contradicted. "Stand up, Jane, and try the new one. I had it made especially for you."

"But why?" she asked.

Max helped her up. "Take a little walk to the wall and back. Try it."

Jane rolled her eyes but took hold of the new cane. She took a step, and then another. The cane was taller. She did not have to stoop at all. A smile tugged at the corners of her mouth.

"Does it feel a little taller?" At her nod, he said. "I realized the first week I was here, you leaned a little too much on your cane. I thought if you had a longer one, you could stand straighter, and your back would not hurt so much from leaning when you walk."

Jane walked to the wall again and back. It was wonderful. "This is better," she said. "Thank you, Max. It is most kind of you." Tears filled her eyes, and she blinked them back. She was touched he had the cane made for her. She could not remember the last time she received a gift from anyone. Neither the duke nor her mother were inclined to remember her, so caught up were they in their own worlds. When she was a child, perhaps her mother cared a little, for she kept her well-guarded, but as she grew older, it ceased. Now, here she was, accepting a beautiful handmade cane from a handsome man for her crippled leg.

Trust him. He shall solve riddles and answer long-ago questions.

Jane smiled. She did trust him. The trip across the room got easier. Jane's shoulder and back relaxed.

"You are welcome, Jane," Max said.

Jane stopped beside him. "This is the best Christmas I have ever had.

Max took her hand in his. "It shall be the first of many."

Their companionship grew and flourished. They spent every waking minute together. Each could not wait to be with the other. Before they knew it, the winter passed, and it was spring.

Chapter Eight

Visitors arrived the second Monday in March. Jane was in the great hall enjoying her breakfast.

Max sat opposite her eating his partridge and eggs with relish. He took a slice of bread as Alfred entered the room.

"My lady, wagons are entering the castle grounds," Alfred announced.

Beware.

Jane set her goblet down. "Who is it? What do they want?"

Alfred stood beside her. He frowned. "Father Brown awaits at the door."

The blood in her face fell to her feet. *Father Brown?* She swallowed. "Did he mention why he was here?" Jane rose. Her hands trembled. Was today the day he came for her? Father Brown was a stalwart Christian soldier and believed an evil spirit possessed her. He led the overzealous in their pursuit to rid the world of evil, witchcraft in particular. Since Jane was the local favorite, she was the subject of his lengthy Sunday sermons. He visited the castle once since Mangus Rathborne died. He came to perform an exorcism.

Jane refused. She tried to reason with him, demanding proof of her wrongs. The vicar damned her to hell. He denounced her as a servant of Satan and counseled the villagers against having any connection with her. He had not stepped foot on Rathborne property since. Why had he come today?

Father Brown seeks to destroy you.

She wiped the perspiration from her brow and reached for her cane.

Max rose to his foot as well. “I shall see to this, Jane. Do not trouble yourself.”

“I will come with you,” Jane answered. If he came to try her for witchcraft, she wanted a chance to defend herself. She followed Max to the front door.

The gray-haired priest turned as they approached. He spotted Jane and held out his crucifix to ward her off. “Stay back, demon. I want nothing from you.”

All is not as it seems.

Jane stepped through the open door and stood on the stoop facing him.

Max stopped beside her. His hand cupped her elbow to steady her. His presence beside her comforted her.

“Father Brown, what a wonderful surprise. How nice to see you again.” Jane held her hand toward him, ignoring the crucifix. “To what do we owe the pleasure of your company?”

Father Brown made the motion of the cross over his breast and stared at her. “I want nothing from you, witch, unless it be a confession. I came to speak to his grace.” He turned toward Max and bowed slightly from the waist. “Your grace.”

Max’s hand fell from her arm. He stiffened beside her.

Jane glanced at Max. “Do you mean Mr. Radley?”

The priest stared at her. “Do not work your riddles

on me! I mean the Duke of Rathborne. Do you not recognize him? He is master here. Your days of evil are over, witch."

"The Duke of Rathborne?" Jane looked around wildly, and then realization struck her. She turned to stone. A million thoughts ran through her head as she faced Max. *"You are the Duke of Rathborne?"* Everything happened in slow motion, like a nightmare she could not escape. Jane stared as if seeing Max for the first time. Nausea rose in her throat. Her heart jumped in her breast. The magnitude of his deception roared through her, and the pain was unimaginable. Her heart broke and shattered into a million pieces. The sharp edges tore her to shreds. Jane resisted the urge to strike Max and run away. Since she could do neither one, she glared haughtily. Her body shook. God, could this day get any worse? She took a step to the side to put distance between them. Once her mind cleared, rage took over.

Father Brown smiled a sarcastic smile. "Sanctify them in the truth," he quoted. He tucked his hands into his bell sleeves and rocked back and forth on his heels. His gaze darted between them.

Max gazed at Jane through hooded eyes. "I am Thaddeus Rathborne," he confirmed.

Jane leaned heavily on her cane. All this time, *Thaddeus Rathborne* was here, and she did not know it.

Your life and his are intertwined.

"Be silent, traitor," Jane muttered. She took another step away from him.

Max's eyes turned liquid silver as he studied her face. He reached a hand toward her, and she jerked away. His hand fell to his side. He turned to the vicar.

"Say your piece." He glanced at Jane with concern.

"I came to perform an exorcism. This servant of Satan has occupied your house long enough. She must agree to be cleansed or be cast out." Father Brown puffed out his chest. "Those members of my flock who you hired to work for you, refuse to leave the security of the wagons until I deem it safe." His beady black eyes swept over Jane. "Twice I have offered to cleanse the witch, and twice she has refused. Until she does, no one will enter this place." He pointed a bony finger at Jane. "I have suffered your presence too long. Now the duke has returned, I will purge this parish of all evil. Peace shall return to this castle and this village."

Jane shook her head as she stared at the vicar, her mouth dry with fear. *Now the duke has returned.* "I am not the evil you seek. There is no witchcraft or black arts practiced within these walls. Nothing of import occurs here." Her voice shook. She gripped her cane and stiffened her spine.

"Do you deny you have an unholy knowledge of things to come?" the vicar thundered.

"As does every mother with her child, many farmers with their flock, and any vicar worthy of his parish," Max answered. He caught Jane's elbow and squeezed.

Father Brown choked. "I am under the influence of the most holy God. These other examples are nothing. They cannot compare to my holy calling."

"I am not the evil you seek," Jane repeated. She pulled her arm from Max's grasp. She did not require Max's help nor his support. Fire burned her throat. He had every opportunity to tell her his identity, and he had not. Her knees shook with the effort to stand. She turned her head to glare at Max.

He met the ice in her gaze with the mercurial silver of his.

Anger roared in her ears. Lifting her chin, she looked down her nose at the vicar, and said, "There will be no exorcism." She turned to go before the tears spilled for all to see. Her knees wobbled as she moved woodenly toward the open door.

Suddenly, liquid fire burned her face and hands. The vicar laughed wildly. Jane turned her head as he tossed the contents of a silver bottle at her person. Jane cried out. The liquid branded her everywhere it fell. She rubbed her face and hands where the liquid splashed.

Alfred left his post beside the door and caught Jane by the arm. He inspected her hands and face. "I will fetch Gertie for you, my lady."

Jane took a step back and then another.

****

Max boiled with rage. How dare the vicar attack Jane! He caught Jane and turned her toward him. Red bubbling blisters appeared where the liquid burned her skin. Max stepped between Jane and the vicar and took the silver bottle from his hand. "What is this?" he asked angrily. He smelled the contents. He caught the cool scent of sage and a delicately sweet scent he could not identify.

The vicar jerked away and held his hands toward heaven. "See my children. Look how the witch writhes and cries as the holy water purges her."

Jane glanced behind the vicar. The villagers in the wagons murmured and pointed at her. "Die, witch, die," they cried.

"What have you done?" Max demanded. With a

muttered oath, he tossed the remaining contents of the bottle on the priest. "Let us see how you like it."

Father Brown stepped to the side to avoid the liquid. He did not move fast enough. It caught him across the face. The vicar shrieked and swore profusely. He rubbed and swatting at the liquid splashes, ignoring Jane and everyone else. Father Brown danced around in pain, howling like a babe.

Jane gaped at the priest and then at Max. "After deceiving me over your identity and lying about your reason for being at Rathborne, you now defend me?" she asked incredulously.

Max gazed at her. "I shall always defend you, Lady Jane. You are innocent in this," he said gently. Then, he turned to the villagers. "Stop this farce!" he roared.

The villagers quieted. They huddled together, whispering amongst themselves. "Is Father Brown possessed of the devil as well?" one woman called out.

Max shook his head. "This holy water is a trick, a mixture of herbs and water. It does not reveal the presence of evil."

"Lady Jane is a witch. The water burned her." the woman replied. The other villagers nodded their heads in agreement.

"It also burned the vicar. It will burn anyone who touches it. It proves nothing."

****

Max's words struck Jane's heart as she struggled with the pain. Why should he care what they thought about her? Jane bit her lip to keep her cries of pain inside.

"Curse you!" Father Brown yelled at Max. "The witch has blinded you to the truth with her evil. You are damned for what you do this day."

"No," Max said, "you are. The villagers can see your superstitions are unfounded. You created the stories condemning Lady Jane of witchcraft. They are all false. Lady Jane is a gentle God-fearing woman." He faced the villagers with his hands on his hips. "Anyone who has aught against Lady Jane shall answer to me. She is under my protection."

There was silence. Everyone stared at Max. "This is my castle, my land, and my village. Everything for miles in any direction belongs to me, as do you. Lady Jane is no witch. Anyone who says any different shall be imprisoned and tried for falsely accusing an innocent. This is my command and my law."

No one moved. Father Brown stared at Max as if seeing him for the first time. Fear chased across his face.

Gertie appeared in the doorway. "Alfred said ye have need of me." She took hold of Jane's hand and inspected the angry red spots. "Deadly nightshade, I am thinking," she said. "Come along, Lady Jane, let us find you something to help with the pain."

Max touched her arm. His voice gentled. "We must talk," he said before Gertie led her away.

Jane ignored him and let Gertie lead her to her chamber. Hot tears rolled down her cheeks. She was such a fool to believe her life could be any different than it was. She threw herself on her bed and covered her face with her hands.

"There, there, my lady. I have just the thing to help you. Give me a few minutes to collect my herbs."

Jane nodded and Gertie left, closing the door behind her.

What in God's name was she going to do? She thought of the last few months since Max arrived at Rathborne and wondered why she had not guessed. He was not the kind of man who took orders. He gave them. It was evident in the way he walked, the way he talked, and the way his presence demanded attention. She sobbed into her sleeve. She remembered every word she said over the past few months. She constantly spoke of Thaddeus Rathborne and how much she hated him. And he? She peeked out at her cream plaster ceiling. He was silent. Once or twice, Max questioned her comments, asking if she had proof of the duke's wrongdoing. Fool that she was, she thought he knew the duke. She never guessed *Max was him!* Was she so lacking in intelligence? And where was the voice in her head? Why had it not warned her of his cunning and deceit?

As if on cue, it whispered. *Trust him. He will right the wrongs.*

Jane threw a pillow across her room. Then another one. Damn him! She hated him. Look what he did to her! Even as she thought the words, she knew they were not true. Max had not caused her accident. She did. He did not send her mother away. She left on her own. He did not kill his father. His father was old and brokenhearted. Jane folded her arms over her chest, unwilling to give more. Max could have come to Mangus' funeral. He could have done that much.

Trust him.

She wanted to throw a pillow at the voice in her head. Jane sighed. What if Max did not receive any of the letters? He suggested as much. She remembered Max's face when she mentioned them. He was surprised. She threw another pillow and buried her head beneath her arms once more.

Your life and his are intertwined. Take courage. He will right the wrongs.

"Silence!" she yelled. Why was her life so complicated? Just when her heart showed signs of recovering, she was betrayed once more.

You must trust him.

"Go away!" Jane yelled. What in God's name was she going to do now the duke was home? She could not stay here. She could never look at Max the same. The man who made her laugh, who came to her chamber to chase away her nightmares, the man who made her feel safe, was also her enemy. Jane buried her head beneath the lone pillow on her bed and cried.

Gertie reentered the chamber with her pouches of herbs. She selected a small one containing dried Calabar beans and crushed them in a small pottery dish. She added a little water and made a paste. "I got these beans from a sailor. He traded me for some poppy seeds. Said he got the beans in Africa." Gertie chuckled. "I took them because they are the only thing I know which counteracts deadly nightshade." She smoothed the paste on Jane's blisters, muttering about the vicar. "Damn fool." She waggled a finger in Jane's face. "Mark my words, he will find some new evil in the village before nightfall." She shook her head. "He has to have some plague or another descending upon us." She wrapped Jane's blisters with clean strips of linen. "But as long as it does not include anyone I care for, he can say whatever he wants." She finished her task and covered Jane with a blanket. "You must lie here and let the herbs do their job." She patted her arm.

"The burning will die down soon. I will be back to check on ye."

****

Damn! Damn! Damn! Max frowned as Jane moved woodenly away. He never meant for her to find out like this. He ran a hand through his hair in irritation. His chest tightened. He would have to speak with her as soon as he got rid of the vicar. He would never forget the hurt in her eyes.

He turned to Father Brown. "Why are you still here? You performed your exorcism. Be gone. Never darken my door again. Know this. Lady Jane is under my protection. You will treat her with respect."

Father Brown's eyebrows rose. "The devil takes care of his own."

Max stared at the old man. "Lady Jane is no more a servant of Satan than I am."

Father Brown stopped rubbing his hands and face. His dark eyes assessed Max. "Perhaps I underestimated the witch's power. Have you entertained any dark feelings or violent thoughts since you came to Rathborne?"

"I am not possessed." Max stared at the vicar's ceremonial robes. An uneasy feeling worked its way through him. Max narrowed his gaze. "What else have you come to do?"

Father Brown stared back. "I came to assess the darkness. The level of evil here must be evaluated. I will perform accordingly." He lifted another bottle from the inside pocket of his robe. "Once I deem this castle free from satanic influence, I will sprinkle it with holy water. Only then will I allow the villagers to enter. I must look after the eternal souls of my flock. You understand?" A glitter of excitement entered the old man's eyes.

Max narrowed his gaze. "There is no darkness here."

"Then you deny me permission to continue my exorcism?" Father Brown challenged. He puffed his chest out and waited.

Max folded his arms. He stared at the vicar until the man dropped his gaze. "Explain this ritual."

"I read from the sacred script commanding the demon to depart. Once I finish, the witch must be doused with holy water and commended to Christ."

"You already doused her, commend her to Christ and be on your way." Max glared at the vicar. Scaring the villagers with tales of evil delighted him. "Once you commend Lady Jane to Christ, you will cease your superstitious prattle concerning her."

The vicar smiled. "Only if she is truly free of Satan's influence."

"Do you doubt the efficacy of your ritual? Or do you enjoy frightening the innocent people of my village?" He took a step toward the vicar. "Whichever it is, you shall have to find something else to preach about."

Father Brown coughed.

Max could see the vicar struggled with giving up his stories of witchcraft. "What else?"

Father Brown twitched. "I must sprinkle holy water on the base of the castle."

Max considered his options. If he denied the vicar, the whisperings concerning Jane would increase. The little man was full of righteous indignation. If he allowed it, the people would feel safe enough to accept his offer of employment.

Max stepped aside. "Douse it with holy water. You will find it changes nothing. I give you my word there is nothing evil or satanic within these walls. But I warn you now. If you speak another word against Lady Jane after this ritual is conducted, I shall hang you from the pillar of your church. Any man or woman who mistreats Lady Jane or lays a hand on her shall answer the same fate."

Father Brown stared into his eyes for long minutes, then nodded his sparse gray head.

"Perform your ritual. I shall watch from here."

****

Jane's tears dried to her cheeks. She lay thinking of where she could go or what she could do. She could not stay here with Max. His betrayal hurt worse than she imagined possible. She must escape. Max planned to go to York to investigate Uncle Harold. So, she must go a different way. Jane closed her eyes. Her father's family lived in Oxford. Lady Lenwood ran the estate after the death of her husband and sons. Jane's father, James, was the last to go. Lady Aldetha Lenwood was the grandmother Jane never knew. Jane's mother was spiteful toward Lady Aldetha, but Jane was not concerned. Her father was a wonderful man. His mother would be nothing less. Jane would go as soon as Max left for York. Somehow, she must hide her plans and her hurt from his watchful gaze.

Trust him.

"I did, and look where it got me," she answered.

Chapter Nine

Max crossed his long legs in front of him and studied her. Jane had dark circles under her eyes. He doubted if she slept at all last night. She refused to look at him and would not let him within six feet of her. He knew he hurt her, and it grieved him more than he thought possible.

"So, I am free of suspicion now the vicar has sprinkled holy water on the castle and commended me to Christ?"

Max nodded, his gaze on her face. "That was the agreement. I hired several people from Rathborne village. Other servants are on their way from the neighboring villages. No one wanted to step foot inside Rathborne until Father Brown pronounced it safe."

Jane rolled her eyes. "If I had the power to cast spells, I would have turned Father Brown into a snake. Everyone would see what he was from the beginning." She picked at her breakfast, eating nothing. "I would have turned you into an eel."

"Why an eel?" he asked curiously. He figured he was a snake in her mind also.

Jane turned to meet his gaze for the first time since she found out who he was. "Because they are worse than snakes. Snakes have dry, rippled skin. Eels are snakes with slimy, wet skin. They are slippery and disgusting."

Max digested her comment. "It was important no one knew who I was while I searched for the ring. I should have guessed someone would recognize me. Now that my identity is common knowledge, I must hurry with my investigation." He was silent for a minute. "I never meant to hurt you, Jane. I planned to tell you. I had not found the right way yet."

Jane threw her goblet against the hearth. It shattered into a million razor-sharp pieces. "I hate you. I wish you had not come to Rathborne. You cannot suddenly appear one day out of nowhere and take over. You never cared before this! Why now?" she asked. She got to her feet. Her beautiful eyes shot blue flames.

"As I told you last eve, Jane, this castle and everything in it belongs to me. I can do as I please." His gaze followed her as she paced back and forth across the floor. Her walking had improved now her back was straight, and she was not bent over.

"You do not own me," she stated vehemently.

"On the contrary, you are my stepsister as well as my ward. I can decide where you go, who you go with, and everything about you. The only way to escape me is to marry, and even then, I must give my consent. Unless you have other family to take you in, I am your next of kin, and you must have my permission whatever you do."

Jane stopped her pacing. "Oh God, you are right." Her shoulders slumped, and she looked defeated. It lasted less than a minute before her anger took over again. "I shall escape." She resumed walking back and forth.

"Where would you go, Jane? How would you travel? The roads are full of peril for a lady alone. You might get lost, or a hundred other very unpleasant things. The best thing to do is to stay here and allow me to make up for the past. You never know," he teased. "I may turn out to be a likable fellow."

Jane's jaw dropped open at his suggestion. "How can you say such a thing? Look at me. I would be whole if all this were different." Jane was beyond furious.

Max studied Jane for another few minutes. "Different does not always mean better," he commented. "I like you the way you are." He meant it. Jane was beautiful, limp and all.

She glared. Jane was not in the mood to listen to reason. Anything he said made her more upset.

"Where would you go if you left?" he asked quietly.

Jane stopped pacing. She narrowed her gaze. "As far from you as I can."

He was silent for long minutes. "Do you have other family?" He needed to know where she would go in case she did something foolish. His heart thudded in his chest at her suggestion. He could not think of her being on her own. It was too dangerous.

Jane shook her head. She sank onto the settee and stared into the flames of the fire. She looked lost and alone.

Max leaned over and took her cold hands in his. "I must travel to York and find Sir Harold. Once my mission is complete, I will make arrangements to take you wherever you wish." He was silent for a moment. "It was never my intention to hurt you, Jane. I apologize from the bottom of my heart. I would do anything to ease your pain. I cannot change what is done, but I can change the future. Give me a chance to make your life better." Max studied her bowed head. "I have come to care for you a great deal. Promise me you will do nothing rash in my absence. I would never forgive myself if something happened to you." When she said nothing, he added. "I have soldiers coming to protect you. There will be workmen and furnishings as well. Rathborne shall be everything it was in the past."

"How long will you be gone?" Jane asked after several minutes.

Max leaned back in his chair. Her question was the first encouraging sign yet. "Will you be saving a dungeon cell for me?"

Jane blushed hotly. "I have the very one especially for you."

Max laughed. "Then I shall hasten my return." He sobered. "Have you forgiven me?"

She glanced up. "There is much to consider." Her blue eyes were cold as ice.

Max nodded. Her comment offered hope. "I would very much like to right the wrongs." He squeezed her fingers as he rose to his feet. "I meant what I said. I care for you, Jane. Promise me you will take care while I am away."

Jane nodded slowly.

Max sighed. "I shall return as soon as I am able." He placed a kiss on her bare knuckles. She shivered in response.

Max smiled. She was not as immune to him as she would have him believe. "Until then, sweet Jane." Max left the room without a backward glance. If he had, he would have seen the tears streaming down her face.

****

Jane had never felt so alone. She argued with herself constantly over the fact. How could she miss someone she despised?

Your life and his follow the same path.

Stop it!

Trust him. He shall right the wrongs.

Jane wished the voice would leave her alone with her self-pity. In truth, she did not know how she felt. Max was kind and gentle. He made her laugh and entertained her with his wit. He was everything she wanted in a man, yet he was her enemy.

He will change everything.

That was certainly true. All the years of blaming Thaddeus Rathborne for every misfortune rose inside her. Max's voice played in her head. *"What if Thaddeus did not know of his father's wish to be reconciled?"* Jane had to consider it. Was she wrong about him? *"You say Mangus wrote letters. How do you know Thaddeus received them? You act as though he read them and created the circumstances which led to your injury. What if Thaddeus had no idea about any of this?"* Jane bowed her head. *"You believe she sent the letters to Thaddeus because she is so…trustworthy?"* Max's voice mocked her.

Jane went for a walk. There were too many voices in her head, and she had to clear them out so she could think.

Give him a chance. Wait for him.

"Mind your own business," Jane told the voice. She went to the garden. It was the only place she found peace.

The first wagons to arrive at Rathborne Castle contained carpenters and an army of maids. They came complete with a housekeeper to assign them their duties. She was a jolly woman named Mrs. Patrick, with graying hair and a quick smile. She was a motherly person, with a sympathetic ear and a pocket full of sound advice. Jane liked her a great deal. Mrs. Patrick came to Jane's room in the evening to rub the soreness from her knee as she told her stories of Scotland and the times she had there before coming to England.

The maids cleaned the castle from the top spires to the dungeon floor. Smoke covered the stones from the fires burning throughout the castle. Jane's chamber was one of the first ones cleaned, and a hearty fire lit to keep her warm. She lay on the freshly cleaned sheets and ran her toes over the fine fabric. It was nice to sleep in her bed again. She had taken to sleeping on the settee in the antechamber for lack of wood to keep the rooms warm. Heat was no longer a problem. The workmen cut plenty of firewood each morning. On the second day, several loads of coal arrived. Candles followed, and the entire castle was once more lit, making it possible to walk the long corridors after dark.

The great hall had been cleaned and aired. Everything shone in the light of the many candles burning in the chandelier. A cheerful fire burned brightly in the marble hearth. The wooden floor gleamed from its recent scrubbing. The polish lent its fresh scent to the newly whitewashed room.

Jane sat still as a stone at luncheon.

You must accept the change.

The voice asked a lot. The emptiness of the castle pressed down on her. It was full of people, but they were all servants. None of them were Max. She stared at his empty seat. She wanted him to be Max, not Thaddeus Rathborne. Max was a friend, a confidant, and a companion. Thaddeus Rathborne was another matter. How could she miss someone she hated? Where was the independent girl she used to be?

She lived alone for three years after her mother left. She had no one to rely on but herself. There was Alfred, Gertie, and Thomas, of course, but they were servants. She counted on them to do their jobs, but they were not her equals. She let Max into her life and look where it got her. All the while they were together, they spoke of the castle and her life, never his. Jane had no idea where Max was the years after he left and now.

Your life and destiny lie with him.

Jane gripped her cup. No. Her path followed a different course. She hoped he delayed his return, so she had time to put some distance between them. She covered the ache in her heart over his betrayal with anger. The more she hurt, the angrier she became. The servants walked a wide path around her.

You must trust your destiny.

"Stop it!" Jane put her hands over her ears. She would not listen. Her destiny was her own. She would not share it with someone who betrayed her trust.

The servants paused. Jane rocked back and forth in her chair, her untouched luncheon in front of her.

Wait for him.

"I will not!" Jane rose to her feet, sweeping the contents of the table to the floor with her cane. The dishes crashed to the floor. Food splashed everywhere. Jane hit her chair with her cane until her arm ached. "I hate him!" Her voice echoed around her.

The silence of the long hall stopped her tirade.

Servants stood still as statues avoiding eye contact. Food dripped from the new table to the polished floor. Broken dishes lie scattered at her feet. An apple rolled behind her chair and stopped.

Jane drew in a long shaky breath. The servants must think her touched. Embarrassment rose to her cheeks. She grabbed her cane and left as fast as she could drag her foot.

Mrs. Patrick found Jane in the antechamber curled on the threadbare sofa crying her heart out. “Dinna worry Lady Jane, his grace will return soon enough.” She patted Jane’s shoulder.

“He lied to me. I hope he never comes back,” Jane answered.

Mrs. Patrick drew back at the venom in Jane’s tone. “Dinna say such a horrible thing! Imagine how you would feel if something befell his grace. You would never forgive yourself. Whatever you think he did, I am certain it was a misunderstanding.” Mrs. Patrick sat beside Jane. “Now, what has you so upset.”

Jane told Mrs. Patrick about Max and the duke. When she finished, there was silence.

“Well, my lady,” Mrs. Patrick said. “I think it best to forgive him. The man did protect you and see you were safe before leaving. He dinna hold the fact you imprisoned him against you.”

“I suppose you are right,” Jane said slowly. She changed the subject then. She was not ready to forgive him.

Later as Jane settled into her soft, warm bed, she considered what Mrs. Patrick said. Max defended her to Father Brown. He ordered her a cane to help her walk better. She glanced at the gleaming cane in the light of the fireplace. She slept in her own bed because of workmen he hired to keep her fires going and servants he employed to clean her sheets and do her laundry. He made sure she had someone to cook for her and food to eat before he left her. He did this for her. Jane threw a pillow across the room. She would not be beholden to the Duke of Rathborne. She would wait for an opportunity, and she would leave.

Stay.

Jane grimaced.

Wait for him.

She put a pillow over her head. "Go away," she said. If the voice had nothing better to say, she did not want to hear it.

The following week, more servants arrived. They now had a butler and an army of footmen. The footmen stood outside the doors and lined the hallways as Jane walked from one part of the castle to the next. Scullery maids and kitchen staff arrived a day or two later, each outfitted in new uniforms. There were so many people bustling around; it was impossible to find a room not already inhabited by another person even if said person was a servant.

More furniture arrived. Just when Jane thought everything was settling down, something changed. Jane went to the gardens to escape the workmen as they broke the furniture out of the wooden crates. The duchess's rose garden was the same as the day she came to Rathbone. It belonged to Mangus' first wife, Margret, and required a lot of care to return it to its original glory.

Every day, things were different. The first was her bedchamber. Another chamber had been prepared for her in the meantime. Jane told herself to be gracious. Mrs. Patrick led her toward an identical chamber further down the corridor kept for visiting family. Cream-colored velvet walls and cherry paneling framed the room. A giant bed boasted a rose floral coverlet. Golden ropes tied back rose-colored velvet drapes. A gleaming side table held a rose porcelain bowl. The scent of flowers filled the air with their sweet perfume.

Jane stared in bewilderment. "When did all this arrive?"

"Och, they've been working on it for a couple of days now. The duke wants you to be comfortable while your room is in repair," Mrs. Patrick said.

Jane stiffened when the housekeeper said Max's name. She walked further into the room. "So, his grace decides what I do and when I do it?" As soon as she figured out a way to leave, she would vanish.

"Dinna be so upset, my lady. I think his grace is being exceedingly kind to think of your comfort. He dinna want any hardship to fall upon you. Look around at the things he is doing for you," Mrs. Patrick urged.

"Well, he is too late. Fancy furniture and servants will not change anything," Jane answered. She gazed at the coverlet. Unable to help herself, Jane ran her fingers over the richly woven fabric. How long had it been since she had seen anything this nice or this lovely? This shade of rose was more beautiful than anything she had ever seen. The elegance of the room took her breath away.

"Would you care for a bath this evening, my lady?" Mrs. Patrick changed the subject as she drew the heavy drapes closed and lit the candles.

Jane sighed. It was not Mrs. Patrick's fault her life

was so complicated. "A bath would be lovely. Thank you." Her back ached from kneeling in the garden. The heat of the water would soothe the muscles in her knee, as well.

Mrs. Patrick nodded at two of the housemaids hovering nearby.

Soon a new gleaming brass tub sat inside the newly finished room. A steady stream of servants carried pitchers of steaming hot water. When the tub was full, Mrs. Patrick sent everyone from the room but the two young housemaids, Mary and Elisa. They helped Jane remove her clothing and step into the steaming water. The maids worked rose-scented soap into a lather and helped Jane bathe. They unwound her hair and washed it. More steaming water rinsed the suds from her hair and body. When Jane finished, the maids wrapped great thick towels around her and presented a heavy velvet dressing robe. Jane dropped the towels and allowed the soft red robe to slide up her arms and the belt to be tightened around her waist. The robe proved to be warm and must have cost a fortune. Jane ran her hand over the sleeve in amazement. It was beautiful. She had never owned anything so soft. The maids brushed her hair before the fire until it was dry.

Mary, thin and quiet with red hair and green eyes, shyly held up a cream silk night rail. Embroidered rose-colored blossoms decorated the neck and sleeves. She brought a new silk chemise and pantalets as well. Jane closed her eyes and allowed her dressing gown to be removed. They helped her into the silk undergarments and drew the night rail over her head. The silk slid against her skin, soft and smooth.

Mrs. Patrick smiled. "They arrived today, my lady.

I have been waiting to see your face since I opened the boxes. Do you like them?"

Jane nodded her head. "They are beautiful."

Mrs. Patrick looked pleased and nodded to the two maids. They covered Jane with the heavy brocade coverlet and drew the curtains around the bed so the footmen could remove the brass tub.

Jane ran her hand over the silk of her night rail. She should be furious Max presumed to buy her a dressing gown and night rail.

As if guessing Jane's thoughts, Mrs. Patrick pulled the drapes back from the bed and said, "His grace is your stepbrother. It is his duty to provide for you. A dressing gown and night rail are insignificant to a man as wealthy as the duke. Accept his gift without judging him."

If only she could. The more the castle changed, the more determined she was to find a way to escape.

It took the workmen a week to finish her room. Mrs. Patrick came for Jane when it was finished. Once they arrived, she opened the door to Jane's chamber and stepped back to allow Jane to enter.

The room was all pale blue, cream, and gold. Jane drew in her breath at the elegant, delightful sight. Pale blue was her favorite color in the entire world. She once told Alfred a silly wish when they were huddled in the antechamber one winter trying to stay warm. The room was exactly as she described it in her imagination to Alfred. How did the duke know? She glanced sideways at Alfred, who stood inside her chamber door grinning like a court jester.

"You told him," she accused.

"I did," Alfred admitted.

Jane allowed herself the pleasure of enjoying the room, for Alfred's sake, despite the fact Max paid for it. She walked slowly across the gleaming wood floor and stepped onto a thick pale blue carpet. The bed was new with a white frame. Angels etched in gold adorned the head of the bed. Curls of gold wound around the bed, inlaid in the wooden frame. Heavy pale blue drapes were tied back at each corner of the bed frame. The same heavy, pale blue drapes hung from the windows along the outside wall. The detail in gold on the cream plaster walls was exquisite. They were highlighted with golden framed pictures of angels and cherubs dancing and playing their harps. A white and gold side table held a blue porcelain pitcher and bowl. Her ivory brush and mirror rested beside the bowl. A round gold mirror hung above it, while a large white wardrobe, also etched in gold, stood along one wall.

It was the coverlet on the bed, however, which drew Jane's eye. Made from fairy fingers right from her dreams, it was pale blue brocade adorned with bunches of cream roses tied together with golden thread. Jane ran her hands over the exquisite design and decided right then that the coverlet was coming with her if she ran away. A pale blue and gold chair stood before the massive fireplace. The room was perfect.

Mrs. Patrick glanced anxiously at Jane from the door.

"Do you like it, my lady?" Alfred asked.

"I could not have dreamed of a more beautiful chamber. It is everything I thought it might be and more," she answered.

Chapter Ten

The following week, an army of gardeners arrived with pots of plants and flowers. Jane stood back as her one place of solitude was overrun by men, each armed with a garden implement and a pot of vegetation. A man named Francis was in charge. He shouted orders and directed the men in various directions. He gave precise instructions on what he wanted to be planted and where.

Jane stood still as her world transformed into something different from anything she had ever known. Tears pricked her eyes once more. With all the servants, maids, cooks, gardeners, butlers, scullery maids, footmen, and the rest of them, her efforts were no longer required. There were so many servants, it was impossible to find anything to do. All the problems and challenges were now being handled by people she did not know. Jane stepped back as a gardener walked toward her with a pot containing a rose. This was the duchess's rose garden, or it used to be. It was natural, she supposed, for them to plant more roses here. It bothered her a great deal that no one asked her opinion or consulted her about anything. She did as much good for the castle and the people in it as the new chairs beside the new dining table. After years of hardship, sacrifice, and suffering, she had become obsolete. Jane gazed around as the army of gardeners swarmed around her performing their tasks, oblivious to her and her pain. No one spoke to her except to say, “Excuse me, miss,” when she got in their way.

Jane wandered inside through the kitchens. It was a bigger disaster than the gardens. Servants ran everywhere. Cook was in the middle of making luncheon, and Jane was in the way. She walked toward the library. Maybe there she could find a moment of peace. It was not to be. Crates filled with expensive volumes littered the floor. While one group of servants unpacked the books, another group put them on the recently polished shelves.

Jane closed the door. The castle was unrecognizable in its transformation. The walls and ceiling were spectacular with their rich plaster detail and painting, but now they shone with the luster of new paint. Tapestries, gilt-edged mirrors, and pictures once more hung from every wall. The castle looked the way it did the day she first walked in, holding tight to her mother’s hand.

As she climbed the staircase leading to the family’s quarters, she stopped outside the duke’s chamber. The door was ajar. Curious, Jane walked closer. She nudged the heavy door open with her cane. Apprehension clawed at her stomach. Workmen were inside the chamber, refinishing the elaborate designs on the walls and the ceiling. A frown wrinkled her brow. Did Max plan to live at Rathborne when his mission was complete? Jane hurried to her chamber to think. She had not considered the possibility. He had been in England for months before he came to Rathborne. He did not consider the castle or his responsibilities important then.

Her anxiety grew. She had to find a way to escape. How could she stay at Rathborne now she knew Max's true identity?

She jumped when Mrs. Patrick knocked on her chamber door.

"Come in," Jane said.

Mrs. Patrick entered, closing the door softly behind her.

She was out of breath. She leaned against the wall fanning her face with her hand before she spoke. "There you are, my lady. I have been looking everywhere for you. There are several tradesmen here to see you."

Jane sat up. "Tradesmen?" Did someone wish to speak with her? A smile lit her face. "Well, where are they? I shall see them at once."

Mrs. Patrick smiled and motioned for her to follow. "We put them in the duchess's dressing room, my lady. There is more room in there."

That sounded ominous. *More room for what?* Jane wondered. She soon found out. Once the door to the duchess's dressing room opened, she realized her mistake. The tradesmen were not here to seek her opinion. They were here to take her measurements. She was the next project. Every chair in the castle had a new covering, and so would she.

The dressmaker was French. Jane was fluent in the language from her years in the nursery. So, she understood the conversation going on around her. His grace, the Duke of Rathborne, ordered a whole new wardrobe. She was to have everything from silk chemise and silk stockings to outer clothing lined with fur. There were to be slippers, fans, ball gowns, day dresses, tea gowns, evening gowns, traveling gowns, riding habits, silk petticoats, silk night rails, gloves, hats, and parasols for every occasion.

Madam ordered Jane onto a small stool where she measured and turned her this way and the other. Madam consulted with her partner, another French seamstress, and wrote notes in a little book she carried around her neck. Bolt after bolt of silk and satin were laid next to Jane's face and draped over her shoulders as the two women spoke in rapid French. It did not take long for Jane's leg to become shaky. She asked for her cane so she could lean upon it. Soon after, they helped Jane from the small stool and seated her in a burgundy velvet chair. The two women finished their discussion quietly, consulting their notes. A pale green silk dress was brought in. Jane had to stand as they removed her worn gown. The women clucked their tongues over the state of her chemise and stays. Jane glanced down. She realized her clothing was old and tired, but surely it was not as bad as the two French women made them out to be.

Jane sat bundled in her new velvet dressing gown and listened to the two women talk. Several seamstresses accompanied the women, and they altered a delicate silk chemise to fit her slim form. They cinched Jane into a new stay, and rolled silk stockings onto her legs, held in place with new satin garters. Several silk petticoats later, they lifted a darker green underskirt over her head and fastened it. Jane ran her hands gently over the delicate silk. Everything was so beautiful. She could not help feeling like she lived in a dream world. A world where she did not belong.

While Jane waited, the green silk dress was altered, and then it was lifted over her head, as well. Jane turned when all the buttons and laces were fastened. A mirror was placed before her. Jane stared at the reflection of a stranger. The last time she was dressed this fine was years ago, before the old duke died, before her mother left, and her world fell apart.

"You look lovely, Lady Jane. The color is so fair. It complements your hair and makes your eyes as blue as the sky above," Mrs. Patrick said.

Jane smoothed the front of her new skirt with trembling hands. "Thank you. Mrs. Patrick." Jane could not look at herself any longer. She did not belong in such a rich fine world. She turned away from her reflection. "I am tired. I want to go to my chamber," she said. The truth was, she wanted to escape the watchful gaze of the French women. They both glanced at her curiously as they worked. Jane knew they wondered why a wealthy man as powerful as the Duke of Rathborne would bother with a woman like her. Jane thanked the women in perfect French. Their eyebrows rose in surprise at her fluency.

She hobbled toward the door then down the long corridor to her chamber. Mrs. Patrick followed; her arms full of clothing. The two maids, Mary and Elisa, could bring the rest of the garments the seamstresses brought as soon as they were finished being altered.

"Does your leg ache, my lady?" Mrs. Patrick asked as she followed Jane into her chamber and shut the door.

Jane sat in the blue velvet chair facing the fire. She wiped the moisture from her eyes and sniffed.

"Och, what is wrong? Why do you weep? You look so fair in your new dress. Why are you so unhappy?"

"I do not belong here, Mrs. Patrick!" Jane wailed. "The castle is no longer my home." Tears streamed down her face.

"What are you talking about, my lady? Rathborne is your home. Why would you think it wasn't?"

"Everything is now so fine and beautiful, the walls, the carpets, the pictures, and the flowers. Rathborne Castle is as it used to be, the home of the Duke of Rathborne," Jane said quietly. "It is no longer mine."

Mrs. Patrick gazed at her quizzically. "And you are his stepsister. Where else would ye belong?" She walked around and pulled a stool in front of Jane's chair. "Surely, you like the new gown. The duke wants to please you, my lady. He wants to make you happy," Mrs. Patrick said. She massaged Jane's knee as she talked. Her eyes were sad as she gazed at Jane.

Jane could only nod. How could she explain her feelings for Max when she could not explain them to herself? She no longer belonged here. The last thing she wanted was to be beholden to Max in any way. Yet, he made it impossible for her to do anything else. She would not wear the clothes he bought, nor would she live in a castle he owned. The voice told her to stay, to trust him, but she could not do it. She would leave as soon as she had a plan. She was not out of options yet. All she had to decide was how to get to Oxford without being detected.

Jane was quiet for the next few days. She spent long hours in her chamber staring into the fire. Mrs. Patrick did all she could to rouse Jane's spirits but to no avail. Jane's new clothes arrived a few at a time. Mrs. Patrick inspected them. She had the maids air them out to remove the wrinkles before hanging them in the white and gold wardrobe in Jane's chamber.

The new gowns were the last straw. Jane could no longer pretend. Everything familiar was gone. Rathborne, as she knew it for the last three years, disappeared beneath the new paint, polish, and furnishings. She was no longer connected to any of it.

It was the arrival of the stable hands and several fine horses, which raised Jane's spirits. They gave her an idea of how to escape. Jane spent the next few days in her room claiming illness. She ordered her meals brought to her. She must save enough to sustain her on her journey. She could not carry food without arousing suspicion. Since one hand held a cane, she would either have to bring the food a piece at a time or ask for help. Jane did not have time for either one of those scenarios, so she ate in her room. Eating enough to satisfy her hunger, she wrapped the rest in cloth and hid it where her maids were not likely to look. After she had enough food stored for a week's journey, Jane dug out some of her old clothing. She did not want to be beholden to Max, and her new clothes would give her away as a lady of quality. She would travel as the wife of a poor soldier and keep well off the main road. Lady Lenwood lived in Oxford, and this is where she planned to go. She knew from stories her mother told that Oxford was south of Cumbria. She figured if she headed south sooner or later, she would find it. She would ask for directions on the way. It could not be too difficult.

Jane rode every day once the horses were properly settled. A little chestnut mare named Bessy arrived with the other horses. Jane was immediately taken with her. She was young, strong, and very gentle. The two were made for each other. Every morning when Jane went out to ride, she carried a little of her food and some clothing. She hid them in a corner of the stable. When Jane was sure she had everything prepared, she retired earlier than usual. It was happening! She would have her freedom. Jane had no idea if her father's family would take her in or not, but it was worth the risk.

Both anxiety and exhilaration raced through her as she slipped from her chamber. She wore her old dark gown and a black cape thrown over her head. It was a new one, lined in fur. Jane reasoned it would be better to take it and repay Max than to freeze on her journey. She wanted to be prepared for inclement weather should it suddenly come upon her. She carried an old pistol in the saddlebag for emergencies. Her cane was bound tightly to her valise strapped on the back of her side-saddle.

Jane rode silently out the castle gate and down the road. She chirped to Bessy once they were away from the castle. She let the mare run, glorying in her freedom and laughing as the cool breeze nipped at her nose and cheeks. It was wonderful to ride away from the castle, away from the pain, and especially from the memories. Jane focused on making as little noise as possible; so she did not see Gertie watching her ride out of the gate and down the road.

****

Max rode hard for York. He arrived two days later. He went to find Lord Andrew Darham first. Perhaps Andrew had insight as to how Sir Harold acquired the location of the English Fleet. Sir Harold was his number one suspect. There had to be a connection between him and one of the admirals with access to the sensitive information.

Lord Darham and himself kept rooms at a local tavern. It was a safe location to conduct their inquiries. Max retrieved the key and let himself in. He stood in the open door surveying the scene with dismay. It was a mess. Every piece of furniture was broken. The contents of the rooms were scattered everywhere. Andrew was nowhere. The room smelled and looked as if it had been vacant the entire five and a half months since Max was here last. He ignored his racing heart. Andrew was the only one who could testify Max was not the traitor. Max picked through the rubble. Andrew was a highly skilled knight. He would not die easily. Max took a deep breath to calm his furious thoughts. He wiped the dust from the window ledge and discovered blood. Did it belong to Andrew or someone else? Max righted a chair and sat down. He studied every scrap of debris until he had the scenario pieced together in his mind.

Andrew waited beside the door as an intruder attacked. A hell of a fight ensued. He killed the intruder and dragged him from the room. Andrew was wounded during the fighting but he was alive. Max found strips of linen near the bed to support his theory. Andrew bandaged his wounds and went in search of the person responsible for his ambush. Andrew would return when it was safe to see if Max left a message. He sifted through the debris until he found a pot of ink in the rubble. Max dipped a broken stick into the ink and wrote *Meet me at the birthing* on a sheet of parchment. He laid it on the bed. It was code for "meet me in London." "Birthing" because it was where they were assigned their mission.

Max figured Andrew would hide out until he

deemed it safe. No one was better at hiding in plain sight than Lord Andrew Darham. At least he was alive. Max wiped perspiration from his brow. Andrew would find him, and together they would exact revenge for this incident.

Max went in search of the proprietor of the tavern to question him. The disturbance in Lord Darham's rooms occurred in October. Max figured it happened the week after his departure. The proprietor required coins to repair the room. The episode cost him dearly, for he lost good customers over the noise. Max paid him six gold coins for the loss of business and another six coins to keep the rooms. Then he went in search of a different room. He did not want to stay at this tavern. Whoever attacked Andrew might still be watching.

Max had been at Rathborne since October. Had the weather cooperated, he would have returned to York months ago. Where the hell was Andrew? Max ordered a bath and washed the dirt of the road from his body. Disappointment furrowed his brow. Nothing on this mission was going as they expected. First, there was the ambush in the tavern, then the assassin, Andrew's disappearance, and now Jane. Max never expected to meet a woman like her. He was tantalized by her, fascinated by her, and bewitched by her. She frustrated him and excited him at the same time. He thought of her soft pink lips and voluptuous body. He wanted more. He wanted to learn all her secrets and see the smile on her face when she looked at him once more. It saddened him that she thought so little of him. He thought of the kisses they shared and groaned. Her honeyed mouth caused him to thirst for more. He remembered how she looked the last time they were together. Covered in blisters from the priest's holy water, she had dark circles under her eyes from lack of sleep and accusation in her gaze. As soon as he found the traitor and turned him over to the king, he would change Jane's world. He would give her something no one else had. He would give her safety and happiness.

Dressing carefully in black, he went in search of Sir Harold Roswell's estate. Max spent the next few weeks making note of everyone who came and went. He kept watch from the trees bordering the estate. Sir Harold went riding every morning, alone. Max followed at a careful distance to see what he did. Three times a week, he visited a bawdy house. He never returned home before dawn. Twice, he rode into the woods and met with a woman in a dark cloak. She waited beside the road in a plain black carriage. Whatever they did, they kept the drapes drawn. Max was unable to get close enough to hear anything. The woman had four outriders who took their job seriously.

The second time, he followed the carriage instead of Sir Harold. The carriage turned into a monastery outside York and did not return. Max was perplexed. He thought the mysterious woman was the courier who brought Sir Harold information. He was wrong. Max went back to his watch outside Roswell Estate to see what else he could find.

Lady Melissa was every bit as bad. She had several lovers and spent her time covering her liaisons with them. Max hunted down each of her lovers and discovered they were all dead ends. A sorrier group of dandies could not be found.

The remaining suspect was Lady Emily. She stayed indoors and hardly ventured out. When she did, she went to the dressmaker or the shops. Her only companion was her lady's maid. Max had to draw a blank for her, too.

He was ready to storm the house and tear it stone from stone until he found the parchment when Sir Harold appeared on his dappled gray stallion. Sir Harold waited inside the tree line of Roswell Estate for several minutes, peeking out in both directions. It was dusk, at the end of the fifth week, and the beginning of May. The weather was warm enough Max left his fur-lined cloak behind. He sat on his horse watching Sir Harold from the forest.

After a while, Sir Harold left the security of his hiding place and cantered away. Max followed. Sir Harold headed west. Once he was outside York, he whipped his horse into a gallop. Max stayed close enough to see Sir Harold but far enough away to be undetected.

Sir Harold stopped at a bridge bordering the next village. He dismounted and walked his horse beneath the trees. A woman appeared from beneath the bridge and hurried up the embankment.

Max stopped. The woman was short and gray haired. *Gertie!* She walked toward Sir Harold and began to talk.

Max rode around behind them and tied his horse. He slipped through the trees until he was within hearing distance.

"How long has she been gone?" Sir Harold asked.

"She left a week ago. She did not know I saw her leave," Gertie's gravelly voice said.

Max stiffened. Were they talking about Jane?

"Did you bring the letter?" he asked.

Max peered from behind the tree. Gertie pulled a folded parchment from her pocket and handed it to Sir Harold. "Do I get me coins now?"

Sir Harold opened the sheet of parchment.

Max froze. *It was the document with the location of the English Fleet!* Gertie had it the whole time.

Sir Harold folded the sheet and tucked it into his jacket pocket. He tossed a silver coin on the ground at her feet.

Gertie scooped it up. She squinted at Sir Harold. "This is not what ye said ye would pay when I told ye I found it in Mr. Radley's things."

Sir Harold struck her across the face. "Do not speak to me in such a tone. Women should know their place. I do you honor by paying you at all. I should whip you for your disrespect."

Gertie spit the blood from her mouth onto the ground. "If ye whip me, I will go to Lady Jane and tell her everything."

Sir Harold snorted. "What can Jane do? I shall have her whipped as well. No one will believe anything either one of you say." He snorted again. "Jane must realize she is a woman. She has no rights, and neither do you." His voice turned mean. "Do not question me again. " He stared at Gertie for a long minute. "I hope you are not stupid enough to double-cross me."

"I will keep yer secrets." Gertie spat again.

Sir Harold climbed on his horse. "Get back to Rathborne and keep your eyes open. I want to know the second Maximillian Rathborne appears."

Gertie tucked her hands inside her dark cloak. "Yes," she agreed.

"Yes, what?" he demanded.
"Yes, master," Gertie said tonelessly.

Chapter Eleven

Jane rode until the sun was high in the sky and stopped beside a stream to eat a little of the bread and cheese she brought with her. She took a drink of water and rested her leg before mounting Bessy once more. She followed the main road but stayed well hidden in the trees. When evening fell, Jane stopped in a nice meadow in the middle of the forest to make camp for the night. Jane knew enough about making fires from days spent alone in the castle to light one. Jane let Bessy drink from the stream and wiped her sides down with a woven cloth she brought along. She had some grain in a sack in the other saddlebag and fed the mare, talking to the horse while she did so. She tethered her mare securely to a nearby tree, and sat on a log beside the fire to eat her bread and cheese. She gazed up at the trees and smiled. She was on her own, and it was marvelous. The tension left her shoulders the further south she journeyed. She hoped Max choked when he realized she escaped him. Jane smiled at the picture her mind made, and wrapping her cloak around her tightly, lay down with her head on her saddle to get some sleep.

She woke as the first rays of the sun warmed the grass around her. Jane sat up and froze. She met the amused glances of Captain Jameson of the Rathborne guard and three of his men.

"How did you find me?" she asked.

They glanced at each other. The captain cleared his throat. “It was not hard, Lady Jane. You leave a wide trail.”

The other soldiers chuckled.

Jane was not amused. She jumped to her feet and hurried to the nearby stream. She hastily washed her face and plaited her hair. She ate a bit of bread and fed Bessy some more grain. The soldiers saddled her horse while she was gone.

“Where are we going, Lady Jane?” the captain asked. “Perhaps we can find a better road for you to travel.”

Jane studied his face. Captain Jameson meant well. “I am not going back to Rathborne,” she warned.

Captain Jameson took his tri-tipped hat off. He gazed earnestly at her. The sun glinted on his dark hair. “I am here to see to your safety, nothing more,” he said. “His grace will be upset if something happens to you. We will see you to your destination.”

He speaks truth.

Jane stilled. This was the first time the voice spoke to her since—she shook her head. Since she learned Max was the Duke of Rathborne. She’d left, despite the voice’s urging not to. No matter. She would get along without either of them. *Damn the duke and damn the voice!* She took a deep breath, gave the captain her most brilliant smile, and nodded. “I travel to Oxford to Lenwood Estates. My grandmother lives there.

Captain Jameson grinned and replaced his hat. His green eyes sparkled. “We will go south, cross country. It is the fastest route.” He nudged his mount forward. “We want to avoid the main roads. We are less likely to draw attention if we do. Stay beside me. Lady Jane. We will see you get there safely."

They rode beneath the shelter of the trees. The second night, a couple of thieves stumbled onto them while Jane slept. She had no idea her protectors slit the throats of the intruders before dragging the bodies off into the trees. They took turns keeping watch all through the night.

Four days into the journey, Jane's knee became tender and swollen. They stopped at the next tavern. Jane asked for a room and a warm bath while the soldiers looked after the horses. The proprietor laughed at the pitiful amount of money she carried and chased her out of the tavern. Lady Jane clutched her cane and walked slowly to the barn where Bessy enjoyed a bit of grain.

"I am sorry, Bessy, but it looks like we shall have to find somewhere else to stay. We do not have enough money to stay here. As soon as you finish your grain, we shall go," she whispered into the mare's ear. Jane leaned her head against the horse and sighed.

The soldiers stepped inside to have a word with the proprietor.

A few minutes later, the proprietor hurried out to the barn, anxious to catch Lady Jane.

"Why are you suddenly able to find a room for me when a few minutes ago you were not so pleasant?" Jane questioned.

The proprietor rubbed his sweaty hands down the front of his dirty apron. "It was my mistake. I did not realize you were the Duke of Rathborne's sister. Forgive me. He is a powerful man. I want no quarrel with his grace."

Jane assured the man she would not hold it against

him and grimaced as she turned to follow him. She rubbed her aching knee and grabbed her cane. So much for escaping Max.

The tavern keeper prepared the best room at the inn. A tub and hot water were hastily brought up the stairs to the little room. Jane sank into the hot water with a sigh. A maid helped her bathe. She took clean undergarments and a night rail from Jane's saddlebags and helped her dress. Then, she took Jane's gown to clean it and left the chamber. Jane fell into a deep sleep as soon as she pulled the quilt up to her chin.

After a hearty breakfast, they were once more on their way. They reached Oxford two days later. Jane rode through the village with curiosity. It looked much the same as the one at Rathborne but with more people. Jane inquired after Lady Lenwood at the tavern and received directions to the estate. It was dark when Bessy trudged wearily up the cobblestone drive to the two-story stone building. Jane slipped to the ground and almost fell.

Captain Jameson hurried to her side. "Are you all right, my lady?"

Jane bit her lip and nodded. She grabbed her saddle and held on until her knee quit shaking, and she could put her weight on it again. Taking her cane from the saddle, Jane walked beside the captain up the steps to the large front door. He knocked and waited.

A white-haired butler opened the door and stared down his thin nose at them. "May I be of service?"

"I am looking for Lady Lenwood," Jane said.

"I am afraid her ladyship is not receiving visitors. You will have to return at another time." The man moved to close the door.

"Wait!" Jane said. "Please. I have come from Cumbria to see her, and I do not think I can go any farther," she said. The pain in her knee made her dizzy.

" 'Tis a shame, miss. As I said, her ladyship is not receiving visitors." The butler frowned at her sternly as if warning her he meant what he said.

"But I am her relative," Jane said right before the door closed in her face.

It opened again, slowly. The butler took a step toward her and looked her over from head to toe with a mixture of disgust and curiosity.

"Her ladyship has no female relative your age, miss. Now, if you will excuse me?" He moved to close the door once more.

"I am the late Earl of Lenwood's daughter, Jane. I must see her. She is my grandmother."

The butler opened the door further and stepped back.

"Please…" Jane began, but she stopped when an elegant lady with white hair dressed in the most extravagant gown Jane had ever seen stepped to the door.

The lady gazed out at her. She held gold-rimmed eyeglasses to her face so she could look Jane up and down. Which she did, staring as if searching for the last piece of a particularly vexing puzzle. "You are James' daughter. Let the girl in, Giles, and show her to the study."

She turned to Captain Jameson and his men. "You may ride around back and stable your horses. Dinner and beds will be prepared. Come to the kitchen when you are ready."

Captain Jameson bowed, hat in hand. "Thank you,

your ladyship."

Jane walked beside the lady to the study. Giles opened the door for them.

The white-haired lady waited until Jane sat down before ordering a tea tray to the study.

Giles bowed his head and left to see to the task, his nose in the air, signifying his disapproval.

"I am Lady Aldetha Lenwood. What is your name, child?" the lady asked.

Jane stared at the lady's dress in awe. It took her a moment to realize the lady addressed her. "Lady Jane Lenwood, your grace. I am pleased to meet you." Her gaze lingered on the dress.

"Do you like my gown?" Lady Aldetha asked.

"I do. It is the most amazing thing I have ever seen!" Jane exclaimed.

The lady sat up a little straighter, a smile tugging at the corner of her mouth. "Did you hear her, Giles? My granddaughter likes my gown. She thinks it is…amazing." Laughter tinkled from her mouth as she repeated the word.

Giles sniffed audibly and sat a silver tray at the lady's knee. "I see she has your sense of…fashion," the butler said as he walked toward the door.

"Yes, it appears she does." The lady laughed again.

Jane listened as she studied the gown. Made of the brightest hue of blue Jane had ever seen, the bodice had vivid embroidery of red, black, yellow, purple, and orange covering the entire thing, front and back. The sleeves were tight and ended at Lady Aldetha's elbow. The full skirt was the same bright blue as the sleeves and around the bottom of the skirt was the same vivid embroidery as the bodice. Jane could not take her gaze from the gown.

"I was trying to emulate a peacock," Lady Aldetha said. "Did I do a good job?"

"Oh yes." Jane took a breath. Lady Aldetha's gown was exactly as she imagined a peacock should look.

Lady Aldetha smiled. She poured them both a cup of tea and leaned back on her plush red chair. "Now explain to me, child, from where did you come? Why do you knock on my door so late in the evening?"

"I come from Cumbria," Jane answered. "It has been a long journey, and I have nowhere else to go."

Lady Aldetha sipped her tea. "Why were you in Cumbria? James died in London."

"We lived in London until Papa died. Afterward, Mama married the Duke of Rathborne, and I have been at Rathborne Castle ever since."

Lady Aldetha nodded. "I believed you were in London somewhere," she said quietly. "Why did you not come to me when the Duke of Rathborne died? Despite the rift your mother caused between James and me, you were always welcome."

Jane glanced at Lady Aldetha. "Mama never spoke of you. The one time I asked about you, Mama said you did not approve of us."

Lady Aldetha set her teacup on the table. "Phyllis did not want me in your life. She was jealous of the time your father spent with me. When she learned she was expecting a child, she demanded James make a choice. He could have either her and his child or me. James suffered a great deal over her ultimatum. I told him his unborn child required a father more than I needed a son. The last time I saw either of your parents alive, they packed their belongings and left for London.

James wrote me of your birth. It was the only time he broke his word to Phyllis. He told me he had a red-haired daughter. I will never forget the day. He wrote he named his daughter Jane and I cried. The granddaughter I could not see had my name." Lady Aldetha smiled. "I do not think Phyllis realized my middle name was Jane, or she would never have agreed. The next message I received was a notice of James' death. I never knew what became of you. Your father was a kind and loving man. I grieved over his death for a long time. I saw his mischief in your eyes the second I laid eyes on you." She studied Jane's face. "I am pleased to put a face to the name after all these years. But tell me, child, why did you wait so long to come to me, and what caused you to do so now?"

Jane gazed at the old lady. Lady Aldetha was her grandmother, and this was the first time they met.

"Mama was with me at Rathborne until the duke's death," Jane bowed her head. "I awoke one morning to find her gone. I chased after her, hoping to convince her to return. In doing so, I fell from my horse and damaged my knee. It did not seem fair to force myself on you with my crippled leg. I thought Mama would come back. For this reason, I stayed and kept watch over the tenants and the castle."

Lady Aldetha took her hand. "It has been years since then."

"I never gave up hope," Jane answered. She whispered the words. When she said them aloud, they sounded so foolish. "Rathborne was my responsibility. How could I leave it? There was no one else." Then Max was there, and she was so busy reveling in his attentions she thought of little else.

“So, what changed that you leave Rathborne now?” Lady Aldetha asked.

“The current Duke of Rathborne, Thaddeus, is coming to live at the castle. I cannot be there any longer. I came to find my father’s family and ask if there is a place for me here.” She did not dare look up. She did not want to see pity in Lady Aldetha’s eyes.

“Of course, my dear.” Lady Aldetha’s face softened. “There has always been a place for you here. There is one condition to my agreement, however. You will call me Grandmama. I will rethink my decision if you address me by any other name. Do we have an agreement?”

Jane looked up. A smile lit her face. “Of course, Grandmama.”

“Well, now we have that out of the way, let us get you a bath and find you something to wear. I am afraid you smell from your travels. Once you are bathed, I shall give you a proper hug.” Lady Aldetha rang a little bell, and Giles entered the room. She gave her instructions and then rose to her feet. She walked toward the door.

Jane grabbed her cane and followed Lady Aldetha. She kept her gaze on the ground. “I worried you would not want me here because of my leg and…”

Lady Aldetha waved her hand. “It is part of you, and you are now part of us, so no more talk about your leg. We are all family here. Do not be embarrassed. Perhaps, sometime, you will tell me the rest of your story, but for now, we have other things on which we must focus our minds. The first thing is a bath and getting you to bed so you may rest after your long journey.”

****

Men servants arrived with a brass tub and placed it in front of the fire.

Lady Aldetha turned to Jane. “We shall discuss this in detail in the morning, Jane. For now, have your bath. I shall return afterward.”

“Thank you, Grandmama,” Jane said. She smiled and curtsied as Lady Aldetha walked away.

“Are the men being looked after properly?” Lady Aldetha asked Giles as soon as they were away from the bedchamber and Jane.

“They are in the kitchen, my lady. I told Cook to give them something to eat. You should listen to their story. Our girl gave them quite a time on the way here,” Giles said.

So, Giles liked Jane. Lady Aldetha smiled. He called her “our girl.” She did not comment. “I imagine Jane did, especially if she is anything like her father.” Lady Aldetha gave a little laugh. She entered the kitchen and motioned for the men to sit when they jumped up at her arrival. “Tell me of your journey,” she invited.

Captain Jameson set down his goblet and told her all that occurred. Every night they chased off villains or animals. Lady Aldetha made appropriate noises. She was amazed Jane dared to travel such a long way, but she was grateful she had. Now she would get the chance to know her only grandchild.

Lady Aldetha returned to Jane’s chamber sometime later. When she opened Jane’s door and slipped inside, she found Jane curled up in the monstrous bed asleep. She had one hand tucked beneath her pink cheek, and a smile curved her mouth. Lady Aldetha tentatively touched the girl's face. She closed her eyes and held steady for several minutes as the vision consumed her. After a time, she opened them again and stroked Jane's curly auburn hair. So that was the truth of it. She saw what she wanted to see. Smiling, she leaned down and kissed the girl. She wondered what James' daughter looked like. For years, she assumed her granddaughter was in London with her mother. Lady Aldetha would search the faces of everyone she passed when she visited London, curious about the girl. She hoped some face, somewhere, would look familiar.

Now, she had a face to go with the name. Contentment stole over her. She had her granddaughter, and she would see to it the girl had a future. She frowned as she considered the girl's limp. It must be dealt with. Several scenarios passed through her mind. She would settle a dowry on her. She had the money, and she would make sure Jane landed a gentleman. With her limp, she would require a fortune to hold her head up amongst the wolves of society. It would take Lady Aldetha's considerable skill to weed out the fortune hunters. They would come sniffing around when they learned the amount of money she intended to settle on Jane. Such things could not be avoided, unfortunately. It was a risk they must take to lure a worthy gentleman to the altar. First thing tomorrow, they would move to their London townhouse for the season. She would take Jane to Bond Street and get her dressed out as befitting her granddaughter. After that, Jane would make her curtsy to the king. With Lady Aldetha guiding her, the girl should be properly affianced within a few months' time. She knew everything of import in the girl's life and knew her course of action was the right one.

Chapter Twelve

Max followed Sir Harold through the trees and back to the main road, determined to get the parchment before it disappeared again. He did not get the chance.

A swarm of men dressed in black descended from the trees and surrounded Sir Harold. Max pulled his horse up short. There were too damn many of them for Max to battle. He swore in frustration as the men pulled Sir Harold from his horse and threw him to the ground. They tied his hands and feet and stuffed a rag into his mouth. An unmarked black carriage rode up in a cloud of dust. They tossed Sir Harold inside, and slammed the door shut. The driver whipped the horses, and the carriage raced off, surrounded by the men in black.

Max sat still beneath the trees. Who was Sir Harold caught up with? The carriage was the same one the mystery woman rode in. The one Max followed to the monastery.

He urged his mount into a gallop. He followed the carriage through York until it disappeared behind the gates of the same monastery as before. Max swore profusely.

He waited outside the monastery for a week. The carriage did not reappear, neither did Sir Harold. There was no other gate into the property. Anyone coming or going had to use the front gate. Discouraged, Max went back to his rooms to get some rest and plan his next move. He slept for a day and a half.

While at breakfast the next day, two men at an adjacent table discussed Sir Harold's death. His body was found the day before in the River Ouse by a local fisherman. Max lost his appetite. Now what? Without Sir Harold, he had no way to track down the traitor. He hit the table and rose to his feet. He wanted proof the bastard was dead.

On impulse, Max bought flowers and went to Roswell Estate. When he knocked on the door, a dour-faced butler answered. The man had white hair and a disapproving scowl. Max offered his condolences and the flowers. The butler took them without a word.

"May I offer my sympathy to Lady Melissa and Lady Emily?" he asked.

The butler led him to a small salon where Sir Harold lay on a bed of velvet in his best clothing.

Only Lady Emily was present. She sat on a stiff chair sniffing into a lace handkerchief.

"His Grace the Duke of Rathborne," the butler intoned.

Lady Emily rose to her feet.

Max approached, his eyes on the pale figure of Sir Harold Roswell.

Lady Emily extended her hand.

Max kissed her gloved knuckle and rose to gaze into her eyes. "My deepest sympathy, Lady Emily."

She inclined her head. "So, you are the Duke of Rathborne and not Mr. Radley. How delightful." She smiled. "Does Jane know?" She did not seem surprised.

"Does Lady Jane know of Sir Harold's death?" he countered. His gaze searched her pale face. She was dry eyed, giving no indication her sniffing was related to any form of sadness. He filed the information away. Perhaps her father's harshness made her immune to his death.

Lady Emily stared for several seconds. Then she shrugged. "I sent word as soon as we were informed." She dabbed her eyes with the lace-edged cloth.

Max studied her.

Lady Emily knew the appropriate response. She just did not feel it.

Max murmured an appropriate platitude. "I expected Lady Melissa to be present. I would wish her my condolences as well."

Lady Emily rolled her eyes. "She is visiting one of her many lovers." She sniffed. "With Papa gone, she has no one to see to it she behaves."

Max nodded. Jane said as much. He made his excuses and left. He returned to the tavern and packed his things. He had to find Andrew. Who knew where that damn parchment was by now? Without Andrew, there was no hope. The king expected them to find the traitor. Instead of finding one, the traitor framed Max as one.

He stopped by Andrew's rooms. Nothing changed. His message was still on the bed where he left it. Max groaned with frustration. Gertie was his only hope. He must return to Rathborne and get her to talk. She knew something. She had to.

Max rode out to the monastery one more time before he left York. A plain black carriage exited the compound and rolled out onto the main road. Max stopped in his tracks and waited for it to pass him. There was one occupant, *Father Brown.*

Max dropped his reins. What the hell was he doing

in York? This was too damn much coincidence for him. Max trotted his horse behind the carriage. Sir Harold, Gertie, and now Father Brown. Which one was the traitor? Who was in command? Sir Harold forced Gertie to call him "master," yet he was dead. Did the vicar kill him, and if so, why?

Max followed until they were away from prying eyes. Then, he rode alongside the carriage and encouraged the driver to stop with the point of his sword. When the carriage halted, Max warned the monk to stay where he was and pulled a quaking Father Brown from the carriage. He tossed the vicar on the ground and leveled his sword above the man's head.

"For the love of God, what do you want?" the vicar asked. His eyes were the size of goblets, and his hands shook where he clutched them to his chest.

"Someone stole a document from my chamber at Rathborne. In following the clues, my investigation has led me to you." Max narrowed his gaze at the trembling vicar. "Who do you work for?"

Father Brown shook his head. "I know nothing—"

Max cut his cheek with the tip of his sword. "Do not lie, old man. The last place Sir Harold was seen alive was this carriage. It took him to the monastery you just left. Explain it to me."

"Sir Harold is…dead?" The vicar's face paled.

Max studied him. "Yes. A fisherman found his body floating in the river. Why were you at the monastery? What is your connection to Sir Harold?"

Father Brown wiped the perspiration from his forehead and the blood from his cheek. "I was taught at the monastery. I know nothing of Sir Harold or his death."

Max leaned toward him. “Why were you in York?” The vicar knew something. His eyes darted side to side, and he sweated profusely.

Father Brown licked his lips.

“Think twice before you lie to me,” Max said. “Lady Jane will see the truth. She will tell me.”

Father Brown laughed. “You will have to find her first. Lady Jane left more than a fortnight ago.”

Max stilled. Then his heart rate increased. “Where did she go?”

The vicar laughed again. “She went south and good riddance to her. My employer wanted news. I came to York to let her know Lady Jane left.” He shrugged. “I will say no more.”

“Your employer is a woman.” Max digested the information. “Why does she care where Jane is?”

Father Brown smiled. “She wants Lady Jane to stay at Rathborne. It was easier to get information with her there. I do not ask questions.”

Max frowned. “All the stories in the village about Jane being a witch, you made up to keep her there?”

“A man has to eat.” The vicar chuckled. “I wished we could have burned her, but my employer wanted Lady Jane alive for a bit more.”

Rage roared in his ears. “Who is your employer?” He had to get to Jane. Who knew what trouble she was in by this time?

The vicar said nothing more. He smiled like a simpleton as if he knew something Max did not. “You will not be able to save her. She has outlived her usefulness.”

Max severed his head from his body with one blow. A weight settled in his stomach like a stone. Jane, his beautiful Jane, needed him. He would find her and save her. He had to. He could not bear to think of anyone hurting her. She was a gentle woman who deserved love and protection. Hell, she deserved happiness and everything which came with it.

The monk on the carriage made the sign of the cross over his breast with a shaking hand. "You have nothing to fear from me," Max said. "Unless you serve the same master as this devil." He indicated Father Brown.

"I serve God," the monk answered quietly.

Max nodded. "Tell the woman who commands you I shall sever her head from her body as I did Father Brown's if she touches one hair of Lady Jane's head."

The monk gazed at Max. He quivered with fear. "I serve only God. I do not know the woman Father Brown spoke of." He averted his gaze from the body on the ground and swallowed. "But if any woman asks after him, I shall relay your message."

"You may go." Max searched the vicar's pockets for the damning parchment. It was not there. Max used every swear word he knew. Where was it? Who had it? And who was the mystery woman Sir Harold visited with? He was certain she was the same woman who paid Father Brown to persecute Jane. Max mounted his horse and rode for Rathborne. He must question Gertie. Perhaps she had the answers he sought.

Max rode through the wrought iron gates of Rathborne the next day. He caught himself looking for Jane as he ran lightly up the front steps and walked inside. The transformation was astounding. Where once the castle was empty, dusty, and cold, now it gleamed with light and warmth. Servants in pressed uniforms hurried past, attending to their various duties. Max crossed the entry hall nodding with satisfaction. It was perfect, exactly the way it used to be. He walked down the corridor with pride, his gaze taking in the paintings, the mirrors, and the gleaming furniture. Freshly cut blooms scented the air with their sweet perfume. Satin brocade side chairs stood here and there, offering comfortable seating as one traversed the corridors. It was the way Rathborne Castle had always been.

Max entered the kitchens in search of Alfred. It was good to be back. He found the butler deep in conversation with Mrs. Patrick. His old face creased with worry.

Alfred stopped when he caught sight of Max. Mrs. Patrick turned to greet him as well.

"Sir," Alfred said, "how nice to have you back. We have an emergency which requires your immediate attention."

Mrs. Patrick curtsied. "Indeed, we do, sir. I am happy, as well, to see you home safely."

"What is it?" Max asked. "What happened?"

"It would be better if we talk in the library, sir." Alfred led the way down the corridor.

Once the three of them were in the library with the door closed, Alfred explained. "We do not know where Lady Jane is, sir. She left a little more than three weeks ago. When we discovered her gone, the captain and three of his men left to find her. We have had no word since." Alfred lifted his old eyes to Max.

"We were discussing whether we should send a messenger to find you. We know how important your errand was, and we were unsure if we should disturb you." He glanced at Mrs. Patrick. "Not only is Lady

Jane missing, sir, but we received a courier from the palace. The king demands you appear and make a report on your progress." He exchanged glances with Mrs. Patrick. "And Gertie was found dead this morning. The soldiers found her body hanging from a tree inside the castle grounds."

Max bit back his curses for Mrs. Patrick's sake. Gertie was his last link to the traitor.

"Why was I not informed of Lady Jane's absence?" Max asked. "I learned of her disappearance from Father Brown in York!" All this time, he believed Jane was at Rathborne, comfortable and warm, with plenty to eat and soldiers to see to her protection. But she was not here. Her whereabouts were unknown. He had to find her and bring her back to Rathborne where she belonged.

"Father Brown?" Alfred asked. "Good heavens!"

"Precisely," Max agreed. "You should have sent a rider the second you knew she left."

Alfred gazed at Mrs. Patrick then back at Max. "We waited, thinking you would return any day. We did not want to risk passing you in the forest. When you did not return as we anticipated, we did consider sending a rider."

Max ran a hand through his hair. "It cannot be helped now." *Jane*. He had no idea where she was. "Do you know why she went?" Max asked again as he paced. Lord, he was weary. He required a bath, some food, and a night's rest before he left for London. He had not made a report to the king since he left for York in October. It had to be done. There was no way out of it. He would look for Jane on the way. She had family near Oxford. His inquiries into the matter turned up the information. Perhaps she was there. He would visit Lenwood Estate as soon as he reported to the king.

"I do not know, sir. Everything was fine, and then she disappeared," Alfred said.

"She was…upset, sir," Mrs. Patrick said hesitantly.

Max swiveled to look at the housekeeper. "What upset her?"

"She felt out of place. She told me Rathborne was no longer her home and did not require her services."

Max sighed. He had so much to make up to her, and the list kept growing.

Chapter Thirteen

"I assume the carriages and my phaeton have arrived?"

"Yes, sir, the conveyances have been here for a week. The horses arrived four weeks ago," Alfred answered.

"Very good. Have four of the best horses hitched to my phaeton. I want a bath in my chamber and clean clothing packed for my journey to London." Max turned to Mrs. Patrick. "Perhaps I could get some dinner before my departure?"

"Of course, sir, I will see to it right away." Mrs. Patrick stopped. "Sir—"

At Max's questioning look, she asked, "What about Lady Jane?"

"I shall find her, Mrs. Patrick, and bring her home," he said. "You have my word on it."

Mrs. Patrick nodded and with a little bob, exited the room.

Max hurriedly bathed. His mind hummed the whole time. Jane was upset; this much was obvious. He had not meant to hurt her by keeping his identity a secret. She got so angry whenever he mentioned the duke's name, it never seemed like the right time to confess. How was he going to convince her he meant no harm? Or that he was not the villain she believed him to be?

As a young man, he fell in love with Lady Catherine Grayson. He fell prey to her wit and beauty, never realizing she was already married, as his father suspected. Lady Catherine worked her charms on him, filling his ears with her practiced lies, and seducing his mind with her body.

"She will tell you anything. Her purpose is to destroy my heir and lay ruin to my house," his father argued.

"To what end, Father? Lady Catherine wants to be my wife. She wants to be part of the family, not destroy it."

"Her father swore to destroy me because your mother chose me over him. He never got over her betrayal. Lady Catherine is steeped in the hatred and anger of her father. She seeks revenge for him. She wants your money, your title, and your honor. Heed my warning, son. She seeks to ruin you, and thus me."

He'd laughed at his father's words. The rest was as Jane told it. He chose the woman. Max went to Lady Catherine after the row with his father to find she was exactly what his father said she was. He found her drunk and naked. Her only adornment a fabulous ruby necklace from the famed Rathborne jewels. She laughed at the pain on his face. She railed at him for turning his back on the money and title. She called him stupid for believing she would ever want a Rathborne. She tore his young heart to shreds. It was a lesson he never forgot. Pride would not let him beg for his father's forgiveness. So, he joined the army as a common soldier, giving his mother's maiden name instead of his father's name.

Jane believed Mangus sent letters seeking

reconciliation. If there were letters, he never received them. When he returned to England years later, he learned of his father's death, but it was too late to do anything about it.

Max stirred himself from the reflections of his mind. He had to find Jane before anyone else did. Max dressed in the clean dark clothing he used for traveling and went in search of Mrs. Patrick.

Sometime later, he was once again on his way. He was heartily sick of traveling, but this time he rode on the high leather seat of his phaeton. Four perfectly matched bays danced in their harnesses as they waited in the courtyard. Mrs. Patrick hurried down the stone steps with a basket of food for his travels. Max thanked her and tucked the basket into the traveling box beside the case with his clean clothing.

"I am worried," Mrs. Patrick confessed. "Lady Jane is too protected to know what the world is like. She would trust anyone who approached her. She would not know all men are not gentlemen."

Max patted the older lady's hand. "I shall find her, Mrs. Patrick." Max jumped onto the seat of his phaeton, and soon he was traveling south at a very quick pace. Andrew would look for him in London. Perhaps he had better luck finding the traitor than Max did. If Jane were there, society would know.

Jane lingered at the back of his mind. Everything Mrs. Patrick said was true. His hope was in the soldiers who followed her. They would see to her safety. He could not bear to think of anything happening to Jane. He searched every face as he passed through villages and towns. Max asked at every inn and tavern for a lady who walked with a cane, but no one knew anything about her. The nights were the worst. When Max closed his eyes, Jane's brilliant blue eyes and sweet smile appeared. He would dream of bandits attacking her, and she could not get away because of the limp in her leg.

When Max arrived in London, he went to Lord Darham's townhouse. The servants had not seen him since he left for York with Max in October. Max went to Andrew's study and left a note detailing all that happened since they parted. Until a body was found, he believed Andrew was alive. Max closed the door to Andrew's study and asked the butler to send word if Andrew returned.

Discouraged, Max drove to the townhouse he kept in London. He poured a whiskey while his servants prepared a bath to wash away the dust of the road. He sipped the amber liquid and stared into the flames of the fire in his study. When King George sent him to find the traitor, his words were, "a lord in my kingdom betrays me to the Spanish King." Max sipped his drink. Did the king know the traitor was a man, or did he assume? Most men thought women were incapable of this kind of treachery. Max was the exception. His experience with Lady Catherine, among others, taught him better.

Max swirled his glass. Where did he look now? Every possible suspect was dead. The only person linking them all was Jane. Jane and Rathborne. He had to find her. He had to know she was alive and well. He had to see the sun turning her hair to fire one more time. He had to see the smile light her blue eyes and then her pink lips. He yearned to hear her voice. Max frowned. Speaking of voices. Perhaps the voices in her head could tell him where to look next. Max went to his chambers and stripped off his clothes. A gleaming brass tub sat before the hearth. He sank into the steaming water with a groan and relaxed in the heat. He stayed until the water cooled.

A manservant entered carrying a large Turkish towel. "Are you going out tonight, my lord?" The servant held the warmed towel out to Max.

Max nodded. "I will pay his majesty a visit. Tell Cook not to prepare dinner for me. I shall eat at the palace."

"Very good, your grace."

Max rose to his feet and stepped from the tub. He allowed the servant to dry him off and help him dress in clothes appropriate for court. He wore wine-colored breeches with stockings the same hue, a snowy white shirt, and a gold embroidered waistcoat. The manservant tied a stiff cravat into an intricate knot, and Max donned his topcoat. The topcoat was cream colored with boldly detailed gold and wine embroidery stitched around the wide cuffs, down the front, and around the bottom of the jacket. It was tailored to fit Max's broad shoulders and narrow waist exactly.

Max drove a set of blacks to the palace. He trotted them into the huge cobblestone courtyard, where he stopped with a flourish. Liveried servants ran to catch the harness of the dancing horses so Max could dismount. He followed the sentry through the elaborate corridors to the throne room. He found King George sitting on his golden throne, resplendent in his royal robes, waiting. The guard announced Max's presence. He waited until he was summoned, then he approached the throne and bowed low before the king.

"You have news?" the king asked sternly.

"Yes, Sire," Max replied. "Although perhaps an intimate setting is more appropriate for this conversation."

King George nodded his head. "Tomorrow at ten. I shall see you in my private apartments." He nodded at his councilors. "See he is on my daily schedule."

Max bowed. "Until tomorrow, Sire."

"You are welcome to join with my other guests. I will wager it has been some time since you enjoyed society," King George observed.

"I never enjoy society, Sire," Max answered.

"Like your father," murmured the king as Max walked away.

Max made his way to the great hall where dinner was served. He tucked in with relish. He listened to the chatter around him, hoping to hear Jane's name. If Jane were in London, he would know before the night was through.

****

Lady Jane Lenwood was a sensation. She was escorted by Lady Lenwood, one of society's leading ladies. Although she arrived in London but a few weeks previous, Lady Jane immediately caught the eye of the handsome Lord Dewhurst. A subject often discussed in the drawing rooms of society's elite hostesses.

The dashing gentleman doted on Lady Jane. He held her arm as she limped along at whatever function they attended, listening carefully to every word she spoke. He was highly protective of her and discouraged other suitors' attentions. There was a healthy throng once society's eligible gentlemen learned of the huge dowry bestowed upon her by her grandmother, Lady Aldetha Lenwood. Not one of the maidens making their debut in London was able to attract the attention of Lord Jonathon Dewhurst, one of this season's most eligible bachelors. He was too caught up in escorting Lady Jane to pay much attention to anyone else.

The envious crop of newly introduced debutantes pitied Lady Jane whether in a salon having tea, in the balcony at the opera, or limping awkwardly into a ballroom. She moved stiffly, leaning heavily on the arm of her adoring escort, her cane at her side. It simply was not fair for someone like her to receive the attention of such a handsome man.

Lady Jane had one of the most beautiful faces anyone had seen. Many of the more desperate lords declared themselves madly in love with her and hoped to be the one to wed her. Lady Aldetha had an excellent nose for sniffing out the fortune hunters who came to call. When she caught their scent, they left so verbally chastised many of them left London, and some left England altogether.

Lady Jane was extremely well dressed. She did not care about the latest fashion. A scandalous notion for any other single female. With Lady Aldetha at her side and Lord Dewhurst escorting her, she walked around in a golden bubble. Society looked on but kept their opinions to themselves. Many of society's leading ladies began copying her unique creations. Soon, everyone looked to see what Lady Jane wore to each occasion.

Her current dress mimicked a red rose from the intricate design of her bodice to the bottom of her full skirt. The fabric gave the illusion of rose petals sewn together to cover her. The bodice of her dress molded her slim form and fell in layered petals to the floor. Her skirt fluttered softly as she danced. The light of the chandeliers overhead caught the spark and fire of the diamonds she wore in her magnificent red hair.

Elegantly dressed nobility filled the white and gold ballroom of the palace. The men wore elaborate waistcoats with heavy embroidery, tight knee-length breeches, and heeled shoes. The ladies wore silk gowns of every shade, their hair piled high on their heads in elaborate designs. Jewels sparkled in the light of the massive chandeliers. An orchestra played the Courante.

Jane blushed and smiled widely at Lord Dewhurst as he twirled her carefully around the floor. Jane's leg was improving. She was able to maneuver through several of the more popular dances without her cane.

Lord Dewhurst pulled her closer and whispered huskily in her ear.

Jane nodded her head shyly, keeping her eyes on the floor. She was getting weary, and a breath of fresh air would be just the thing. She allowed Lord Dewhurst to lead her onto the terrace and down the wide stone steps to the garden below. Jane pretended she did not investigate every man's face hoping to see Max. She pretended she did not miss his laugh and the way he made her feel when he was nearby. She was safe with Max. A feeling Jane had not experienced since he left.

Lanterns were set along the garden path. Jane gazed at the beautiful flowers and the lights dotting the way as they walked. What she would give to be at Rathborne right now walking in the gardens with Max. She sucked in a breath inhaling the scent of roses, lilacs, and honeysuckle. If she closed her eyes, she might believe she was there with him, instead of here with Lord Dewhurst.

Once they neared a sparkling fountain well out of sight of the ballroom, Lord Dewhurst stopped. He drew her roughly into his arms, imprisoning her against him.

"I am determined you shall be mine and mine alone," he said thickly, his mouth settling on the side of her neck. He licked her delicate skin with his tongue.

Panic pounded in her veins. Alarm beaded on her forehead. She pushed against him to get him to release her. "Sir, you take too much liberty! Let me go!" She protested as his mouth moved up her neck to her ear. His hot breath smelled of liquor, making Jane want to gag. She quickly looked side to side. They were alone and too far away for anyone to hear her scream. Too late, she realized her predicament.

"I have not taken near the liberty I intend to!" he threatened. "I am going to make you mine one way or another, even if I have to toss your skirts right here in the garden. I need your dowry more than you can possibly know. The thought of all your money fires my blood. Once I have taken your virtue, your grandmother will have no choice but to give you to me. The dowry shall be mine!" he said. Then, his lips come down on hers!

Jane opened her mouth to scream. Lord Dewhurst's thick tongue thrust inside. His hands grabbed her skirts. Jane shoved at him with all her strength. Her heart raced. She knew she could never run away. Her only chance was to fight. She pushed against his chest, turning her head from side to side. He grabbed her hair in one hand and forced her head still.

Jane bit down on his lip with all her might.

Lord Dewhurst drew back in alarm. "You bitch!"

Bile rose in her throat. "I am going to be sick," she

warned.

He wiped the blood from his lips and pulled her hair, forcing her head backward. "I will make you pay for that," he said between clenched teeth. "I do you an honor, bitch."

She struck him with both hands, clawing any part of him she could reach. She would not fall prey to the man's evil plans. Lord Dewhurst had been charming until now. He listened to her opinions, held her arm when they walked together, and protected her from the attentions of other suitors. Now she understood his real purpose in being so agreeable. He was ugly, cruel, and evil. Nothing remained of the dashing young lord of the past couple of weeks. His kisses were hot and sloppy. His mouth was *everywhere,* and Jane fought the nausea rising in her throat. This was nothing like the way it was when Max kissed her. Sickened by the man's intentions, slobbery kisses, and groping hands, Jane stomped hard on Lord Dewhurst's toe, making him loosen his hold on her. She pulled an arm free and made a tight fist. She was going to hit him so hard he would forget who he was!

Suddenly, Lord Dewhurst was torn from her and sent flying backward into the rose bushes behind him.

****

"You shall die for this!" Max roared.

He'd caught a glimpse of the pair as he entered the ballroom. His heart skipped a beat. God, she was beautiful. The red of her dress should have clashed with her hair, but it did not. Instead, it caused her to stand out like a light in the darkness. He was drawn toward her like a moth to the fire. He frowned when he realized she was not alone. Lord Jonathon Dewhurst led Jane out onto the terrace.

Max strode toward the door. Friends and acquaintances stopped him several times. When he reached the terrace, they were nowhere in sight. Then Jane screamed. Rage fired his blood. He ran down the path to the fountain. There he found Jane being assaulted. Max tore the amorous lord from his sweet Jane and tossed him into the rose bushes as so much rubbish. By God, the bastard would pay for touching her.

Max turned to Jane to ensure she was all right. Her face was pale. Her hands shook where they clasped together in front of her. The man would die. Max turned to the fool stumbling from the rose bushes.

Lord Dewhurst stepped out onto the path.

"I demand satisfaction," Max said and punched him in the face.

Lord Dewhurst crumpled to the ground, unconscious.

Chapter Fourteen

"What are you doing alone with a man in the garden?" Max asked furiously. "Do you not know when you allow one of these young idiots to lead you outside alone, you can be ruined?" He ran a hand through his hair. "Good God, Jane. What if I had not come along?"

"He asked if I wanted to go outside for some fresh air," Jane said. "I did not think—"

"Correct. You did not think," Max said. "From now on, if you require fresh air, come to me. I will help you. Never let a man touch you again."

Jane took a step back. "Why are you here?" she asked, her voice trembling. She dreamed of him, saw him everywhere she looked, thought of him throughout the day, remembered the feel of his arms around her and his lips on hers, and then remembered who he was.

"I came for you, Jane." Max's tone gentled. He brushed a tear from her cheek with the pad of his thumb. "Do not cry. This time, I was here to rescue you. In future, do not be so foolish." He put an arm around Jane's shoulder and drew her close.

She stood stiffly, allowing his caress. Her body vibrated at his nearness. The trickling fountain was the only sound in the dimly lit garden. "Why have you come? How did you find me?"

Max stepped back. "I came because I care what happens to you. What were you thinking to leave the protection of Rathborne?" He looked her over from head to toe as if to assure himself she was unhurt.

Jane gazed down at the ground. "Rathborne is not my home. It is yours." She let the sound of the water calm her. The smell of the roses scented the air, and a cool breeze blew against her heated cheeks. Then she thought about his answer.

"You care for me?" she asked. Her gaze rose to his, searching for an answer. Her unruly heart skipped a beat. She missed him. She had not forgiven him for keeping his identity a secret. But she could no longer hate him as Thaddeus. She was intelligent enough to know he was not to blame for all she laid at his feet.

"Of course, I care," Max answered. "You are my ward and my responsibility."

Jane's heart sank. Her gaze dropped to the stone path beneath her feet. "Is this all I am to you?" What was he doing at the palace? Jane turned away from him.

Max narrowed his gaze as if confused. "What other reason is there?" He caught Jane's arm. She meant to pull free, but Max tightened his grip.

What other reason indeed. Every cell in her body urged her to hit him. "I do not require your assistance. Lady Lenwood is my guardian now," Jane said. "She is my family. Please step aside. I will go to her." Her chin went up a notch, challenging Max.

Max stood watching her face. "We shall go to your grandmother together. I will escort you."

"No," Jane said, rebellion in every line of her body. Who did he think he was to simply grab her arm and start giving out orders?

Yes," Max said at the same time. He stared into Jane's eyes as they fought a battle of wills, neither one willing to back down.

Jane flounced her shoulder in rage. She wanted to punch Max right in the face. She wanted to punch him for leaving her. She wanted to punch him for breaking her heart. Most importantly, she wanted to punch him for only caring about her as his ward. Jane flounced her shoulders again. Here she was, pining over him, and he thought of her as his ward. She ended up slipping and would have fallen except Max caught her around her waist.

"Are you going to behave while we search for your grandmother, Jane? If you keep on as you have, you shall lose your balance and injure yourself. In which case, I shall simply have to pick you up in my arms and carry you through the ballroom," Max said.

Jane was livid. "You would not dare!" she challenged. Every inch of her frame stiffened with rage.

"Oh, but I do." Max accepted her challenge. Before Jane could react, he swung her lightly into his arms and strode toward the terrace steps and the dancing inside.

"Put me down!" Jane yelled. She hit him with her hands, but she might as well have saved her strength for all the good it did. "Put me down this instant!" she yelled again.

Max leaned down and whispered in her ear. "If you raise your voice again, I shall have to silence you."

Jane gasped out loud. "You would strangle me?"

"No, I shall kiss you. It would be most effective in silencing your delicious mouth." He smiled wickedly.

Jane struck him again, but Max caught her hand. "Careful, love, or the entire ballroom will not only see me carrying you in my arms but will also witness a most passionate kiss between the two of us. If you open your mouth again, I shall be happy to prove my point."

Jane snapped her mouth shut. She had nothing to say. She did not doubt he would do as he said. Humiliated at being manhandled by Max, and concerned about what society would say, Jane closed her eyes to gather her strength for the ordeal ahead. She was not used to the stares and whisperings.

As she closed her eyes, Jane immediately became aware of the purely masculine scent of Max. For a minute, she was back at Rathborne, just her and Max in front of the fire. She breathed in deeply, smelling sandalwood, the starch of his cravat, cigar, and Max. Jane wanted to weep over the memories his scent evoked but now was not the time.

Then, it hit her. The vision filled her with its erotic promise. Suddenly, she was in bed with Max, naked. His scent was all around her. He rose over her and gathered her close in his arms. The heat of his body melted her resistance. The strength of his embrace molded her body to his. He kissed her lips and stroked inside her mouth with his tongue. He was everywhere, over her, around her, and inside her. Pleasure burst through her. Heat shot through her bloodstream. Her breathing quickened, and rapture such as she had never known permeated her. Jane gasped aloud, shuddering at the intensity of the scene she experienced.

"Jane."

Her eyes popped open. The cool of the evening brushed against her heated cheeks. She looked around. Music floated around her. People's voices drifted in and out. The scent of roses teased her nose. She was at the palace, in Max's arms.

You shall be lovers.

Panic assaulted her. What if Max guessed the reason for her discomfort? Jane patted her hair and tried to look normal.

Max stopped before entering the ballroom. His silver eyes bored into hers. His gaze traveled from her face to the rapid rise and fall of her chest. “Are you well?”

“I am quite all right. Unless you count the fact I am being manhandled by someone I violently dislike,” Jane lied. She was proud of the way she kept her voice even.

“You do not speak the truth. You do not dislike me. Quite the opposite, I would say. Judging from your heavy breathing and the delightful blush I see on your cheeks, you were thinking about me, thinking of us together. I can see it in your eyes. I feel it in your trembling body.”

Jane gazed at him in alarm. How did he know?

Max chuckled. “Do not worry, love, I shall not tell.” He stepped inside the crowded ballroom before she had a chance to answer him.

****

Every person stopped what they were doing as the wickedly handsome Duke of Rathborne carried Lady Jane Lenwood in from the garden. He held her close to his chest as if he carried something most precious. Lady Jane pasted a serene smile on her face. She nodded at everyone they passed as if being carried by the most eligible bachelor in England was a natural occurrence. Several of the ladies stared at Jane with jealous indignation.

“How does she do it?” Max heard one lady ask. “How can the Duke of Rathborne want her? He is so beautiful. He could have anyone. Why Lady Jane? She is so beastly. I do not understand it."

"Perhaps she has put some sort of enchantment on him, so he does not know of her flaws," another lady suggested. "My maid told me the peasants in the village below the castle where she lived believe Lady Jane is a witch."

The ladies turned toward the procession with varying degrees of envy.

"If she is a witch, I shall ask her to make a potion for me. I do not care if I do not get the most handsome man in England to pay his addresses to me, as long as I get one in the ranking somewhere," the first young lady said. Several of the other girls nodded in agreement.

The whispers rose around the room, and soon the whole ballroom was abuzz with the scene. It stopped when the Duke of Rathborne gently sat Lady Jane on an elegant settee next to her grandmother and turned to face the ballroom.

He glared at the crowd, as he turned to Lady Aldetha. "Good evening, Lady Lenwood." Max kissed the hand she extended toward him.

****

At the slight touch, Lady Aldetha froze. Her eyes widened at the scene before her. Then it was gone. She smiled up at the duke. "Good evening, your grace." Her sharp eyes noted the deep flush on Jane's cheeks and the way Jane's arm curled around the duke's neck as he carried her. She smiled as Jane drew in a deep breath, right before letting go of Maximillian as if his nearness comforted her. So, this was the missing piece. Lady Aldetha understood now, and it delighted her.

"May I call on you?" Maximillian inquired, his silver eyes gazing at Lady Aldetha questioningly.

"But of course," Lady Aldetha smiled. She could not be happier with the scene they were making. By morning, talk of the Duke of Rathborne and Jane would be all over London. "Shall we say tomorrow, for tea?"

"I shall be there," Max kissed Lady Aldetha's extended hand once more and turned to make his exit.

Lady Aldetha sat back. Maximillian took his leave, ignoring the hum of excited whispering. They were the talk of the town. Lady Aldetha hid a smile. Jane did not realize what she revealed with her attitude. She was in love with the Duke of Rathborne, although she may not admit it. Lady Aldetha sighed with contentment. Everything would work out. She could not hope for a better outcome.

Lady Aldetha turned to Jane. The fake smile she plastered on her face since entering the ballroom in the duke's arms was fixed permanently in place. Furious, Jane sat tall and stiff beside her. Her granddaughter did not like being the center of attention nor of everyone's conversation. Jane ducked her head to hide the blush staining her cheeks. Lady Aldetha patted her hands. It was time to go home. Nothing more could be accomplished tonight. What an altogether fabulous evening.

****

Lady Phyllis Rathborne smiled with malice. She kept her fan in front of her face to avoid detection. So, Maximilian was back in London and making a fool of himself over Jane. Lady Lenwood had the satisfied gleam of a matchmaker who made the pairing of the century. Lady Phyllis never liked the old bat. Jane was the only one who did not look happy. She sulked next to her grandmother, her arms folded tightly over her chest. This was interesting. Any girl would be flattered to have Maximillian's attention. So why did Jane act as one condemned?

Lady Phyllis caught sight of Max's face as he walked out. She was stunned. Maximillian wanted Jane. It took her a minute or two to digest the information. Her pride came to her rescue. She had plans for him. The only way she could control Rathborne was if Maximillian were dead. Now she knew he wanted Jane; Jane must die too. Maximillian had to be going crazy, wondering where the parchment with the details of the fleet was and why everyone who knew anything died. Lady Phyllis smiled with satisfaction. It was marvelous to return some of the pain she suffered for years. Maximillian would never have Jane. She would keep her just out of reach. Then she would kill her while Maximillian watched. Lady Phyllis licked her lips with anticipation. Once she got her hands on the Rathborne wealth, she would show the men in her life what she thought of them. No more blind obedience, no more sexual favors, and no more reporting everything she did. She would be the boss and do what she wanted.

But first, the destruction of Rathborne. There was more than one way to obliterate a man and his legacy. Maximillian was one of the wealthiest men in England. Not only did he inherit the land, castle, and tenants belonging to the Rathborne name and title, but he also had a diamond mine. The story was Maximillian joined the army after his fight with his father. He met and befriended a young man there. When the fighting ended, they decided to see the world. Together the two of them traveled until they reached Brazil. Maximillian invested all his army pay into a diamond mine, and his friend traveled on without him. The other partners in the mine died of smallpox a few years later, leaving Maximillian the sole owner of one of the richest diamond mines in the world. Sir Harold failed to find the document Mangus made for her. He had years to search Rathborne and bring it to her. Now, it was too late. Phyllis sent men to kill him for his incompetence. She would have to find the document before she could claim Rathborne.

Chapter Fifteen

Max stood legs braced wide apart. His hands were at his side. He held a rapier in his right hand as he faced Lord Dewhurst in the park. The early morning light settled softly on the vegetation warming the earth with its rays. Silver droplets of dew gleamed on the shimmering emerald leaves of the trees. Max waited for Lord Charles to signal for them to begin. His physician stood on his left, beside his valet. Lord Dewhurst's physician and second stared at them from across the way.

Lord Charles nodded.

Max nodded in return and lifted his rapier. He hated duels. He wished the morning were over so he could see Jane. First, he must teach this bastard a lesson for touching her. He saluted Lord Dewhurst and took his stance. "On guard."

Lord Dewhurst charged. Max deflected and stepped to the side. The young fool had no idea who he fought. Max stepped aside three more times as Lord Dewhurst trampled his way back and forth across the green. Max cut the side of his face.

Lord Dewhurst's eyes widened when he rubbed his cheek, and his hand came away bloody. "You will be sorry. My father will see you hanged."

Max shrugged. "Any man who interferes will be shunned. This is a duel of honor, and I will have satisfaction." He deflected two more blows. The boy had no training. His thrusts were short, and his attacks were wild and uncoordinated.

"I do not know why you want satisfaction. Lady Jane is a cripple. I took her time after time. There is no honor defending her." Lord Dewhurst's words sealed his fate.

Max stabbed him through the heart. "You lie. Lady Jane is yet a virgin."

Lord Dewhurst fell to the ground with a thud. His face streamed with perspiration. He looked wildly around for help. None was forthcoming. His eyes glassed over. "What?" he asked.

Max stepped up to his body. "You touched the wrong lady."

Lord Dewhurst died a second later.

Max handed his sword to his valet and waited while Sir Charles and the physicians examined the body.

"The Duke of Rathborne has satisfaction," Lord Charles announced. He shook Max's hand. "It was a clean fight."

Dewhurst's physician bent over the body as Max walked away. Max looked up, and his gaze clashed with Jane's. He frowned. The location of the duel was a secret. It was not the sort of thing a woman should witness. But Jane was not an average woman. He did not have to ask how she knew where he was. The voices in her head no doubt told her. He studied her face as he got closer, hoping for a clue on her mood. She stood frozen amidst the trees, staring at the body of Lord Dewhurst. Lady Lenwood's carriage waited on the cobblestone road behind her. He stopped two feet away.

"Jane," he acknowledged and waited for her to speak.

****

Jane swallowed the lump in her throat. Max fought a duel of honor on her behalf. Lord Dewhurst's body lay on the grass covered with a blanket. Her hands shook. For years she dreamed of a champion who would defend her honor. It happened. The thing she did not know was if he fought for her as Max Radley or the Duke of Rathborne? To him, it might not make a difference. But to her, it did. She would prefer he fought as her friend rather than her guardian.

Jane met his gaze steadily. "Why?"

Max stepped closer and lifted her chin so he could gaze into her eyes. "He insulted you and your honor. I am your protector. Lord Dewhurst answered to me for the wrongs he thrust upon you. Now everyone knows the fate they shall suffer if they offend you."

Jane dropped her gaze. He fought as the duke and her guardian.

"I will not allow you to be treated with disrespect." He studied her face. "This is no place for a gentle lady. I shall see you this afternoon for tea." Bowing slightly, he turned and walked away.

Jane waited until he was gone before she returned to her carriage. She mulled the situation over.

The voice woke her in the wee hours of the morning. Darkness still covered the sky.

He is in the green in the park. Go to him.

There you are," Jane said to the voice. "Where have you been?"

His enemy comes. Help him.

Jane sat up. "All right, I will. Why do you talk to me sometimes and ignore me the rest of the time?"

There was silence. “Did you leave me because I ignored you and left Rathborne?” Her head was quiet. Jane sighed and slipped from her warm bed. There could be only one reason for Max to be in the park at this hour. He dueled with Lord Dewhurst. She dressed hurriedly and sent for her grandmother’s carriage.

Jane anticipated a wounded Max when she arrived. She quickly realized Max was the better fighter. His fighting style was fluid and graceful, while Lord Dewhurst’s resembled a stampeding cow. Jane stood back in the tree line. She wiped her damp palms on the side of her gown and used her kerchief to remove the sheen of anxiety from her brow. Max was not dead. He was not wounded. He danced on the green evading the wild thrusts of his opponent with ease. She sucked in a deep breath and stiffened her knees to keep them from wobbling. Her heart rate returned to normal, and she was able to think clearly once more. Why had the voice sent her if Max was not in danger?

Jane stiffened when Lord Dewhurst said she was not worthy of a duel of honor. He bragged about taking her virtue. Max killed Lord Dewhurst with one thrust of his rapier. Jane’s hands trembled violently. Max could have killed his opponent at any time but decided against it until Lord Dewhurst spoke of her. She knew by the swiftness of Max’s retaliation. Jane leaned against a tree for support. For the first time in her life, she knew what it was to have someone care. Jane dropped her chin as tears filled her eyes.

He needs you.

“Why send me to the green? He was not wounded.”

Others come. You must be prepared.

****

Max was shown into the king's private study at ten o clock sharp. He poured a glass of whiskey and took his seat before the hearth. King George kept him waiting the better part of an hour. Max was not concerned. He spent the time thinking of Jane. She was surprised he fought for her. The look on her face told him as much. He did not like the notion she considered herself unworthy. Yet she did. What did he care of her twisted knee? It was Jane he loved, every part of her. She deserved far more than she had been given.

He swirled his glass. Max recalled the look on Jane's face the previous evening when he called her his ward. Did he dare hope she thought of him as something more than the hated Duke of Rathborne? Had she forgiven him? He realized when he thought he lost her, she meant more to him than he previously thought. He loved her. She occupied his thoughts and his heart. Her place at his side must be permanent, for he could not envision his life without her. He would marry Jane and make her his. Oh, he realized she was angry with him. He read it in her beautiful blue eyes. But there was also something else. For a minute there, outside the ballroom door, Jane was quite excited. Her heavy breathing and the pounding of her heart gave her away. She trembled in his arms. Was she having one of her visions? Maybe she saw the two of them together on their wedding night. A smile tugged at his lips. If she did, it probably rattled her composure more than a little.

Father Brown said Max would not make it to her in time, and Jane had outlived her usefulness. Max did not doubt the threat. Someone killed Sir Harold and Gertie.

The killer was not Father Brown. Max's enemy was out there waiting, planning for his demise. Without the protection of Rathborne, Jane would be a tool to get to him. The only way he could protect her would be to keep her by his side.

When King George appeared, Max filled him in on the meeting in York and Lord Darham's disappearance. He mentioned the document with the English Fleet but left out the part about the Rathborne insignia.

King George scratched his chin. "Sir Harold met the end he deserved. We wanted to hang the traitor ourselves, but it cannot be helped now." He gazed at Max. "Well done, Maximillian. Once you find Lord Darham, I shall reward you both."

Max frowned. "I do not know who supplied Sir Harold with the information on the fleet."

"We do," the king announced. "Sir Edward Matthews was found dead in his townhouse earlier this week. A confession letter was on his desk. All is well." He studied Max's face. "We have a new assignment for you. One we think you will enjoy."

Max looked up. "Sir Edward is too much of a coward to commit suicide," Max murmured. Once again, he lost a suspect.

King George made a steeple of his fingers. "Sir Edward would prefer to hang in private than in public. He betrayed us by allowing the information to leak from his office. He confessed to losing it. His was a just end."

Max bowed slightly. "As you say, Sire." He considered Sir Edward. He could not be the killer. He never left London. Max frowned. Unless he hired someone to do it for him. Mauldrin Kane came to mind.

The king studied him through half-closed eyes. "We are satisfied with the outcome. The case is closed. Sir Harold is the traitor. Sir Edward supplied him with information. Both men have met their end. All that remains is for Lord Darham to return. Once he makes his report, it shall be forgotten. This is cause for celebration." He rang for a tea tray and turned back to Max. "The new assignment we have for you is marriage." King George sat back in his elegant damask chair, his gaze on Max's face.

"Marriage, Sire?" One did not deny the king.

King George nodded. "Yes. We want you to take a duchess and ensure the continuation of the Rathborne line. The Rathborne's have been a great support to the throne for generations. We cannot allow the line to die out." He accepted the slice of lemon cake his servant handed him. "It occurred to us this past week if anything happened to you, we would have to find a new caretaker for Rathborne. Since you are the last."

Max stared at the floor, his mind whirring.

"Now you have saved England once more, you must save the Rathborne line. It is our royal command you take a duchess before the summer's end." He nibbled on his cake. "We hope to hear news of a new heir by this time next year."

Max was silent for several minutes. Marriage was his next move to protect Jane. A picture of her laughing face flashed across his mind. Max bowed to the king. "I am delighted to serve you."

King George held his hand out for Max's gesture of allegiance. "We thought you might."

Max left the room, his thoughts on the conversation. The real traitor was still out there.

Nothing ever fell neatly into place. When it did, it aroused his suspicions. Max reached the end of the corridor and turned left toward the front of the palace. He knew it was not over.

Max's mind wandered to Jane. They had much in common, an easy friendship and the same sense of humor. She was comfortable to be with. She had wit, charm, and a good mind. He enjoyed the time they spent in conversation. She would make an excellent duchess and mother. The passion and attraction between them would be pleasant to explore. He relived their kiss in his mind and heard the sounds she made in the back of her throat. She was curious and passionate. Max ran lightly down the palace steps. He would teach her all the pleasures they could give each other. Pulling his gold watch from his waistcoat pocket, he glanced at the time. He had one hour before he joined Lady Aldetha for tea. Smiling widely, Max thought of all the things he wanted to do to Jane as they joined to make an heir. Once she was his, he would spend his life making up for the wrong in her past.

****

"I will not go down, Grandmama. I know you have gone to a great deal of trouble for me, but I do not wish to see the Duke of Rathborne again." Jane folded her arms obstinately. She did not want to come face to face with Max ever again. She could not get the erotic vision of him and her out of her head. It replayed on her way home from the park. This time with more detail. They would never be twisted up together naked like they were in her vision. It hurt too much to think about, and she had to protect her heart before it became involved. She wanted no more visions. The only way to ensure it never happened again was to limit physical contact. Without the touching, she could control what she saw and hopefully control her destiny as well. Besides, she did not know if she could hide her thoughts and feelings if it happened again.

Lady Aldetha frowned. “He is the catch of the season, dear, and the wealthiest man in England. His bloodlines are impeccable. You can do no better than the Duke of Rathborne.”

Jane dipped her head. “I know. I heard it often enough from his father and my mother. They lectured for hours on the purity of the Rathborne legacy.” Tears filled her eyes as she looked up. Besides, how could she contemplate anything with him when he thought of her as his ward?

“What is it? Why do you cry when you are honored by such a wealthy and powerful man? Any number of ladies would gladly walk in your shoes,” Lady Aldetha said. She rose from her seat beside the fire and sat on the edge of Jane’s bed.

Jane swallowed the lump in her throat. “He thinks of me as his charge.” She twisted her fingers together.

Lady Aldetha smiled. “Is that all?” She stroked Jane’s red hair, her gaze thoughtful. “Have you forgiven him for being the duke?

Jane sighed. “I do not know if I want to. When he came to my rescue last eve, I asked why he was here. He said he came because I was his responsibility.” A tear betrayed her. Jane wiped it away impatiently. “When he was Max, we were friends. We talked, laughed, and had good times together. Now that he is the duke, I am a burden. I hate him for lying to me.” Jane threw herself backward onto her bed and folded her arms over her eyes. She acted like a child, but she did not care.

"Jane, my dear girl, many of the nobility travel incognito these days. It is safer to give a family name to those unknown to you than to give your title. The Duke of Rathborne did nothing wrong in giving you his family name," Lady Aldetha reasoned. "As for the other, do you think the duke defends every ward as fervently as he defends you?"

Jane moved her arms. "He has other wards?"

Grandmama nodded. "Maximillian brought several children from Brazil. They were orphaned when their parents died of smallpox. He keeps them in a home he purchased for them. They have a governess and a tutor, as well as an army of servants to care for them. All of London knows of his kindness."

Jane digested this. "I am sure Max cares for them the same."

"Are you? Yours is the first duel Maximillian has fought in defense of a young lady."

Jane shrugged. "Perhaps if one of his other wards were a young lady, he would do the same."

"I disagree. Two of his orphans are young ladies. They came out last year. They are both married to charming lords. Maximillian protected them, but he did not take a special interest as he does you."

Jane said nothing.

Lady Aldetha smiled. "Have you forgotten all he has done for you, child? I shudder to think what would have become of you if he had not shown up and cared for you last winter. His actions are commendable." Lady Aldetha studied Jane curiously.

Jane sat up. "It was winter. We were snowed in. He

was wounded, and I took care of him."

"Yet he spent a fortune returning Rathborne to her original glory. He did not do it for himself."

"That is exactly why he did it. He is used to having nice things. Rathborne is his castle," Jane muttered defensively. Grandmama had fallen prey to the duke's charms.

Lady Aldetha surveyed Jane through her gold-rimmed spectacles. "Do you honestly think a man as wealthy and powerful as the Duke of Rathborne challenges every man to a duel who touches something he should not? No, Jane, he demanded satisfaction because of you."

Grandmama believed what she said.

Jane dropped her chin.

"You must forgive him. Now, come downstairs and serve tea. We must see what the duke has to say," Lady Aldetha coaxed.

Grandmama was determined. Lady Aldetha had gone to great lengths to help her, and Jane could not disappoint her. Jane looked around for her gloves and put them on. If she had to meet the duke for tea, she would wear gloves as a precautionary measure. "All right, Grandmama. I shall come, and I shall try to behave."

****

Max stepped from his shiny black carriage drawn by perfectly matched blacks at exactly five minutes after three in the afternoon. He knocked on the shiny brass knocker attached to the heavy oak door of Lenwood Townhouse at seven minutes after three. He wore an elegant black top hat, wine topcoat, and black breeches, his long legs encased in shiny black boots.

His elegant marble-handled cane gleamed as he followed Giles into the blue sitting room where Lady Aldetha entertained callers. The ladies sat on a pale blue settee in the center of the room. A marble fireplace stood behind them. The walls were cream plaster with gold detail. A gleaming marble table stood before them. Lady Aldetha waved him toward the facing settee.

Max bowed over Lady Aldetha's hand, kissing her knuckles. His attention was drawn to Jane. She sat with her hands folded in her lap. She wore a lavender tea gown that heightened the delicate flush of her cheeks and drew attention to her wide blue eyes. Her glorious auburn hair was piled high on her head. Wisps of hair curled around her neck and face giving her a soft, elegant look. She wore pearls around her neck and in her ears. Ropes of pearls gleamed in the light as they moved in and out of her glorious red curls. Max frowned. She should be wearing the Rathborne amethysts. They alone would do her justice. Soon she would be his duchess, and he could adorn her with jewels of his choosing.

Jane refused to meet his eyes. She extended her hand for his greeting.

Max kissed her gloves and took his seat directly across from her. He noted the gloves and hid a smile. She saw them in bed together last night at the ball. He would stake his castle on it.

"Your gloves are delightful, Jane," he said. "So stylish, and yet I do not recall seeing you wear them before. Are you avoiding the bare touch of hands, or are you acclimatizing to London fashion?" She rewarded him with a glare and a blush that spread from her neck to her hairline.

Lady Aldetha poured Max a cup of tea, adding a cube of sugar. "Bare hands are frowned upon in polite society, but I miss it. One can learn so much more without gloves," she commented as she handed Max the teacup.

Max kept his gaze directed at Jane. She avoided eye contact and took the cup of tea her grandmother handed her.

"So, what brings you to London, your grace?" Lady Aldetha asked, sipping her cup of tea delicately.

"I came to speak with the king," Max answered. He blew into his cup to cool the hot beverage. The scent of the tea filled the air. He'd had a busy day so far. A sunrise duel, a meeting with King George, and finally tea at Lenwood Estates. He looked forward to this meeting most of all.

"Oh? Nothing serious, I hope," Lady Aldetha said.

"His Highness suggests it is time for me to find a duchess," Max answered, his eyes on Jane.

She sat silent. Her hand shook when she lifted the teacup to her lips.

Max smiled.

Lady Aldetha sipped her tea. "Do you have someone in mind for the position, or are you getting used to the idea?"

Max gazed at Lady Aldetha a long moment. The lady was certainly direct. They both understood why he was here. The question was, did Jane? "I come to formally ask your permission to take Lady Jane as my wife," Max's voice deepened when he said Jane's name. He set his cup on the table, and prepared for battle. His Jane had a temper, and she would use it. But he was not concerned.

Jane looked up. Her eyes were miserable. "I must decline your proposal. I have decided to remain unmarried."

"Jane!" Lady Aldetha said sharply, setting her teacup down, as well.

"I will only marry for love. This is my answer." Her chin rose a notch in challenge.

Max smiled. He expected as much. His Jane was stubborn, too. Max leaned back on the settee and crossed his long legs in front of him. One way or the other, Jane would be his duchess.

Lady Aldetha gazed firmly at Jane until Jane dropped her chin. A delicate blush rose to her cheeks.

"I was not aware I spoke to you, Lady Jane. I was speaking with your grandmother," Max said lazily, his gaze intent on the heart-shaped face before him. Her blue eyes flashed with anger and rebellion. Max turned to Lady Aldetha. "As I was saying, I have decided to take Lady Jane as my duchess. This is a matter of honor, after all." Max idly played with the handle of his cane as if they were chatting about the latest social event.

Jane's eyes narrowed dangerously.

Lady Aldetha turned to Max. "I pray you forgive my granddaughter, your grace. We are privileged by your presence and grateful you pay your addresses to her. Jane does not understand what an honor you bestow upon her. She has a volatile temperament. I am afraid it may take some time before she acquires a gentler disposition."

Max nodded his head. He doubted several years would do anything for Jane's disposition. Jane had a fire which was quite intriguing.

Lady Aldetha picked her cup up once more. She sent Jane a warning look. "So, you have decided on taking Jane as your duchess? I do hope, your grace, you are not put off by Jane's refusal."

"On the contrary, Lady Aldetha, I am very aware of Lady Jane's disposition. I expected as much. We were snowed in alone together for several months last winter and know each other quite well."

****

Jane's gaze shot up in surprise. Alone? The two of them? She gazed at Lady Aldetha in alarm. Max made it sound like they spent the entire winter alone. Fear clutched her chest. She could not marry Max. Her heart was too involved. He would destroy her. Grandmama would not believe him, surely. "We were not alone, Grandmama, there was also—" Jane began hastily.

Lady Aldetha held her hand up for Jane to be silent. "The two of you were alone? For months?" Lady Aldetha questioned. "This would be at Rathborne Castle?"

Max nodded. "It was impossible to get in or go out of the castle. The ice and snow lasted for weeks. It got so cold we ended up sleeping together in the antechamber to conserve heat." Max smiled smugly as Lady Aldetha's eyes widened at the picture Max painted.

Jane sat up straight. The rat! She could see what Max intended. If Grandmama believed her virtue had been compromised, she would insist on Jane's marriage to Max. "This is not true!" she yelled. This could not be happening. Jane's hand trembled so violently she set her cup down to keep from spilling her tea.

"Of course it is. Do you deny we slept in the

antechamber together?" Max asked, his gaze piercing her to her core.

"No, but—" Jane spluttered.

"Do you deny we shared the same settee to conserve heat? Do you deny we used the same blanket at the same time?" Max questioned with a wicked glint in his eyes.

Why was he doing this? Of course, they shared the settee, but they sat on opposite ends. They *were* wrapped in a quilt to stay warm, but they were well chaperoned by having Alfred, Gertie, and Thomas present. It was not as if they were naked doing whatever men and women did together when they were naked, but this was the picture he presented.

"Oh my!" Lady Aldetha exclaimed. Shocked, her hand rose to her bosom. "Is it true, Jane? You were alone with his grace, sharing his blanket and—" Lady Aldetha gazed questioningly at Jane, her cheeks pale. "You must tell me the truth, child, even if you are embarrassed or afraid of the consequences."

"I was," Jane answered, "but we were not alone, Grandmama—"

Lady Aldetha held her hand up for silence again. "Thank you, your grace. I am grateful to you for bringing this to me in private and offering to do right by my granddaughter. I shudder to think what should happen to my poor Jane if word of our conversation reached the ears of society. I understand you extend the offer of marriage to Jane out of honor, and so I accept your proposal. We shall plan a grand wedding to take place immediately. Not in haste, to draw attention to us, but as quickly as we can."

Max nodded with apparent satisfaction.

Jane sat still in horror. She looked around for a means of escape, but Lady Aldetha placed a hand on her arm.

"Jane, dear, you are to accept his grace graciously for his kind offer. I shall leave you two alone for a few minutes as I discuss with Giles the wording for the engagement announcement in tomorrow's banns," Lady Aldetha said. She smiled as she sailed across the room toward the door.

Max stood up once Lady Aldetha left the room. "Come, my dear, let us seal our engagement with a kiss." He held a hand toward Jane.

She ignored it. "How can you do this?" Jane asked. "How can you lie to my grandmother and make her think we…that you…you bedded me?" Jane finished weakly.

"Is that what I did?" Max asked innocently. "Your question is rather odd because I thought I told her we spent the winter alone together, which we did if you think back on it."

Jane jumped to her feet, indignant. "You know what I mean!" she yelled. "You deliberately made it sound like we were in a bed together." Jane's voice dropped to a whisper. She did not want Lady Aldetha to hear her talking to Max.

"We were in a bed of sorts," Max reasoned. "After all, you did sleep there, did you not?"

He was enjoying her discomfort. Jane could see his amusement, and it made her furious. "Why do you ask Grandmama for my hand? What happened to your search for a traitor? You cannot want to marry me." Jane switched the subject of their conversation on him. "You only care for me as your ward, remember?"

****

"I ask for your hand because I want you as my wife." Max frowned. "My search is at a standstill, and this is a conversation for another time. I do know your life is in danger, and I cannot allow it. What better way for me to protect you than as your husband?" He waited for her to say something. When she was silent, he added, "I missed you."

Emotions chased across her face. Still, she said nothing.

Max sighed. She meant much more to him, but it was all he was willing to give her at the minute. She put him through hell when he returned to Rathborne and found her missing. Fear such as he had never known settled around his heart. He was sure Jane caused his fear with her inability to take care of herself. He had his second moment of torture when he spied Jane in London, at the palace, engaged in a kiss with some lecherous fool out in the garden. His satisfaction at killing Lord Dewhurst was all-inclusive. Jane belonged to him. He knew she would never agree to be his wife without a push from her grandmother. Max studied her through the slits in his eyes. He did not doubt she intended to fight him over this marriage, but he would not take no for an answer. They belonged together. He could see it if she could not. Her vision should have convinced her. Max pulled her into his arms and lowered his head. He sealed their engagement with a soul-consuming kiss.

Chapter Sixteen

London buzzed with the news. The Duke of Rathborne was to be wed. He married the unsightly Lady Jane Lenwood. They appeared together for the first time at the palace. The king planned an elaborate engagement ball to celebrate the occasion. King George made the announcement in court the day after the banns were read.

The Duke of Rathborne wore a heavily embroidered navy-blue topcoat. His snow-white cravat was tied in an impossible knot. His waistcoat gleamed gold beneath the millions of lights suspended over the massive ballroom. He wore navy-colored breeches and stockings. His feet were encased in the newest style of heeled shoes. He was a magnificent specimen of manhood, standing a head taller than most of the men in attendance. His broad shoulders filled out his jacket in such a way the ladies sighed with delight over the manly picture he presented.

Lady Jane Lenwood appeared at his side, her slim figure draped in light pink silk. Her gown had a low square neckline adorned with dark pink roses. Bell sleeves fell from the tight bodice and ended with a cascade of delicate lace at her elbows. She wore a satin belt adorned with dark pink roses around her tiny waist. It was the skirt that caused the ladies of the court to look at her in wonder. For Lady Jane did not wear the panniers that were so fashionable at the time but instead wore her skirt full and longer in the back, creating a small train as she walked. The same dark pink blossoms that circled her waist and adorned the neckline of her gown were embroidered on the bottom of her full skirt. She was a fitting match for the duke, were it not for the lady's limp.

****

Jane allowed Max to help her as they descended the stairs to the ballroom.

"Smile, love, or those watching will think you are not happy with our impending nuptials," he whispered into her ear.

"I am not, as you well know," Jane whispered back.

Max stopped their descent and tilted her chin up so he could look into her blue eyes. He leaned in close. "This matter stays between us. Do not drag the gossips of London into our disagreement."

Jane swallowed at the intent in his eyes and nodded her head. She would behave while they were in public, or he would sweep her into his arms and give her very public, extremely passionate kisses for everyone to see. He made sure she understood the consequences.

Max smiled tightly and placed a chaste kiss on her upturned lips.

Jane blushed to the roots of her hair when the king cleared his throat to get their attention.

"Let us begin the dancing Rathborne. You shall soon have Lady Jane all to yourself." King George chuckled with amusement.

Max bowed toward the king and continued leading Jane down to the ballroom. He swung her into his arms and pulled her close against him once they reached the dance floor. Jane placed her hand on his shoulder and let him lead her in the dance, her traitorous body responding to the closeness of his. The strains of the music floated around them. Jane was aware of Max's heat. Scenes of the vision danced inside her head. Max's muscular body rising over hers, the passion of his kiss, his hands everywhere, and the pleasure she experienced when he joined their bodies together. Jane dipped her head so Max could not see the longing in her eyes. She wished with all her heart he stayed Max Radley, her companion, confidant, and friend. She could not look at him the same now she knew he was the Duke of Rathborne. Such things were foolish to dwell on, but she could not help it. She needed a friend to tell her what to do and help her through the troubled times ahead.

"What has you frowning so, love?" Max asked in her ear. "Are you in pain?"

"No," Jane answered. "I am thinking."

Max frowned. "Are you worried about the wedding?"

"No," Jane said. "Grandmama said it was nothing to worry about."

"I shall be gentle. There is no reason to fear me or our life together." Max caught her against him. His lips hovered over hers.

Jane shivered with desire. She shook her head to rid her mind of its erotic thoughts.

Another comes who seeks your life.

"There will be men among the crowd to see to my safety." She said the first thing which popped into her mind.

“I will see to your safety,” Max said. “I am your fiancé, and it is my duty to see to your happiness.”

“The traitor is not dead.” Jane stared into his eyes.

“I know.” Max turned Jane around in the dance. “Do you doubt my ability to protect you?”

Jane sighed. “No.” She doubted her ability to protect her heart. Her vision had been correct after all, despite her denial. Max would be her husband, and there was nothing she could do to stop it. The future terrified her. The traitor wanted Max dead and the destruction of Rathborne. The traitor wanted her dead, too, but Max was a fierce fighter. He would keep her safe. Her only consolation was Rathborne. Once they were married and living at the castle, things should be simpler. At Rathborne, she knew her way around, accepted who she was, and understood what was required of her. At Rathborne, she would see the traitor coming.

Max led her to a chair once the dance was over and went in search of the king.

Jane spent the evening in a blur of congratulations and introductions. The bright lights and brilliantly colored gowns of the ladies danced before her eyes. Her head whirled with confusion. Everyone wanted to meet her and give her their best for her upcoming marriage. She closed her eyes and wished for a quiet corner to gather her thoughts. Perhaps there, her head would stop spinning. She looked around for Max and caught sight of him sitting next to the king, deep in conversation. She motioned for a lady’s maid and asked for an escort to the lady’s privy. The maid helped Jane down the maze of corridors and inside a small room and closed the door behind her. Jane sank onto a nearby chair and bowed her head. When the room quit spinning, Jane contemplated her future. There was nothing to be done. Max and Rathborne were her destiny. The voice in her head confirmed it.

With a sigh, Jane left the little room and turned to go back to the ballroom. Cautiously, she walked down the corridor; her limp pronounced from all the dancing.

A footman appeared at her elbow with a note. "I was asked to find you, my lady, and give you this."

Jane took the note and read it.

I have something of import to tell you. Come to the library. I will be waiting. PR

Jane read the note again. She did not know anyone with the initials PR. Jane stood uncertain of what to do.

"I am to escort you to the library, my lady," the footman said.

Jane nodded her head and took the footman's arm. He led her to the library and held the door open for her to enter. He shut the door quietly behind him.

Jane let her eyes adjust to the darkness of the room. Only a few candles lit the interior besides the large fire in the hearth.

Danger. Beware.

Jane turned. There was a dark blur behind her. Pain exploded in her head, and everything went black.

She woke on the floor. The room was full of smoke. It stung her eyes and burned her throat. Jane blinked rapidly, trying to focus. Tears leaked from the corner of her eyes, and her head ached. She sucked in a breath and put a hand over her mouth, resisting the urge to cough. A man moved around the room. He was a small, thin man with dark hair. He wore a thick sweater and dark coarse breeches. He tore the drapes from the windows and ripped the cushions from the chairs. He had his back to her.

He came to kill you. He makes the room appear as if there was a fight.

Jane's hand trembled. She wiped the perspiration from her forehead. Max. She needed Max.

He will burn you alive.

Jane closed her eyes and focused on Max. She put every ounce of strength she had into calling him.

Max, please help me. I am in the library.

She said the words in her mind, willing them to fly to Max's ears. Her arm and side ached. She rolled slowly onto her stomach and looked around for her cane. It lay on the floor to her right, just out of reach. She glanced at the man.

He muttered beneath his breath, cursing as he worked. He did not know she was conscious.

The man is dangerous. Beware.

She inched her way to her cane.

He pulled books from the shelves and tossed them on the floor.

Hurry. Hurry.

The man looked around and grabbed a chair.

Jane swallowed. He was evil. The air was thick with it.

The man broke a leg off the chair and held it in the flames until it caught fire. Smoke billowed from the hearth, making it difficult to breathe.

Jane's heart thudded in her chest. She reached for her cane, her gaze on the man. She caught the tip of it with her fingertips and pulled it toward her. The cane rattled on the wooden floor.

The man looked up. "So, yer awake." He laughed.

A cruel high-pitched sound. He held the flaming chair leg to a pile of pillows and cushions. Smoke billowed up as the fabric burst into flame.

"Why are you doing this?" Jane shuddered as the flames grew higher.

The man turned toward her. He held the burning chair leg in front of him as he approached. He laughed. "Fer gold. If I kill ye, I get more."

Jane stiffened. "More? What have you done?"

The man laughed. His beady black eyes glimmered in the light of the fire. "I kill people."

Jane shivered. Fear shimmied down her spine. "Who?" The smoke rose, making it difficult to see his face. Jane was on the floor, where the air was clear. She inched her cane into position. As soon as the man got close, she would trip him with it.

The man's laugh split the smoke. "Yer cook screamed like a baby."

Jane stilled. "You killed Gertie?" Her heart rose to her throat. Her mouth went dry.

The man's face appeared in front of her. His eyes gleamed. "Among others." He stepped closer.

Jane quaked in reaction. "Who else?"

He shrugged. "Does it matter? You will soon see them in hell." His gaze moved over her face. "I been looking forward to this all day."

Now!

The man took a step, and Jane swung her cane wide. The thin little man tripped and fell hard. The burning chair leg skidded across the floor. Jane reached for it. She could just touch the tip of the leg.

The man groaned and rubbed his head.

Hurry. Hurry.

She stretched her body as far as she could and grabbed it. She glanced at the man.

He pushed his head up from the floor, scowling at her. "Yer going to die!" He rose to his feet and rushed at her.

Jane sat up and swung the burning leg with all her might. She knocked him off his feet.

When he landed, he shook his head and sat up.

Anger surged through her. Her vision of Max tangled up with her in bed danced in her head. If this weasel killed her, she would never know what it was to mate with Max. "I am not going to let you hurt me!" She swung again and hit him on the side of the head.

"What tha—" He blinked and fell forward.

Jane trembled in reaction. She dropped the burning leg and shuffled backward as fast as she could. The weasel lie face down on the floor. Blood dripped from a wound the chair leg made. Her hands shook. The settee with the pillows was ablaze. Red flames licked the draperies. The room was sweltering. Jane looked up at the latch. The door was locked.

"Jane!" Max's voice was on the other side of the door. The latch rattled.

Move. Cover your face.

Jane moved back and buried her face in her arms as the library door splintered into a hundred different pieces. When she opened her eyes, Max stood before her.

His gaze took in the room in one sweep, and then he was beside her gathering her into his arms.

Jane touched his face and was instantly transported to a different time and place. She stiffened and then slumped against him.

****

"Max."

Max looked up. He could have sworn he heard Jane's voice. He studied the ballroom. She was nowhere in sight. He made his excuses to the lord he conversed with and searched for Lady Aldetha. Her grandmother might know where she was. He found Lady Aldetha sitting alone, gripping the head of her cane.

She looked up as he approached. Her lips were pinched with agitation. "Something is wrong. My granddaughter is in trouble. You must find her." Lady Aldetha touched his sleeve. "I sent footmen to the gardens and the dining hall. Jane is not there."

A large stone settled in Max's stomach. "I will search the corridors. Send footmen to the antechambers." Max hurried off.

He strode through the corridors looking in every room. There was no one around but the servants. When he asked after Jane, a young footman told him a lady paid him to give Jane a note and escort her to the library. Max thanked the man and hurried to the library, hoping Jane was still there. He smelled smoke the second he turned the corner. It billowed under the door. Max froze as the implications swam through his mind.

"You will not be able to save her." Father Brown's voice played in his head. Anxiety tightened his chest. He failed her! Max ran to the door and tried the latch. It was locked. He kicked the door with all his might. The door split, and he strode into a smoke-filled room. His gaze darted here and there and settled on Jane sitting on the floor at his feet.

Chapter Seventeen

She shuddered and shivered in his embrace.

Max glanced at her face with concern. He strode down the corridor with Jane in his arms, yelling for help. Manservants appeared, and Max indicated the library behind him. "Get some buckets of water and sound the alarm. The library is on fire."

Menservants raced to get the fire under control.

Max found an antechamber free of guests and sank onto a settee holding Jane close.

She was pale, and her eyes were glazed over. Jane moaned and tucked her head under his chin. She huddled against him as if she were freezing with cold.

Max stroked her hair and whispered encouraging words in her ear. He knew what ailed her. She was immersed in a vision of epic proportions. The only aid he could offer was to hold her as it drained her of her energy with its fierceness. When she went limp in his arms, Max felt the side of her neck for a heartbeat. It was faint but steady. Thank the gods. His own heart started beating again. Max held her close and kissed her forehead.

For long minutes she remained still as death. Then, her eyes fluttered and opened. She gazed at him in confusion. "Max?"

"I am here, Jane. Everything will be all right. Hold still for another minute until you get your strength back." He stroked her back to soothe her. Max closed his eyes. For several god-awful moments, he thought he lost her.

Jane leaned against him. She rested her cheek against his chest and breathed in deeply. Her tears soaked his shirt.

"Jane, what is wrong?"

"Nothing." She sighed and rose unsteadily to her feet.

Max stood and offered his arm for support.

Her legs wobbled. Tears dripped down her cheeks. She gazed at him in confusion.

It was too much. The need to protect her surged through him. Dammit to hell! He should have noticed how long she was gone. He scooped her up and sank back down on the settee. "Do not cry, love. I am here."

She shoved against his chest and tried to move off his lap.

"You must give yourself a few more minutes to recover." He tugged her back into his arms. "Why did you leave the ball?" He hoped she trusted him enough to tell him what vision held her prisoner to such an extent.

"I needed the privy. When I came out, I got lost."

Max nodded slowly.

She dropped her gaze and said nothing more.

"You have not had a vision so intense before. What did you see?" he asked gently. "Are you in danger?"

Jane looked up. "It is nothing. I saw part of a future event. Until the rest is shown to me, I have nothing to say."

Max gritted his teeth silently. What had she seen? Why would she not share it with him? Hell, she would not even look at him. Jane usually brought her troubles to him. At least, she had when he was Max Radley. She must get used to the idea that he was the same man with whom she'd spent the winter. Once she did, she would confide in him once more. Max sighed. He would give her time.

"Come, love, we must get you home to bed so you can rest your knee," Max said.

Jane nodded her head weakly.

Max sent a servant to the ballroom with a message for Lady Aldetha. Then he carried Jane out to his carriage. He laid her gently on the thick velvet seat and covered her with a soft blanket. He tapped on the roof with his cane to let his coachman know they were ready and studied Jane's face as the carriage traveled down the narrow cobblestone lane.

"How is your knee?" he asked gently.

Jane opened her eyes and gazed at him. "Do you genuinely care how my knee feels? You do not need to pretend when we are alone."

Max leaned forward and lifted her chin. "I truly care how your knee feels, Jane." His mouth came down on hers. He kissed her gently, tenderly. His lips and tongue teased her until she opened her mouth. With a groan, Max slipped his tongue between her lips. His hand cupped the back of her neck to steady her against the onslaught of his sensual assault.

****

With a whimper, Jane wrapped her arms around his neck and pulled him closer, returning stroke for stroke as his tongue plundered her mouth. After the vision she just experienced, she needed to feel the steady beat of his heart. *They* were in danger. Rathborne was in danger. Jane trembled with fear. She needed him to hold her tight until all else ceased to exist. She reveled in the heat of his body next to hers. There was only her and Max like it had been the winter before. All she could think about was Max, the way he felt, the way he smelled, and the way he touched her. She was shameless in her desire for him.

He picked her up gently and sat her on his lap. She gasped when her backside met his arousal beneath her. He was so hard, so muscular, and so warm. Max stroked inside her mouth repeatedly. His hand found her soft full breast. He squeezed her gently. Jane whimpered loudly and tightened her arms around him. Her nipples were hard, pressing against the fine silk of her chemise, wanting Max's attention. Jane had never experienced anything like the emotions Max created inside her. Jane could not get close enough, and Max must feel the same way. She wanted to forget everything she saw and heard. She would drown out the cries with Max's growls against her lips. She would erase her powerful vision in a cloud of scandalous delight. She wanted to submerge herself in Max and the sensual, forbidden things he did to her. He moaned when she squirmed against him and dropped a large hand to clamp her hips in place. He stroked his tongue along hers and rubbed her taut nipple beneath the fabric of her dress and chemise. Jane cried out with rapture, arcing against him to get more.

****

Max's mouth went dry with anticipation as he reached for the laces on the back of her gown. He pulled them free and pushed her gown off her shoulders. He made quick work of her stays. He tore them from her body and tossed them on the seat beside Jane. He stared into her slumberous eyes as he reached for the neckline of her chemise. He could see her full breasts through the thin silk. Her nipples strained against the fabric. Slowly, he pushed her chemise off one shoulder and then the other. Jane put her hands over her breasts to hide from him, but he caught her slim wrists with one hand and gently kissed her palms.

"Show me, Jane," he said huskily. "I want to see all of you." He bent his head and kissed her gently on the lips as he pulled her hands slowly away from her breasts. His gaze heated. Max tilted her face up to his. "You are beautiful, Jane, so exquisite, and so perfect. Let me show you how enchanting you are." He gazed deep into her eyes and then slowly lowered his gaze. She was what every woman should look like without their clothing. God, she was beautiful. Max stared at her full round breasts. They were perfect. Her rosy nipples stood erect like sweet berries ripe for sucking.

He kissed her soft lips and reached for the fullness of each breast. He squeezed them and measured their weight with his hands. His thumbs rubbed back and forth over her erect nipples. Jane shook with sexual excitement. Heat flooded between her legs. She squirmed against him, breathing raggedly. Max plundered her mouth fully. Suddenly he wanted to feel Jane against his naked chest, her skin against his. With shaking hands, he removed his topcoat and cravat. He dropped them to the floor. His shirt followed.

Jane rubbed against him. She looked down in surprise when his chest hair tickled her sensitive nipples. She gazed at his muscular chest with its dusting of dark hair and trembled

Max groaned when she rubbed her chest against him. He wanted to lay her back, part her legs, and plunge inside her. He throbbed with need. She was perfection, and soon he would show her how much he wanted her. Jane quaked against him. He stared at her. Her hair framed her face with glorious red curls. Her eyes were closed, and her face was flushed. Her pink lips panted with the rapid rise and fall of her chest.

"God, you are so beautiful." he rasped. He stroked her back with a soothing, circular motion and bent his head toward her breasts.

****

Jane gazed into Max's eyes and saw the fire burning there. He wanted her! He was not disgusted at the sight of her. He was here, looking at her naked chest, his eyes heavy with passion. He had not turned away. Instead, he was stroking her back and kissing her with an urgency that reached the pit of her stomach. Excitement hummed along her spine with every touch of his knowing hands. He felt so good, so warm, and so male. She wanted more.

Max gazed into her soul as he slowly bent his head to her breasts. She thought she died of pleasure when his lips closed around her nipple, and he began to suckle. She cried out, arcing against him. He pulled her deeper into his mouth while his hand tugged on her other nipple. Heat flooded her body. The space between her legs ached. She squirmed against him, anxious to feel more. His hands and lips worshipped her. Jane closed her eyes and leaned back, giving him full access. Max lifted his head and pulled her other nipple into his mouth. Ecstasy swept through her and settled between her legs. Moisture gathered there. Jane arced against him, rubbing her bottom against his swollen member. Max groaned out loud.

"Max," Jane whispered huskily, her legs restless with desire. Her breath coming fast. She wanted Max inside her, filling the ache. Max lifted her and laid her back against the soft velvet seat. He pulled her skirts up and parted her legs. Jane thought she would die if he did not touch her soon. Then he settled himself between her legs. Jane's forehead broke out in a fine sheen of anticipation. "Max," she groaned. When his male member pressed against her throbbing core, Jane shuddered. She was incapable of thought. She lifted her hips and rubbed her pelvis against him, shaking with need.

"Shhhh," Max whispered in her ear. "I will take care of you." He rocked back and forth against her. "Do you like what I am doing to you?" he asked. His hand slid under her skirt and up the inside of her thigh.

"Yes." Jane gasped, trembling violently as his hand inched closer to her heat. "Touch me, Max. Please touch me."

He tugged her drawers down her legs and slid his finger between the folds of her femininity.

Jane's breath hissed from her parted lips. "More. I want more. Max, please. I am going to die if you do not touch me."

He took her mouth in an open kiss, plunging his tongue into her sweetened depths as his fingers probed the lips of her mound. Jane could no longer breathe. She was faint with anticipation. Then his finger touched her swollen, aching sheath. Dizziness assailed her. Max stroked her tongue as his finger slowly penetrated her. Jane came off the bench grasping his shoulders. His finger penetrated deeper. Jane shuddered. She pulled her head back to suck in a breath. She had never been so alive. Her arms grasped his shoulders in a death grip. "Max, please. Please, Max," she chanted.

He pulled gently away to catch her nipple in his mouth. He gazed deep into her eyes as he suckled. His finger withdrew and then slid inside her again. Jane whimpered. He slid his finger in and out of her, creating a rhythm. Jane's trembling increased with the tempo of his rhythm. Then he slid two fingers inside her. Jane fell backward, oblivious to all else but the feeling of his fingers stroking the heated ache inside her. It was so good. She lifted her hips to take more of him inside. Her body shuddered and spasmed around his intrusion. She did not know what her body reached for. She only knew she did not want Max to stop.

He worked his fingers in and out quickly, increasing the tempo. Jane fell apart in his arms. She screamed his name, splintering in a million jagged pieces. Max stroked her again and again. She shuddered violently with each thrust of his finger. It went on and on. Jane thought she died and went to heaven. When the last tremor stopped, she lay limp in his arms. Her hair stuck to the sides of her face. Her cheeks flamed with color. She smiled up at him and blushed, not knowing what to say.

Max's silver gaze rested on her heaving chest and then her parted lips. He smiled into her eyes. "Was it good, love?"

"Oh yes." She took a deep breath. "Were we mating? I thought," she blushed. "Well, I thought a man had to be naked too."

Max's gaze was hooded. "This was but a taste of

what we shall enjoy on our wedding night. You are yet a virgin. I merely showed you what your body is capable of."

Suddenly, Max stiffened. He took a quick peek from behind the heavy drapes covering the carriage window. They were turning down the street by Lenwood Townhouse. Max drew back slowly, pulling Jane tightly against him. "We are at your grandmother's house, love," he said regretfully. "We shall finish this another time."

Jane gulped in air to calm the racing of her heart and pushed her body from his arms. She pulled her pantalets up and tugged her chemise back over her chest. She picked up her stays. She never imagined a man could make her feel the things Max did. Her mind was alive with curiosity and wonder.

She turned her back so Max could lace up her stays. Her body trembled with the aftermath. She tugged her gown up and put her arms through the sleeves. Max had his shirt on and was buttoning up his waistcoat. She turned her back one more time so he could tie the laces on her gown.

"You are certainly good at getting a lady in and out of her clothing," she remarked.

Max kissed the side of her neck. "Only yours, love."

Jane did not want to dwell on how he became so skilled. She hugged her middle. His other women were no doubt beautiful and…normal.

Max turned her face toward him as the carriage came to a stop. "I have not been with any woman since you threw me into the dungeon. You are the only woman I want." Max held her gaze, his eyes earnest and sincere. She believed him.

Chapter Eighteen

The wedding took place two weeks later. London society declared it the social event of the season. It was not every day the wicked Duke of Rathborne took a wife. For a man so perfect to choose a crippled girl was scandalous. Not only was Lady Jane disfigured, but she was also the daughter of a mere earl. Thaddeus Rathborne could have his pick of women. His breeding and social standing were impeccable. Many speculated Lady Jane must hold something over him. They supposed she knew some dark secret and blackmailed him into making her his duchess. There were a few who whispered about spells and witchcraft, convinced the duke was not in his right mind. Whatever the reason, high society agreed, it was most unusual.

Those individuals lucky enough to receive an invitation to the wedding gloated to friends and acquaintances. Those who did not receive an invitation pretended otherwise to maintain their social status while secretly wondering why they were excluded from the guest list. A great many seamstresses spent long hours sewing last-minute gowns. Florists were emptied of their inventory as the orders poured in. Chefs spent long hours in preparation for the grandest of feasts following the ceremony. The wedding was scheduled to take place at ten o'clock. Hundreds lined the streets between the Duke of Rathborne's London townhouse and the cathedral hoping for a glimpse of the handsome duke and his bride. The excitement was overwhelming. King George would be in attendance during the ceremony. The Duke of Rathborne was the king's favorite vassal, and his highness had a singular interest in the marriage.

Lady Jane Lenwood stood quietly by the window of her chamber. She, alone, was unmoved by the excitement and hustle of everyone around her. She stood in her wedding finery looking out with unseeing eyes. She had no idea what tomorrow would bring or any of the tomorrows after. In truth, she did not know anything to speak of and wondered where her life would take her after this. She was alone, unsure of herself, and more than a little afraid of what lie ahead. For days she had neither eaten nor slept, and the dark circles under her eyes bore testimony of the fact. The images of her fierce-some vision the night of her engagement party kept her up at night and haunted her when she succumbed to slumber out of pure exhaustion. She languished in a pool of melancholy, unable to climb out. She had no idea how to stop it all from happening. The only person who knew of her gift of sight was Max, and he was the one person in whom she could not confide. Even the voice in her head deserted her. So she sat and stared into the fire or lay on the bed in her chamber, as she struggled with her knowledge of the future.

They had not discovered who the traitor was. The weasel who lit the king's library afire escaped and was nowhere to be found.

The king questioned Max extensively about the fire. It was unthinkable someone should enter the palace and try to burn it to the ground. He added extra guards for tighter security.

Max spent little time in her presence since that night.

She missed the sound of his voice and the feeling of security which settled over her when he was near. Jane wondered if he regretted what happened in the carriage on the way to her grandmother's. She did not, and she thought of it often after she went to bed. It amazed her she allowed such intimacies, especially when she knew the outcome. Jane sighed.

Even the arrival of her beautiful wedding gown, made of the most delicate lace from France, cut simply and adorned with the palest of pink flowers around the neck and hem did little to raise her spirits. Lady Aldetha ordered delicate satin slippers and silk undergarments embroidered in the most exquisite fashion. Nothing brought so much as a smile to Jane's face. She wore her auburn curls high on her head and threaded with diamonds that sparkled like fire in the light. A heavy diamond necklace was clasped around her neck, large diamond earrings adorned her ears, and a magnificent diamond tiara sat upon her head. She was stunningly beautiful, and yet she did not care one way or the other.

"Perhaps you are nervous, dear. It is quite normal to be anxious on your wedding day," Lady Aldetha suggested.

"I am not nervous, Grandmama. I am simply unsure of my life and what awaits me," Jane said softly.

"Are you nervous about the wedding night?" Lady Aldetha wondered. "I remember my wedding day. Mine was a marriage of convenience. My parents arranged everything. I knew nothing of the Earl of Lenwood until my wedding day. I had only been alone with the man once immediately following our engagement. He placed a diamond ring on my finger and gave me a chaste kiss. And suddenly, there I was, married. My mother took me by the hand and led me down the hall to the bridal chamber. I was so nervous I tripped and ripped my beautiful gown. My mother gave me her advice as she helped me prepare for bed and left me alone to my imagination until the earl appeared." Lady Aldetha sighed. "Do you wish for me to speak with you about what to expect in the marriage bed?"

"Nay," Jane answered. Whatever happened, Max would see to her needs. It was the after and all the afters that followed. She must find a way to change the future, or she would end up a penniless widow with no home before the year's end. Rathborne would be lost, and the people who relied on her would starve. There was only death and destruction in her future, and she did not know how to change any of it. She resolved to never share Max's bed after the vision she saw. The strength of her feelings for him frightened her to death. Every person she cared about died or left. Max would be no different. She fought the wedding, hoping that the future would change if she did not follow through with it. Max would live, Rathborne would be safe, and the people who relied on her would grow old, secure in their future. Yet here she was, heading for the place she fought to avoid. If she could not stay that vision, how could she stay the one haunting her now?

"If it is not the bedding or the wedding, what is it? Come, child, you can tell me. Let me help you with whatever has you so forlorn."

“I have been so miserable, Grandmama,” Jane confessed.

Lady Aldetha smiled wryly. “I could tell.” She glanced pointedly at the wilted plant beside her granddaughter’s bed. “I thought I told Giles to remove all the plants to the greenhouse until all this is settled.”

Jane looked up. “What?”

“Never mind,” Lady Aldetha said, adjusting her shoulder. “Please continue.”

“I have a problem, Grandmama, and I do not know the answer to it,” Jane said.

“Well, whatever it is, I am quite sure between the two of us, we can figure it out.” Lady Aldetha sat in the chair facing the fire and waited for Jane to continue.

“You might think me quite silly—”

“My dear, say it. I am made of stouter material than you suppose.”

Jane clasped her hands together. Did she dare tell her grandmother about her gift of sight? She glanced at Lady Aldetha while she considered it. Lady Aldetha met her gaze frankly, her eyes wise and thoughtful.

“I am…different…” Jane began.

Lady Aldetha looked at her leg pointedly and then back at Jane. “I can see as much, Jane. It has not been an issue before this. The Duke of Rathborne knows about your knee. He offered for you anyway. We both know he would not have if he were put off by you. Why worry now?”

Jane rolled her eyes. “I do not speak of my knee.” She took a step toward Lady Aldetha.

“Then what, child?”

Jane took another step toward her and sank onto the floor at her feet. Resting her head in her grandmother's lap, she blurted it out. "Sometimes I see things, Grandmama, things about the future, things which are about to happen. I cannot explain how or why. I only know I do. Sometimes, all I have is knowledge. Other times, I see things as if I were there. I am transported to another time and place where I see, feel, hear, and smell everything around me. It is frightening. Then I am back in the present, doing whatever it was I did before the vision came." Jane waited for her grandmother to scoff and tell her it was all in her mind like Alfred and Gertie had at first. She did not dare look up.

Lady Aldetha's hand stroked the curls from her face softly. "You have the sight." It was not a question. It was a statement made with wonder and amazement.

Jane looked up. Her grandmother was not shocked or afraid. She was not even surprised. She had a faraway look in her eyes as she stroked Jane's face.

"You have seen something which frightens you?" Lady Aldetha asked quietly.

Jane nodded.

"How long have you had the sight?" Lady Aldetha asked.

Jane shrugged. "The first time was the morning after Mama left."

"What happened right before? What were you doing?" Lady Aldetha asked, her eyes searching Jane's face.

Jane explained what happened. She could hardly breathe. It hurt to remember her mother's desertion.

Lady Aldetha nodded her head at Jane. "You inherited my powers, child. It usually passes from mother to daughter. I cannot tell you how happy it makes me James passed it on to you." Lady Aldetha smiled. "The reason you see on certain occasions and not on others is because of your emotional involvement with the other person. Did you ever know anything about any of the servants? I am asking about the ones closest to you."

Jane nodded, thinking hard about what her grandmother was saying. "You see things too?"

"Yes, dear, now let me finish. You have *knowledge* for someone you know and care for but do not necessarily love. When you receive sight for someone you *love*, it is more than knowledge. It is a vision involving all the senses. The deeper you love the person involved, the more vivid the sight."

Jane stilled. "You are right, Grandmama. I did have knowledge when it came to Alfred, Gertie, or Thomas." She frowned. "I heard the voice when Mama left. There was no vision. I just knew." She gazed at her grandmother in confusion. "Why did I not see anything? I love Mama."

Her grandmother nodded. "Yes, you love her. But in that moment, you felt betrayed and abandoned. Those feelings blocked your sight." She studied Jane's face. "Have you had a full vision?"

"Oh yes. The visions I have involve—" Jane broke off. She saw who attacked Max the night he came to Rathborne. She saw the assassin enter the grounds. She also watched Max's fight with the assassin and knew to warn him of his fighting technique. Jane pushed to her feet. She paced to the window and back. "It cannot be. I will not believe it. It cannot be true!" Even as she said the words, she knew them to be false.

"What is not true?" Lady Aldetha asked. A smile

lurked around the corner of her mouth.

Jane refused to answer, her brow furrowed in thought. “I think, Grandmama, you are right. In most circumstances, the depth of sight is related to my feelings about the other person except in one instance, the Duke of Rathborne. My visions involving him do not follow any of the rules.” Jane nodded as she said the words. This had to be it.

Lady Aldetha smiled. “Why do you suppose you have visions for him and no one else?”

“I hoped you had the answer. When I have them for him, I *live* in the visions. I hear, smell, feel, and taste everything! They are so intense I shake with reaction. When they are over, I do not have strength to breathe, let alone walk.”

Lady Aldetha gazed at her steadily. “Has it occurred to you that you love him, and this is why they are so powerful?”

“No!” Jane stood still. “I do not think so. I do not love him. I hate him! He lied to me and considers me a burden. How could you suggest it is love?”

She wrung her hands as she paced back and forth. When one loved, the heart became involved, making it vulnerable to breaking. She could not allow herself to feel anything for Max until she solved the future. To do so would be the end of her. He would destroy her soul.

Lady Aldetha shook her head and changed the subject. “What have you seen which worries you so? I can tell it involves the duke.”

Jane walked back to her chair and sank beside her. “He will be hanged for treason. His lands and money will be forfeit to the crown before the year is out unless I determine how to stop it! The thing is, I do not have much more information. My sight this time was centered on Rathborne. I was there when I received word of his plight. They hanged him before I got to London." Jane looked up at her grandmother. Tears glistened on her lashes. "I do not know how to stop it. I tried to stop the wedding and failed. So, how can I stop his death?"

Lady Aldetha leaned forward. "Give me your hands, child."

Obediently, Jane leaned forward and held her hands out for her grandmother to take. Lady Aldetha dropped her head for a minute or two.

Jane stared, fascinated. There was no sign of the tumult she went through when she saw things. One would suppose her grandmother nodded off, so still was she as her vision took over.

At last, Lady Aldetha looked up. "It will be all right, my dear. You will be given what you require when you need it. "

Jane gazed at her in amazement. "How can you say such a thing? And how did you hide the fact you were somewhere else?"

Lady Aldetha squeezed her cold fingers. "My visions are correct. I say you and Maximillian shall get through this with fine colors. You shall have to trust me on this point. As for how I did it, it is a little trick I learned when I was young. Instead of fighting the vision as it comes, embrace it."

"There is another thing, when I stand in my mother's room, voices speak to me, but I cannot understand them." Somehow the voices were related to Max and the traitor. If Grandmama had the sight, maybe she knew how to decipher the voices.

"Listen to me, child. You must not fight your feelings. When you do, your gift is blocked. When your feelings flutter all over, your gift comes and goes. Once you control your feelings, you will be able to control your gift, as well. Make peace with your mother in your heart. Make peace with Maximillian. When the voices or the visions come, allow them to flow over you and through you. Breathe in deeply and let the sights and sounds fill your soul. They are given to you for a purpose. Soak them in until they become part of you. Let them imprint upon your mind and heart. Only then will you understand what you must do."

Jane nodded her head. She would try it next time. Maybe an answer would present itself. "I thought if I stopped the wedding, Max would escape whatever puts him in jeopardy."

"No, Jane. Such is not the case. This is part of the plan. Max's life rests upon you becoming his duchess," Lady Aldetha said with conviction.

Jane's shoulders slumped. "I hoped it would not be so."

Lady Aldetha shook her head. "You have been given a great gift, Jane. You must forgive Maximillian. Sort your feelings. Let the gift guide you. Let it become you."

"Why can I not see what happens in my own future?" Jane muttered. "When I ask, I see nothing. The voice tells me if I am in danger, but that is all."

Lady Aldetha caressed her cheek. "The sight is given to aid others or warn you. It will never work for any other purpose. Therefore, I can see your future, but you cannot."

Jane was defeated. She nodded her head once more

in acquiescence. There would be no reasoning with Grandmama. Now Lady Aldetha saw whatever it was, she had no recourse but to follow through with the wedding.

"There is something else," Lady Aldetha said. "Let me see your knee, child."

Jane lifted the hem of her skirt to her thigh and rolled down her silk stocking. She tugged on the bottom of her silk pantalets until her bare knee was visible. "The scarring is grotesque, is it not?"

"Not for long," her grandmother replied. She placed both hands over Jane's injured knee and closed her eyes.

Heat filled Jane's joint. It grew until Jane gasped aloud. "Grandmama, that hurts!"

Lady Aldetha opened her eyes. She smiled. "You will no longer need your cane. You are healed. This is my wedding gift to you."

Jane stared at her grandmother. Then, she looked down at her knee. The scarring was gone. The angry red soreness had disappeared as well. "How?" she asked in amazement. She rose to her feet. For the first time since her accident, there was no pain. Jane took one step and then another. She turned in amazement to Lady Aldetha. "I can walk."

"Yes, my dear. Be careful how you make it known. We do not want anyone to question it."

"Can I heal too? Is it something I must learn?" Then she stopped. "If you could do this the whole time, why did you not heal me when I arrived at Lenwood Estates? Why settle such a large dowry on me? I could have found a husband without it."

Lady Aldetha chuckled. "Because society is a pack

of wolves. I wanted you to know the man who married you, loved you for yourself, flaws and all. The dowry was for your self-confidence. It gave you equal footing. If you were known as an heiress, more doors were open to you."

"It also attracted fortune hunters," Jane said, shivering as she recalled Lord Dewhurst's sloppy kisses and fumbling hands.

"One touch, and I could tell what they were about," Grandmama declared.

"And Lord Dewhurst?" Jane questioned.

Lady Aldetha laughed. "He was a necessary evil. I used him as bait for the man you were meant for. I was unaware it was Maximillian until he appeared."

"Grandmama!" Jane exclaimed.

Lady Aldetha shrugged. "The only way to get a man to realize he wants something is to take it from him." She turned to look at the door. "We do not have much time. You must be wary, Jane. The women in our family have the power. We have the gift of sight, and each of us receives our own unique gift. Mine is healing. You have yet to discover yours. Keep it secret, my girl. Others will not understand."

Jane nodded. She knew that only too well.

"The carriage is here, madam," Giles announced from the doorway. Then he turned to Jane. "Lady Jane, you make my old heart skip a beat with your loveliness. The Duke of Rathborne marries an angel this day."

Jane looked up in surprise. Giles did not compliment, and for him to do so now was balm to her aching heart. "Thank you, Giles."

He nodded with pride as Lady Aldetha placed the heavy veil over Jane's head and secured it in place.

Jane took his arm, and together they went down the stairs to the waiting carriage. Lady Aldetha followed along behind.

Chapter Nineteen

They rode in silence to the church. Each lost in thought. When the carriage stopped at the cathedral steps, Lady Aldetha placed a hand on Jane's arm.

"I know you have misgivings, Jane, but Maximillian is a good man. He will see to it you are well provided for. If I were not convinced this is your destiny, I would not have agreed to this marriage no matter what stories he told," Lady Aldetha said.

Jane gazed quietly at her grandmother. She leaned forward, lifted her veil, and kissed the older woman's cheek. "Thank you for all you have done, Grandmama," she said and stepped from the carriage, her long train trailing behind her.

Her grandmother stepped from the carriage and took her arm. Since they had no other relatives, Lady Aldetha gave her away. Jane walked slowly up the stairs and stopped, waiting for the strains of the wedding march to begin. A bride's maid handed her a bouquet of tiny pink roses, matching the delicate pink design around the neck and hem of her lace gown. Jane grasped the flowers as if they were a shield to protect her in battle. When the organ began the wedding march, Jane made her way slowly toward the altar. She held Grandmama's arm and lectured herself silently as she forced her feet to take one step and then another. She had the overwhelming urge to run away as far and as fast as she could. Grandmama's words of conviction rang in her ears. Jane continued to walk one step at a time, her eyes on the floor.

****

Max stood waiting, dressed in his formal best. His dark uniform was resplendent with gold braids and heavy with medals of honor. He wore his dark hair combed neatly back from his high forehead and tied at his nape with a black ribbon. A gleam of admiration lit his dark eyes as he gazed upon Jane for the first time in her wedding finery. His heart skipped a little with anticipation. This exquisite creature was all his. He would show her how beautiful she was tonight when he took her into his arms and made sweet love to her, as he had wanted to do for such a long time now. What had been weeks seemed like centuries. It had been hell on earth to be so close these last few days and not touch her. After what nearly happened in the carriage, he would not risk touching her again until she was his. Then and only then would he allow the passion raging within him to come forth. He had come close to losing his control the last time. Thank God the carriage dipped as it turned onto the long road in front of Lenwood's London townhouse. Had it not, he would have taken her there on the soft velvet seat. He could still hear her whimper and feel her shudder in his arms as she found fulfillment. She heated his blood with one look. His body throbbed for her. This day could not pass fast enough for him.

****

Jane would not look at him, so she missed the heated look he gave her. Her gaze was unseeing as she stared down, unable to meet his eyes. She did not want to read the coldness she knew was there. The cool interior of the lofty cathedral pressed down on her. Jane shivered, despite her determination not to.

Since the night of their engagement, Max had been distant, aloof, and withdrawn. Jane wondered if Max regretted his choice of bride. The courtiers' whispers filled her ears. Max required a wife to satisfy the demands of the king. Once wed, the ladies confided behind their fluttering fans, he intended taking other women to his bed while Jane languished at Rathborne. After all, she grew up there, and who would know the castle and the people better than she did? She was the perfect candidate for the job. Jane sighed. It was as they said. Maximillian Rathborne was the only man alive who found her attractive. What did he see in her others could not?

She reached the top step and stood beside Max. She bowed her head, resigned to her fate, as the clergy droned on and on about the sanctity of marriage. Jane sighed with passiveness. She remained stoic throughout the ceremony, repeating her vows in a meek, quiet voice, her face expressionless. She was lost in a sea of unreality and floating in the mist of desolation. There had to be some way she could change the future. If marrying Max was part of the way she saved him and Rathborne, let it be so.

****

Max glanced at her several times in concern. Since when had Jane become docile? When the service concluded, and they were pronounced man and wife, Max drew Jane's unresisting form into his arms for a chaste kiss. He lifted the heavy veil and stared down at her. Jane refused to look at him, her body limp in his arms. Max frowned. This was not what he anticipated when he considered their first kiss as man and wife. His Jane was full of fire and life. The limp form he held could pass for a doll, so lifeless was she.

"What is wrong?" Max whispered into Jane's ear as they began the long walk down the aisle of the cathedral toward the open door. "Are you ill?" Anxiety deepened his voice. Perhaps the strain of such a large gathering was too much. Jane was quieter and more withdrawn than he had ever seen her. It concerned him a great deal.

She was silent.

Max swung an arm around Jane's shoulder and pulled her tight against his side as the congregation threw rice and well wishes at them. He noticed she did not have her cane. He slipped his arm from her shoulder to her waist and eased her down the long red carpet toward the heavy oak door of the church. He smiled at the crowd while keeping Jane's face protected against his wide chest. "Come." he said urgently, "We go to the palace to dine with the king. Once we have appeared and satisfied his majesty, we can escape and go somewhere quiet. Then, you will tell me what troubles you."

Jane did not respond, nor did she pull away. She simply let him lead her wherever he had a mind to with a half-witted smile pinned in place. Her expression remained as it had throughout the ceremony. He threw open the door and drew Jane out into the sunshine.

Max frowned again. "Are you in pain? Tell me, darling, what can I do to help you?" he asked tenderly. "Where in God's name is your cane?" He turned Jane toward him and tilted her face toward his.

"In the carriage, but I do not need it anymore. I can walk on my own."

Max frowned. "How can that be?"

The crowd cheered as they exited the cathedral. Flowers, rice, and rose petals were thrown in their direction. The breeze blew cool against the heat of the sun. Max gazed down at Jane.

"I cannot explain. Just believe when I say I can walk." She looked at the throng of well-wishers. "It does not matter, anyway. We have no future together, so it makes no difference."

Max stilled. "How can you say this? It makes a wonderful difference. I see us enjoying a blissful future. I cannot believe you are healed. Our lives shall be richer for it. What have you seen, Jane, to convince you otherwise?" She never spoke of her vision the night of their engagement. What had she seen?

Jane did not answer.

Max caught sight of several ladies leaning heavily toward them, hoping to hear more of their conversation. This had best be resolved in private. Whatever ailed Jane, he would soon know. Max had no need to be the subject of any more gossip. Jane was the love of his life, and he would not allow anyone to hurt her. Max turned toward Jane and swung her up in his arms. His mouth came down on hers to silence any protest she might make. He strode toward their waiting carriage. His patience was at an end.

****

Jane hit Max's shoulders with her fists to convince him to release her, but to no avail. His lips remained firmly pressed against hers, his arms holding her tightly against his chest. She changed tactics and bit him. He drew back, his eyes mere slits as he gazed down at her.

"Let me go!" she whispered furiously once they were inside the safety of Max's new carriage.

Max lifted his head, his gray eyes dark with anger. "Why do you strike out at me?" he asked. "You and I both know you like my kisses. You usually beg for more. What has happened that you try to draw blood with your teeth? This is not what I anticipated from you on our wedding day. First, you are as limp and unresponsive as a linen towel, and then you fight like a caged animal."

Jane stared into his glowering face. "What *exactly* did you anticipate from me on our wedding day, *your grace*? We shall enjoy a blissful future now my knee has healed? What would we have had before?" Jane asked, her face inches from his. She had no idea why she was suddenly so angry with him. "Why should my knee make any difference to our marriage? Having the use of it does not change my feelings about you or the things you have done."

She was helpless and frustrated. She had only a short time to solve the riddle of Max's endangerment. It was late summer. She had until the leaves turned to find the answer. She had to keep a clear head, or her marriage and his life were over. How could she relax her guard when so much depended on her?

"What is it I have done, exactly?" Max questioned, his voice silky soft. He leaned in close, his breath blowing across her cheek.

A shiver went down Jane's spine at the warning in his voice. Recklessly she answered. "You deceived me when you came to Rathborne Castle, calling yourself Max Radley instead of Maximilian Rathborne," she began. "I took you in. You had all winter to tell me who you were, but you did not! Then you left me alone at Rathborne. When I came to London to see my father's family, you followed and lied to my grandmother about what occurred the winter we were together. You convinced her I was compromised, thus, forcing me to marry you. No one asked me what I wanted. You only care for me as your ward. You wonder why I strike out at you?" she asked incredulously. She made no mention of the real reason she was distraught, the riddle of her vision involving Max. Instead, she focused her anger and frustration on other things, giving vent to her feelings. She bit her lip and gazed out the window.

Anger darkened his gaze. "I offer no apology, my lady," Max said silkily. "I did give you my true name upon my arrival. I am indeed Max Radley. Although, this name is not as well-known as others. Tell me, my love, at what point should I have revealed I was the hated Duke of Rathborne? After you so kindly put me in the dungeon on my arrival? Or after you so eloquently decided what my fate would be if I were he? Rot in hell, throw me to the wolves, freeze in the storm, and starve to death were on the list. After listening to you rant so vehemently against me, I was not inclined to give you my full name and title. Having partaken of your reluctant hospitality, I did wonder what my fate might be should it be known I was the wicked Duke of Rathborne."

"I would do so again if I had the chance," Jane muttered.

"I did have all winter to tell you the identity you knew me best as," Max continued softly as if she had not spoken, "but then I would never have gotten to know you as you are, my beautiful Jane. You would have thrown me back in the ghastly dungeon or worse. I preferred to stay upstairs where there was some semblance of warmth. As for your grandmother, I assure you she would have turned me out on my ear if she were not in favor of our match. In truth, my suit pleased her ladyship a great deal. She knows I will see to your protection and welfare. She had no fear I pretended interest in you for the generous dowry she bestowed upon you. A dowry she donated to the orphanage upon the signing of our wedding contract. I do not require your money or Lady Lenwood's. I am a wealthy man. I do care for you but not as my ward. Something you shall soon see for yourself." Max smiled smugly. "I do believe the whole affair worked out to our mutual satisfaction." He picked up one of Jane's slim hands and proceeded to remove her glove, one finger at a time.

"It may have worked out to your satisfaction, but not to mine," Jane said stiffly. She would not surrender to the warmth spreading through her at the touch of his fingers against her skin. Max picked up her other hand and removed its glove, also.

"This is something I shall remedy soon, my love." Max bent his head and placed his hot mouth against the palm of her hand.

Jane jerked back.

His hands held her steady as his lips kissed and licked hungrily over the sensitive skin of her wrist, moving slowly up her arm. Jane's breath came fast between her parted lips as heat pooled into her belly. She ought to pull her arm away. She was still upset, and she did not want to submit to the sensual heat Max wove around her.

When his lips and tongue reached the crease in her elbow, a cry escaped the tight seam of her lips. She wanted to hold it in and not let him know how good he made her feel, but it escaped. She remembered too well what happened last time. Max lifted his head and stared into Jane's eyes. A smile tugged at the corners of his full mouth. He bent his dark head toward her. She shivered with desire when his hot mouth devoured the side of her neck. By the time Max reached her ear, Jane was whimpering against him. Max tugged her onto his lap in answer and sealed her lips with his. His tongue plundered her mouth as a starving man would devour his first bite of bread.

Jane wound her arms around his neck, oblivious to all but her desire to be closer to Max. She forgot everything else but the feel of his tongue stroking the inside her mouth and his hands roaming the curves of her body through the fine lace of her wedding gown.

His hands found the lush curves of her full breasts. Jane pressed against him, a cry escaping her as the pleasure pulsed from her throbbing nipples to the very core of her. Molten heat flooded her bloodstream, setting her on fire. She needed more. She shifted against him wanting to feel his shaft against the pulsing ache inside her.

Max groaned out loud as her shapely backside rubbed against his throbbing manhood. God, how he wanted to be inside her, pulling out and plunging in again, deeper and deeper, faster and faster, until they both screamed with the force of their release.

A knock sounded on the side of the carriage.

Max lifted his head as reality returned.

The carriage stopped inside the cobblestone courtyard of the palace. Wedding guests waited inside for them to appear. King George arranged a magnificent banquet in honor of their wedding.

"I am sorry, my love, we have arrived at the palace. We shall have to finish this later tonight in our chamber. For now, we must attend the king."

Jane jerked back. Of course, the wedding, the king, the dinner. How could she have forgotten herself in such a manner? She intended to remain so cold and aloof Max realized the mistake he made in marrying her. She married as her grandmother said she must. Grandmama did not say how long the marriage must last. Perhaps if Max gave her an annulment, her vision would not come to pass. If an annulment were the answer, the kissing and touching had to stop. Hastily Jane removed her arms from around his neck and patted her hair. Then she discovered she sat on his lap and hastily slipped off onto the red velvet seat beside him. She flushed with self-loathing for giving in to his kisses. Jane's spine stiffened as the sensual haze dissipated and reality returned.

"It seems I have forgotten myself, your grace. It shall not happen again. I have no intention of sharing a bedchamber with you tonight or any other night. I will thank you to keep your hands to yourself from now on. You may be well satisfied with this match, but I am not. I have no interest in furthering any connection between us," Jane said frigidly. The sooner he understood she was serious, the better.

****

"I am far from satisfied, my Jane," Max answered silkily. "As you have said, neither are you. This is something which shall have to wait until we are alone in our chamber tonight. Make no mistake, my love. We shall share a bedchamber tonight and every night. You will not be sleeping alone for some time. I intend to make sure we are both very satisfied. Even if it takes the entire night, I will not rest until I hear you cry out my name as I fulfill every need in your delightful body. Only then will I be satisfied." Max smiled into her startled blue eyes. He nodded with satisfaction at her dismay. If his little Jane believed he would remain outside her chamber, she was mistaken. He had every intention of bedding his delightful little wife. She was not as immune to him as she would have him believe. If he were not sure of the attraction between them, the carriage ride from the cathedral to the palace would be proof enough. Oh yes, he would be bedding his wife tonight. It would be mutually satisfying, despite the little lies she told herself. The sooner she realized he meant what he said, the better for them both.

****

Max climbed out of the carriage and held his arm out to Jane. Jane sat stiffly, fighting with herself to remain calm despite the panic clawing inside her. He was determined to bed her! Terror caused her heart to beat quite erratically. She would not be able to stop him. But what could she do? There had to be some way to protect her heart, but how? Letting him touch her and kiss her was a huge mistake. She could not think when he was so close. Perhaps she should focus on his deception. It was easy to hate him when she considered all the times he could have told her who he was. She grew close to him during the winter they spent together, and it was all a lie. She must focus on obtaining an annulment, and the future she saw in her vision would change. It had to. She would hate him if it were the last thing she did! She could not afford to feel anything differently if she were to save him. She required a clear head. It was simple. Jane fought with her conscience over whether to make her point and disembark without taking his arm.

Max leaned toward her and whispered. “Let us keep our arguments between ourselves. Look how everyone watches.”

Jane gazed around her. Max spoke the truth. The courtyard was full of carriages and guests coming to dine with the king. They observed everything the newlyweds did with interest. Anything Max or Jane said or did would be repeated until society gave its verdict on their marital status. Jane pasted her most brilliant smile upon her face and took Max’s arm, allowing him to help her from the carriage. He tucked her arm securely into his, and together they walked into the palace leaning toward each other as if they were already lovers. Society must never know the true state of their marriage, for Grandmama’s sake as well as theirs.

Chapter Twenty

Max's dark gaze never left Jane all night. It was heated and focused. Every time she laughed, an answering smile touched his lips. His gaze was adoring, hungry, and watchful. The lady cut her fine linen napkin to shreds. She sat at a distant table where she observed the Duke of Rathborne and his new wife with hostility.

What Max saw in Jane was beyond her understanding. After all, he had no real affection for her. How could he when she was so hideous? Max had to have some reason he married the bitch. The king commanded him to marry. But why Jane? Then she shrugged. What did it matter? Her aunt promised her a vast fortune in payment for her part in the plan. Soon Max would be dead, and Jane would be widowed and an outcast. Rathborne would be hers. She would receive a portion of Max's diamond mine to live on. The lady smiled. She would have the life she deserved. It was only a matter of time. She looked pointedly away from the disgusting sight the newlyweds made and glanced idly around at the other guests. She caught sight of Lady Melissa scowling deeply with her hands fisted at her side. She looked ready to commit murder. Lady Melissa believed she was better than any of her female relatives. My, how the times changed. The lady smiled. Karma was a wonderful thing.

****

Halfway through the evening, Max caught Jane by the hand, and together they bowed before the king, making their excuses for an early departure from the festivities. Laughing, the king waved them away.

Max helped Jane into the waiting carriage, and soon they were off. They were expected to have a honeymoon, and Max could think of no better place to spend it, than his country estate. It was remote and secluded. Both of which were needed for the battle ahead with Jane. He realized she was angry with him for the way he coerced her grandmother. He also knew the depth of her hatred toward him for the things she supposed happened in the past. Both of which Max intended to straighten out. He required time, space, and seclusion from the watchful eyes of society as he did so.

Jane was a beautiful woman inside and out. She was his wife and would belong to no other. Contentment stole into his heart as he gazed at her. It was a feeling which grew with each passing moment. It was so right to be here with her. Max considered it providence the evidence led him to Rathborne last winter. Otherwise, he would have never seen the sweet, gentle nature his wife hid from the rest of the world. He glanced at her now to judge her mood. She appeared to be engrossed in the passing countryside as they journeyed north. He could not fault her for her performance at the palace. Every time she caught his eye, she smiled. Her beauty took his breath away. She appeared complacent in the eyes of society. He wondered what her mood would be when they were alone at last. He did not have to wait long.

"Where are we going?" Jane asked.

"To my country estate," Max replied.

Jane stared at him, suspicion in her gaze. "I will not share your bed," she stated emphatically.

"Then I shall share yours," Max answered. "There is a communicating door between our chambers. It does not matter whose bed we end up in. We could sleep in your bed tonight and my bed tomorrow night. My estate in the country has fifteen separate chambers. We can try them all if you like." He grinned, hoping to lighten her mood.

"If you hope to drag me to Rathborne, bed me until I am with child, and then leave me there to mold whilst you return to court and take a mistress, you shall be sadly mistaken. I have no intention of being secreted away in Rathborne, nor do I have any intention of bearing you an heir." She held her chin high as she stared at him.

Max leaned back in his seat; his eyes gray slits as he studied her defiant face. This was not his Jane speaking but someone else. "You repeat court gossip. Are you so afraid to share my bed and learn of the pleasure we can give each other that you use their words against me?"

"I am not afraid of you or of going to your bed," Jane answered. "I simply refuse to allow you to bed me. I do not intend to be a malleable little wife forgotten in the wilds of Cumbria whilst you are elsewhere. I want an annulment. I want my freedom. We both know this was a mistake." Jane's color was high as she met his stare.

"Do we? You do not wish to share my bed, yet you want me to bed no other. Why is this, do you suppose?"

Max inquired lazily. His eyes sharply focused on Jane. She wanted him the same as he wanted her. He could see it in her eyes when she looked at him. He read it in the way she held her breath when he got close. He knew it by the way she breathlessly said his name and felt it when she leaned into him as they walked, her body rubbing against his like a purring kitten, begging to be stroked.

“I mean what I say, Max. I will not share my bed with you. I want an annulment.” Jane turned away to stare out the window.

“You speak of things you know nothing about,” Max answered. “When you share my bed, Jane, you shall use me to ride the wave of sexual pleasure over and over until you scream out my name in such an intense climax you feel as though you have shattered into hundreds of little pieces. I shall do the same. Your body shall use my body, as much as my body shall use yours. This is the way men and women have made love together for hundreds of years. It shall be the same for us. Your body was made to pleasure mine, and my body was made to pleasure yours. Together we shall climb every peak of sexual excitement and ride every wave of physical delight possible until we collapse into each other’s arms soaked with sweat and weary with sweet fulfillment,” Max said. He undressed her with his eyes, remembering her beautiful body as he slowly looked her over. He stared at the blush on her cheeks with satisfaction. Her eyes snapped with brilliant blue color. At last, his Jane acted like herself. He could deal with her when she was angry and mad as hell. He could deal with her when she spouted her nonsense about how much she hated him, but he had no idea what to do with the docile, limp Jane he encountered earlier at their wedding.

****

Max's eyes blazed a heated path from the tips of her toes to the crown of her head as he spoke. Jane's face burned with color as the images of their naked bodies twined together filled her mind. She shook her head to rid her mind of the vision she had of this day, and of the night to come. She remembered her pleasure in the carriage. She saw Max rise over her again and closed her eyes. She felt the heat of his body, the ecstasy of his penetration. Would it be so again? Her resolve slipped. This would be her one chance to know what it was like to be with Max. The smoky, sensual look he gave her made her wonder if he was thinking about how she looked naked. Her breathing became erratic as she considered what he said. Her anger dissolved in the fervor of the fevered images burning her mind.

Max's gaze lingered on her cheeks. When his gaze held hers, her breath caught. Max was thinking about the two of them naked. She could see it in his eyes. Her heart rate increased as his eyes moved over her again, more slowly this time. He stared at her breasts, and Jane groaned out loud as she remembered the feel of his hot lips closing around her swollen nipple as he suckled. She glanced at him and found him focused on her lips. White-hot desire flooded her body. He looked up and gazed deep into her eyes. The mercurial silver of his made Jane squirm in anticipation. All she could think about was Max. She wanted to stroke him until he burned as she did. She wanted to feel his lips and hands on her body. She wanted to feel the depth of his penetration as he mated with her for real.

The carriage turned through the wrought iron gate of his lavish country estate. The horse's hooves clopped along the tree-lined curved cobblestone drive. They stopped in front of the sprawling two-story stone home. Jane gazed out the little window. It was beautiful. Flower beds, manicured lawns, graceful trees swaying in the gentle breeze. There was a silver lake in the distance. She turned back to the house. A red carpet ran up the middle of the sprawling stone steps. The staff lined the steps, eager to meet their new mistress.

Jane dropped her gaze to her hands in her lap. She wanted Max. She wanted him deep inside her. She wanted to feel his lips closing around her nipples while he drove into her. Her stomach quivered with anticipation. She wanted him to teach her all the things his husky voice promised.

The door to the carriage opened, and a liveried footman bowed to them both. "Welcome home, your graces."

Jane sucked in a breath. Max must never guess how much his words disturbed her. The images in her mind branded her for all time. She glanced at his face. He had his head turned toward the window. She got to her feet and pasted a serene look on her face, hoping she hid her reaction successfully.

Max took her trembling arm in his. "Soon, my love, soon," he whispered in her ear.

Jane flushed bright red at his words but held her head high. Max escorted her up the steps, introducing the staff as they went. She greeted each person with a smile and a nod, genuinely pleased to meet them. Max nodded with satisfaction.

Once inside the foyer, Jane looked around her new home. The room was lavishly decorated with gleaming marble floors, gilt-edged mirrors, mahogany side tables, crystal-cut chandeliers, and flowers everywhere. A heavy gold chandelier hung from the richly plastered ceiling. Jane swallowed nervously. Max was a wealthy man, wealthy and powerful. She would do well to remember the fact.

Max took her by the elbow and steered her through the foyer to the grand staircase beyond. "We shall get settled in our room and perhaps freshen up after the drive from London." Max's eyes roved up and down her body with a hungry look.

Suddenly she was frightened. "I think I shall stay right here, thank you," Jane retorted, feeling unsure of herself. What if she disappointed him? It was one thing to think of all the things she wanted to do, and another to take his hand and go do them. Now, she was his wife. There would be nothing to hold him back.

Max's gaze was predatory. She had to think. If she went up the stairs with Max, all chance of an annulment would be gone. Their earlier conversation repeated itself in her head. She took a step back, hoping to put some distance between them, but Max was having none of it.

He slid his arm around her slim waist and guided her to the stairs. "We must remove your wedding gown, my love, and make you comfortable. Come with me. I want to show you the master suite." His voice was husky with desire. His tone deepened, and it dragged at Jane like a shot of whiskey, warming her through. Her legs wobbled like jelly.

"I do not believe I am in the least interested in the

master suite. I think I would rather have a tour of the stables or the gardens? Yes, the gardens would do nicely. I should like an extensive tour of the gardens before dinner if you do not mind," Jane said hastily as she stood at the bottom of the curved staircase. She required space to think. His presence disturbed her resolve. If she made the wrong choice, she lost everything, including him.

Max studied her through the narrow slits of his eyes. "But I do mind, my dear Jane. I mind very much. You see, I am determined to make you more comfortable before dinner." His wicked gaze stared hungrily at her chest. He scooped her up in his arms and took the stairs two at a time. Jane started to protest, but Max silenced her words with his lips.

He slid his tongue between her lips and fed on the honeyed sweetness of her mouth. Jane's fear ebbed away and a delicious heat spread through her like molten lava. Maybe there was another way. If she let him bed her this once, she would know what mating with him was like. Perhaps a vision would come while they were joined, showing her what to do to save them all. She shivered in his arms. Grandmama said the wedding was important. Perhaps the bedding was as well. She would allow herself this one night.

Max entered the master suite and kicked the door shut with his heel. She had a hazy impression of a heavily masculine room done in navy and maroon velvet. Max set Jane gently on her feet, in the center of the room next to a giant bed with a navy coverlet. His arms held her tight. Butterflies tickled her stomach as Max's hands found the laces at the back of her gown and loosened them quickly. He dropped her gown. It fell into a pool of silk at her feet. Then his hands were on her corset, ripping it from her body and dropping it on the floor beside her gown. Her petticoats followed as well as her silk stockings. Her chemise and silk drawers dropped to the floor with the rest of her clothing. Jane moaned aloud as Max caught the fullness of her rounded breasts in his palms and rubbed his thumbs over her taut nipples. She arched into him with a cry of desire. Max made quick work of his clothing, and then he laid Jane back against the silky sheets. She shivered against the coolness on her back. Max covered her with his hard, hot body, spreading her thighs with his knees as he settled atop her.

The hard length of his manhood pressed against her stomach. Jane looked up in alarm. He was too large! He would tear her to shreds if he—

Max swooped down and pulled a nipple into the heat of his mouth and suckled. The liquid fire in her belly poured into the juncture between her legs, and an ache started to throb at her core. She arched her back, wanting Max to take more of her into his mouth, and he did. Jane's head thrashed back and forth as he turned his attention to her other breast, suckling her nipple as he had its twin. His hand slid between their bodies, and he rubbed the sensitive nub within the silky folds of her sex.

Jane's body was on fire. She cried out as his fingers probed and rubbed against her. She remembered how it was before and wanted to feel the same soul-shattering pleasure. The ache in her core throbbed insistently. Jane thought she might go mad if he did not touch her there. Then his finger was there, pushing into the silky folds of her opening and then pulling out again. Heat pooled around the thickness of his finger. Max penetrated her with his finger mimicking the mating act. Jane thrashed against him. Her forehead beaded with sweat.

"Please, Max, please." She kept repeating over and over. She had to have more.

"I wanted to go slow, to give you time to prepare, but you are ready for me now, are you not, my Jane?" His fingers worked in and out of her slick heat while he lavished one breast and then the other. Jane was mindless with desire. She panted against him, begging him to fill her.

Max covered her whimpering mouth with his. He slowly eased into her. She was so wet, so tight, and so hot. He hoped to God he did not come once he was seated inside her. He hardened at the husky pleading in her voice. He wanted to plunge inside her and take her hard and fast, but he could not. He wanted her first time to be good. He pushed forward slowly, one agonizing bit at a time. He moved down to suckle her breasts. Sweat dripped from him as he fought to control the lust pounding through him. He stopped when he felt the resistance of her virginity. Max placed a searing kiss on Jane's lips as he pushed forward in one quick motion.

Jane gasped as he filled her. The pain was but a pinch, and then the pleasure took over. She bit his shoulder and cried his name.

Max started to pull back, afraid he hurt her, but Jane grabbed his buttocks and pulled him to her, holding him fast in place. She moaned as excitement took over her body. She rocked her hips against him. He felt so good. She rocked faster, bringing her hips higher to take more of him inside. She was not disappointed. Her insides quivered with rapture. The friction of his hard member rubbing so high inside her transported her to a world of bliss such as she never knew before.

"Max!" she said urgently as she moved against him.

It was too much. Max levered himself onto his elbows and moved with her in a rhythm as old as time. Jane screamed his name over and over with the rocking of their bodies. She wrapped her legs high around his waist and rode the wave of rapture he created. It rose high above her, peaking. Max surged forward again and again, his muscular body gleaming with sweat as he fought for control. Then it happened. The wave crashed over Jane, shattering her in a million brilliant pieces. She clawed at his back, screaming with the ecstasy of fulfillment. Max rode the wave, pushing into her harder and deeper, and then his own release rocked the very foundations of his world.

When the last ripple of their lovemaking ebbed away, they lay sated and satisfied. Their sweat-soaked bodies wrapped tightly together.

Jane lifted her head and gazed into Max's eyes. "Is mating always like this?" she asked in wonderment.

"No," Max answered.

Jane's eyes widened. "Is it better, usually?" she wondered. After all, this was her first time, and she was not particularly good at it.

Max chuckled. "It does not get any better than what we just did together, my dear. If it did, I'm afraid I should soon be dead."

Jane frowned at his words. " Why?"

"Because I intend to repeat what we did quite

often. If bedding you becomes any better, I do not believe my heart could take it. You see, my curious Jane, what we share is something few people find. We were made for each other, my dear, and even if our minds refuse to accept it, our bodies already know it."

Chapter Twenty-One

They stayed at their country estate for two weeks, enjoying the solitude. To Jane, the quiet meant she had time to think. She made excuses to be alone. An annulment was out of the question, now. They came together several times a day and sometimes throughout the night as well, getting little sleep. Jane marveled at the way her body responded to Max's knowing touch. Each time was better than the last.

She had no idea what to do to change the future. Surely the reason she lay awake at night had to do with Rathborne and not its master. How could she feel so many things for him at the same time? The passionate feelings which arose within her every time Max took her into his arms and showed her the pleasure her body was capable of battled with the fear that consumed her over the future. She spent so many years hating him and blaming him for the things wrong in her life. How could he show her such tenderness and devotion when he knew how much she hated him? She hated herself for giving in and letting him touch her, kiss her, and make love to her. He distracted her in so many ways when she should be coming up with a plan to save him, to save Rathborne. When they were in bed and Max caressed her, it was so easy to pretend they were the same two people who spent last winter together, just Max and just Jane. There was no such thing as duke's, wealth, treason, or death. There was only the two of them wrapped up together, enjoying the pleasures their bodies gave each other. Jane did not want to think about what would happen when they were once again part of the rest of the world. For then, her time to solve the puzzle would run out. She must save Max. In doing so, she saved Rathborne.

The voice in her head had been unusually quiet. Jane frowned. Grandmama's voice played in her head. *"But in that moment, you felt betrayed and abandoned. Those feelings blocked the vision."*

Jane sighed. She walked around the flower garden. She stopped beside a three-tiered fountain and gazed at the silver water. The scent of roses filled the air. The sun shone down on the water creating a blinding array of colors. She let the cool water trickle through her fingers. Perhaps the reason the voice was silent was she had not sorted out her feelings for Max. She thought of the way he looked up and smiled when she entered the room, the way he caressed her cheek when he whispered in her ear, and the way he leaned toward her when she spoke to him. Her heart fluttered in her chest. Max cared for her. It was there in his eyes. He would not let anything or anyone hurt her. When she was with him, she was safe. If she were honest, she would admit he was nothing like the man she hated for years. Butterflies danced in her stomach when she thought of the way he held her in the night and made love to her. Jane swished the water. Max deserved the benefit of the doubt. She would listen to his side of the story. Somewhere between her memory and his, the answers lie.

Later that night, after an especially energetic and

satisfying coupling, Jane lay in Max's arms thinking. "Why did you not come to Mangus' funeral?" she whispered into his shoulder, unaware she spoke the thought aloud until he answered.

"I learned of my father's death when I returned to England," Max said softly.

Jane frowned. "How can this be? If you did not receive Mangus' letters, where did they go?"

****

Max lay quiet as he contemplated the dangers of pursuing this conversation. One wrong word, and Jane would disappear behind the wall of ice she built around her heart. He was afraid she might not come back out. "I do not know. It was my understanding he never wanted to see me again. So, I stayed away."

Jane nodded her head. "Do you suppose they were sent to someone else by mistake?" she asked.

Max dared not breathe. This was the first time Jane considered there might be a different version of what happened than the one she told, the one where he was the villain.

"I do not know. It is something I am determined to investigate once we are returned from our honeymoon. I never considered my father might have a change of heart until the day I met you and was accused of indifference to my father and the family name." Max dipped his head toward her soft cheek nestled in the crook of his arm and placed a kiss there.

"We shall discover where the letters went and what happened for your mother to run away in the night. I am convinced there is more to the story." Max knew he was playing with fire and risking the tentative peace between them, but he wanted more than her pretense of civility. He wanted her to trust him and turn to him with her troubles. Nay, he wanted her to love him. He wanted every part of her to belong to him without question.

Jane fell asleep soon after, exhausted by the fervor of their lovemaking, her slim body wrapped tightly in Max's arms. Max gazed down at Jane's beautiful face and sighed with contentment. She gave him such peace. Jane murmured and snuggled into his chest a little deeper. He held her close and soon they were both fast asleep.

****

Ten days later, they drove toward Rathborne. The path through the forest was wider, and Max's carriage made good time. As they neared the castle, Jane gazed out at the familiar spires and smiled. She missed her home. She missed Alfred and the others. It was nice to be back in familiar surroundings. They arrived late afternoon.

Mrs. Patrick hurried to greet them. Her ample face wreathed in smiles as they stepped from the well-sprung carriage and walked up the stone steps to the heavy front door of the castle.

"Your grace," she said with a curtsy to Max. "Your grace," she said again with a curtsy to Jane.

Jane's gaze caught on the colorful leaves blowing across the stone steps. She froze in panic. The blood left her face. It was fall. Every emotion she had during that fateful vision came rushing over her at once. She was now the Duchess of Rathborne! She was here at Rathborne Castle! Time was not on her side. The leaves were turning. The king's messenger informing her of Max's death and the seizure of Rathborne Castle arrived in the fall. She had little time to save them both. If she did not, he would die, and she would be penniless and alone. Mrs. Patrick, Alfred, Thomas, and the rest would be sent away to find other employment. Rathborne would once more become overgrown, unkept, and falling to ruin. Her hands trembled violently. Bile rose in her throat. Jane looked around for a place to sit. Max caught her around the waist and helped her into the entry hall. He led her across the corridor and into the antechamber, where he gently set her back onto a gilded chair that stood nearby. His face was a mask of concern.

"Do not touch me!" Jane whispered furiously. She wiped the perspiration from her forehead. O God, what would she do without him? She swallowed the nausea rising in her throat. Jane wrapped her arms around her stomach and rocked back and forth in anguish. She would not be able to live without him. If he hung, she would die. She knew what the future held. What had she been thinking to waste the precious time she had? She had to figure this out.

Max crouched beside her and wiped a tear from her cheek with his finger. "What is it, love?"

Love, he called her love. Panic clawed at her insides. He could not love her. They did not have the time. She could not be his love or anything else until she secured their future together.

"Nothing," she lied. "Just go. I do not want you near me." She could not think with Max so close. Jane sucked in a deep breath, strengthening her resolve. She forced her emotions to the soles of her boots. She had to put some distance between herself and Max before she succumbed to the honeyed sweetness of his touch and lost everything. It would be too easy to throw herself into his arms and beg him to take them back to the country, where they were safe. She could not. Being here at Rathborne meant it was the beginning of the end. She must focus her energy on saving them before her time ran out. She leaned back and turned her head away from him.

Max rose to his feet. His gaze was glacial. "Let me help you to your room, Jane. The journey has overtired you."

Jane glared at him. "Mrs. Patrick can help me. I do not require your assistance, sir. Now unhand me this instant. Your touch repels me." Why could he not just leave? She wasted a fortnight learning of pleasure with him when she should have been thinking of a way to save him. She needed the voice in her head, not Max. It was weeks since it last whispered to her.

"As you wish." Max bowed stiffly from the waist and stalked out.

Mrs. Patrick frowned at Jane once Max was out of earshot. "Tsk, my lady, why do you speak so? Surely you can see his grace cares for you. He was only trying to help."

"I do not require his help, nor do I not want him to care for me. It will be better for us all if he does not," Jane said bitterly. Trepidation held her in its steel vice. She trembled with agitation. She needed time and solitude to examine her feelings.

Mrs. Patrick helped Jane to her feet and down the hall to the newly refurbished rooms belonging to the Duchess of Rathborne. Once inside the lavish lavender and mauve room, Jane climbed onto the large, overstuffed bed without sparing the beautiful room so much as a glance.

Mrs. Patrick placed a delicately woven lavender blanket over Jane. Her hand brushed the auburn curls from Jane's cheek. "We were terribly worried when you disappeared as you did," Mrs. Patrick scolded gently.

Jane shrugged. So much had happened since then. "I was all right. I went to my grandmother. She took me in and cared for me."

Mrs. Patrick cleared her throat. "We were happy to hear of your marriage to his grace. He is a good man, Lady Jane. He will take care of you."

Jane did not bother to answer. She knew Max was kind and gentle. It was best to let everyone believe she hated him rather than reveal the truth of her worry. "I do not have a mother, Mrs. Patrick. Because I do not have a mother, she could not be at my wedding, nor could she do for me the things mothers do when their daughters marry. The man I married is responsible for all the suffering in my life. Tell me, Mrs. Patrick, how am I supposed to feel?" Jane asked grimly. Her heart beat sadly in her chest. Tears spilled over onto her cheeks.

Mrs. Patrick looked at Jane quietly. "Perhaps when you have rested and had something to eat, you will feel kindlier toward him. He has done so much to see to your comfort and happiness."

Jane lifted her swollen face. "He has done much to see to my anguish as well."

And if he died? It would be her fault.

Mrs. Patrick clucked her tongue at Jane. "His grace is the best of men. Perhaps one day you shall know the truth, but you must be willing to give him a chance."

Mrs. Patrick left the chamber, closing the door behind her.

****

Jane fell asleep a few minutes later, her body exhausted from the journey, her mind exhausted from the battle raging within her. She did not awaken when Max gently removed her clothing and slid her carefully beneath the silken sheets. He moved into the bed beside her and pulled Jane's unconscious form into his arms, tucking her head under his chin. Skin to skin, the heat of his body soon warmed Jane through, and she cuddled closer, murmuring with satisfaction at his nearness. She wrapped her arms around him as if she never wanted to be apart again. Max smiled thinly. At least she wanted his touch in her sleep. What caused her violent reaction earlier? Was it because Rathborne brought back old memories? Or was it something else? Was it the vision she had the night of their engagement? She had not mentioned it again. Neither had he. He hoped she would come to him on her own. Perhaps she was overtired from traveling, and being at Rathborne reminded her of her years of suffering. He pulled her sleeping form tighter against him and kissed the soft auburn curls as he sighed. It was going to take a little longer than he supposed to woo his little wife.

Chapter Twenty-Two

The days fell into a sort of routine. Jane did all she could to avoid Max during the day. At night, he pulled her into his arms and made sweet love to her. Sometimes, she resisted. Other times, she did not. His kisses excited her, and she forgot her worries as she let him lead her down the sensuous path he wove with his lips and fingers. Jane wondered why he continued to want her when she took every opportunity to lash out at him during the day. Somehow, he did, and instead of the passion growing weaker, it blazed hotter and hotter. Jane went over and over the vision she received the night of her engagement party. The one thing which stood out in her memory was the season. The messenger came with the summons to court in the fall. Max was convicted and hanged within a fortnight of the summons. Jane tried and tried to have another vision, but nothing happened. The circles under her eyes got darker as the days flew by. Every day more leaves turned brilliant shades of orange, yellow, and red. The air turned crisp, and the winds began to blow. Jane was powerless to stop what she knew was coming.

****

A few days later, it happened. King George demanded Max's presence in London. Max searched Jane's face when he read the summons to her at dinner. She paled. Her hands trembled as she set her goblet down. She did not say a word. She nodded slightly to let him know she understood, and then she got up and left the great hall.

Max sighed and reached for a glass of whiskey. He knew his wife was upset, but he could not ignore a summons from the king. He sat before the great hearth, watching the fire as he sipped his whiskey. If not for her passionate response to his kisses during the night, he would despair altogether. For weeks now, she was either sullen and quiet or angry and volatile. At night, she begged him to touch her, to hold her, and to make love to her. He should be content with the passion they shared, but he wanted more. He wanted her smiles, and he wanted her laughter. He wanted her kisses, and he wanted her trust. Most of all, he wanted her heart. Max stared for a long time into the flames. What must he do to prove his innocence, his worth? He sent men to investigate Jane's claim that his father sent letters begging him to return to Rathborne, but they found nothing. No one knew anything about the letters. Max rubbed his forehead with his hand. Every inch of progress he made following their marriage was undone the second they reached Rathborne. It was worse than the first time they met. Then he was a stranger, and she was suspicious and cautious. Now, she regarded him as the enemy. What had she seen that she would not share with him? This was not a good time to leave Jane alone with her memories, but leave, he must.

Jane was asleep when Max slid into bed beside her and pulled her into his arms. She awoke when he kissed the side of her neck and pulled away angrily.

Max stilled as Jane rolled away from the heat of his body. "I cannot ignore a summons from the king."

She did not reply.

Max sighed with frustration. "Will you be here when I return?"

"I shall think about it. I do not promise you anything."

"I shall find you, wherever you go, and I shall bring you back," he warned. "You belong to me. I shall let no other have you, not ever."

Jane wrapped the quilt around her to ward off the cold and whispered in response. "Forever is a long time. Much can happen between now and then."

Max pulled her tightly against him, his mouth coming down on hers angrily. He licked at her mouth, and when she started to protest, he thrust his tongue into the honeyed recesses and stroked her tongue with his. Soon Jane writhed against him, begging him to enter her and stroke the fire burning within her.

"Say you are mine," Max said into her ear as his fingers worked in and out of her tight sheath.

Jane arced against him. "Please, Max, take me now, please."

"Say it, Jane. I need to hear you say you are mine," he insisted. Perspiration broke out on his brow as he held himself back from what they both desperately wanted.

"I am yours, Max! Now, Max, please!" she cried with frustration.

Max plunged into her with one powerful thrust. Jane screamed at the pleasure his fullness brought and wrapped her legs around his waist. He rode her hard and deep, thrusting faster and faster until they both shouted out their release. Jane's fingers clawed frantically at Max as she rode the waves of pleasure he brought her. When the climax finished surging over them, they lay wrapped together, their slick bodies glistening in the firelight of the master chamber. Max drew the heavy brocade coverlet over them both and pulled Jane back into his arms.

"I shall die if you do not return," Jane confessed, worry in her voice. Then she repeated the words louder this time. "No, that is not true. I shall not die. I shall hunt you down and kill you again. I will make you suffer as no man has suffered before. You shall be sorry you left me." Her voice became a whisper. "Then I shall die."

Max smiled slowly. This death threat was the most encouraging thing she said since their wedding. "I shall be careful to maintain life until I return to you and our bed," Max assured her. He wanted to sing aloud. Jane cared. His heart relaxed, and he pulled her closer. "I shall return as quickly as I can."

****

She stilled. This was it. She knew he would not return as soon as he said the words. Unless an answer presented itself quickly, this was the last time she would see Max or lie naked in his arms. His deep voice rumbled beneath her cheek. His heart beat steadily beneath her ear. His warm breath drifted across her cheek. The thought of him going to London terrified her. What if she never found a way to save him from the king? Jane shivered violently against him. Tears spilled onto his chest. Jane blinked in rapid succession. The last thing she wanted was to explain to Max why she wept at his leaving. She had been so awful to him in her search for a way out. What if he found someone else while he was in London? She could have been kinder and gentler in her attitude toward him. Now, her time was over. Max would leave at first light.

"Such a thing is not possible," Max said as if he could read her thoughts.

"What?" Jane asked.

"I do not want anyone else when I have you," Max answered. He kissed the top of her head.

He believed she wept over the possibility of him taking a lover while he was in London. Although her conscience was guilty over her treatment of him, it was of far less consequence than being unable to save his life. She wiped the tears away. She would not give up. She would fight for Max and Rathborne until the last second. She would find a way. She had to. Jane fell asleep soon after, exhausted but determined.

In her sleep, she dreamed Max journeyed to London. When he was delayed in his return, she went to find him. Max was not at their country estate, nor was he at their London townhouse. In vain, she searched the locations where he should have been, but she could not find him. She called his name aloud as she searched all over London. When at last she found him, he was in bed with Emily, their white naked bodies twisted together in sharp contrast with the red sheets of her bed. A hangman stood over the bed holding a noose. Emily laughed when Jane entered. She bragged about Max being in her bed. She kissed him while Jane looked on. Then she took the noose and slipped it over Max's head. Her mother appeared and pulled the handle. The bed dropped away. Max hung from the gallows while both women laughed.

Jane woke with a start in the early hours of the morning. Fear dampened her brow. Her fine night rail was soaked with perspiration from the frenzy of her dream. She cried aloud when she realized Max had already departed for London. She was alone.

Jane sat up in the large soft bed. The sheets were cold and empty beside her. She screamed Max's name aloud, wishing he were close enough to hear her and come rushing back. The sound of her screaming echoed around the empty chamber. Tears streamed down her cheeks as she realized how alone she was without Max. Hoarse from screaming, Jane pulled the bedclothes over her head and curled into a tight ball. The loneliness of the bed and the castle pressed down on her as she wept. Pain ripped her apart, and panic seized her throat. Jane grabbed the pillow where Max had lain and held it to her face. She could smell him on the fine linen. She choked as she realized she loved him! She loved him with all her heart and soul! Now, when she finally accepted it, she lost him.

"I love you, Max," she said aloud. Jane buried her face in his pillow once more and stiffened. Her present disappeared. She was at Rathborne with Max in a different time, a different place. Jane dared not breathe. After months of trying to see the future and being unable to have so much as a premonition, it happened! A vision came at last! Jane leaned back and breathed it in. She soaked it up as her grandmother said, letting it roll over her and through her. She let it become one with her. She was transported to several different times and several different places. Each time, she let her feelings flow free and used every sense she had to gather information about what she was being shown. She received answers to so many things and found different answers to things she believed she knew. It was a vision of magnificent proportions and clarity.

It was only later, her course presented itself to her mind. There was a way! Jane sat up as the truth struck her heart. Slowly she slid from the high bed. The chill of the morning shivered over her arms and down her back. Jane walked through the communicating door to the duchess' suite and pulled her soft robe over her freezing body. She walked to her fireplace and stood looking down at the flames. She had to hurry to London. The first thing was to gather what she could from Rathborne. The rest she could take care of on her way.

Jane stood still.

Look in the wardrobe.

Bemused, she walked over and put her hands on the latch. Once she did, the present disappeared. She stood in the same room, but she was not alone.

"I hate you. I wish I never married you." Her mother's voice echoed in the silence.

Jane turned her head. Her mother stood a few feet in front of her, wearing only a sheet.

"So, you cuckold me with my enemy? Why Phyllis?" Mangus' voice questioned.

Jane swiveled around. The voices she could not understand before were now clear. Mangus stood in the door with a sword in one hand. He waved it toward the window behind her.

Jane turned. The drapes were parted, and the window was thrown open. Someone just left the chamber. Her mother had a lover, and Mangus caught them together!

"Why not? How does it feel to know something which belongs to you has been given to someone else,

someone you loathe?"

Jane held her breath.

"What are you talking about, Phyllis? I gave you everything I had." Mangus's voice bounced off the walls.

Her mother's laughter floated around her. *"What did you give me, Mangus? Everything belongs to him! Thaddeus inherits the castle, the land, the title, and the money. You have given me nothing, not even your heart."*

Jane's breath hitched. That was untrue. Mangus loved her as much as it was possible for him to love.

"I hate him. What has he done for any of this?" Her mother's voice rose.

"He is my heir, Phyllis." Mangus' voice sounded resigned. As if they had this conversation before.

"And I am your wife. I have given you more than he ever has. For eight years, I have born your fumbling attempts in my bed. I have allowed you to take my body whenever you demanded it. I have suffered your foul breath and saggy, wrinkled skin. I cannot abide your touch. You disgust me."

Jane gasped. Her hand covered her mouth. Good lord!

Mangus' face turned red. *"Why him? Of all the men around, why commit adultery with the Earl of Downing? Why take him to your bed when any number of men would oblige?"*

Her mother's laughter tinkled through the room. *"So, you would know the hurt I feel every time you speak about Thaddeus. He left you, Mangus. He deserves nothing. I am the one who should inherit. I earned it."*

There was a pause. *"We have discussed this. Women do not inherit, as you well know. What would you have me do, Phyllis? I signed the document giving you the right to make decisions for Rathborne if anything happens to Thaddeus. I made you caretaker upon his death if he dies without an heir."*

"Yet you write Thaddeus every day begging him to come home," her mother whined.

Jane stared at her mother's face. It was twisted with jealous rage.

"*I saw you write the document, and I saw you sign it. I want to know where it is. Where did you hide it? I will not be cheated, Mangus."*

Mangus' sigh filled the chamber. *"The document is safe."*

"Why not give it to me?" Her mother faced him with her hands on her hips.

There was another pause. *"I do not trust you. Once Thaddeus returns, everything will be better."*

Her mother's scream of fury echoed around the chamber. Jane put her hands over her ears to block the sound.

"I hate you, Mangus! Thaddeus will never have Rathborne. It is mine. Thomas fulfills me in ways you never have. He asked me to go to Europe with him. I have decided to accept. You will never be the man he is. Margret must have been dim-witted to choose you over Thomas."

Jane could see her mother toss her head in defiance.

"Why did you marry me, Phyllis? You could have married any number of men."

Her mother's voice dropped to a sneer. *"I thought*

you knew. I married you for your money and Rathborne. Make no mistake, Mangus. It will be mine..."

The voices died away. Jane awoke on the floor beside the wardrobe. She was alone once more. Tremors shook her body. Now she understood why Mangus burned the contents of the castle. It was not because of Max. He burned it to spite her mother.

Now the channels to her sight were open, she was flooded with voices and visions. Jane wiped the perspiration from her forehead. She closed her eyes and fought to control her emotions. After a minute, she rose shakily to her feet. She looked at the latch to the wardrobe. Did she want to know more? She had a hard time coming to terms with what she already knew. Jane bit her lip.

Find the document giving Phyllis control of Rathborne.

The wardrobe loomed before her. It was connected to her mother and the secrets of Rathborne. She did not care what passed between Mangus and her mother. She did care about Max. She had to save him. Taking a deep breath, Jane grabbed the latch and opened the door. Her own gowns hung there. She closed her eyes. Voices filled her mind.

Suddenly her mother was there. Jane took a step back. It was another vision.

Her mother carried a packet of letters. She closed the door to her chamber and walked toward the wardrobe. She looked around to make sure she was alone and reached to the back where her old cloak hung. She took the cloak out and slit the lining. Then she tucked the letters inside.

Jane shook her head. When she regained her senses, she was once more on the floor of her chamber. She never knew why she kept her mother's cloak. Perhaps it was because it was all she had left of her. When Jane took over the duchess' chamber, she left the cloak hanging where it was. She had not moved it since the day she found it. The day her mother left. Now, she reached into the far corner and pulled out the old cloak. It was heavy on one side. Jane's heart rate accelerated. She slid her hand into the slit in the lining and pulled out a handful of letters addressed to Max. *He had not received the letters because her mother never sent them!*

Jane's hand trembled as she found letter after letter tucked into the lining of the cloak. So, this is what the voices tried to tell her.

Find the document.

Jane turned around, looking at every corner of the room.

Find the document giving Phyllis control of Rathborne.

Where would Mangus conceal it? Not in the duchess' chamber, that much was obvious. Jane wandered back to Max's chamber and inspected it with new eyes. Where would Mangus keep something important? Especially if he did not want her mother to find it? She wandered around the room. The one thing constant from generation to generation was the bed. Jane leaned on it. Her gaze was drawn to the wall opposite the bed. Of course, the late duchess' portrait. The one with the diamond necklace and the red silk gown. If she could just find the portrait…Jane felt the vision coming. She laid down on the giant bed and let it take over her mind and body.

Chapter Twenty-Three

Two days later, Jane was ready for her trip to London. She smiled widely. She knew how to save Max. She planned to leave in the early hours. Jane blew out the candle by her bed and slipped beneath the silken sheets of the large bed in the master chamber. She rolled to Max's side and laid her head on his pillow. It smelled like him. The scent of his sandalwood soap lulled her to sleep. She was safe and warm.

Suddenly, she sat up. Someone was in the castle.

Danger is close. Hurry.

Jane slipped from the bed and donned her velvet dressing gown. She padded to the door and looked out. The soldiers were making their rounds. "I must call the soldiers," she whispered.

You must find a weapon. There is no time.

She picked up the candlestick from her bedside and blew it out. Grasping it firmly, she felt her way down the corridor and hid in a doorway where she would not be seen.

He comes.

She waited.

A few minutes passed, and the intruder came into view. *He was the same man who tried to burn her in the palace!* His eyes shifted back and forth. He held a wicked-looking blade in front of him as he snuck toward the master chamber.

Jane waited until he was in front of her, then she struck him with the candlestick. He groaned and fell to the floor. She sighed with relief.

"Help me! An intruder is in the castle!" Jane called. Soldiers shouted out the alarm. Jane stared at the man on the floor for a second. Who was he? What did he want? He must know Max was not here. No one would dare enter the castle if Max were present. She pushed the man over onto his back with her foot. Blood seeped from the curved mark left by her candlestick. The man was dressed in black. His knife lay beside him. Jane picked it up and tucked it into her dressing gown pocket. The soldiers were coming. Their footsteps thudded on the stone floor. She turned toward the sound. Something hit her on the head, and Jane went down. It was the last thing she knew.

****

Max wasted no time traveling to London. He wanted to see what the summons was about and go back to Jane. He had no idea what the king could want this time, but he would solve whatever it was as quickly as possible. He could not let Jane out of his sight for long. She might leave him again. It had been extremely hard to leave her sleeping so innocently in his bed. It was not something he intended to do ever again. He meant what he said last evening. If she left, he would follow her. He would never stop looking for her until she was back at Rathborne and in his arms where she belonged.

Max wheeled into the courtyard in London in a record-breaking eight days. His team of bays heaved from the pace he put them to. Max took a minute to pat them on their backs as he handed his reins to the servants who ran to assist him. One hour later, after a quick bath and a change of clothes, Max stood before his king and bowed.

King George gazed down at Max. Displeasure evident in the frown he wore.

"Sire." Max bowed low before the king. "I am at your service." He waited expectantly. Something was wrong.

"At last, you are here. We wondered if you would answer our royal summons after the report we have been given about you and the charges brought against you." King George eyed Max with suspicion.

Max frowned. What was all this? "I do not know of any charges against me, Sire. It is my pleasure to answer any royal command your highness makes of me. I am your loyal servant, and only you do I serve." His deep voice echoed around the throne room.

King George sat quietly for a minute. "We have heard there is another you serve and to whom you give your loyalty," he said. "I summoned you here to question you on the matter."

Max waited for the king to continue. Who accused him, and what were the charges? Max stood at attention, his hands clasped behind his back.

"Do you conspire with Phillip V of Spain against us?"

Max looked hard at the King. "Why would I do such a thing, Your Highness? I have proven my loyalty to England and the crown many times. I have risked my life in the field of battle and forsaken all for king and country. I am only interested in peace and the balance of European power. Now that I have a wife, I desire to raise a family in peace. I would not risk losing those I love to the horror of war."

The king was not impressed. "You make a good speech, Maximillian. We have trusted you more than most lords in my kingdom. We sent you to find this traitor. Now, we find you commit treason against us. We have a witness who testifies you met with the Spanish on English shores. You paid diamonds to join their cause. Sir Harold Roswell caught you in the act and confronted you. You killed him to cover your guilt. The priest in Rathborne Village learned of your sin and asked for confession. You slew him too. Your cook caught you sending correspondence to the Spanish. When you discovered her, you hung her from a tree in your courtyard as a warning to the others who serve you."

Max stood still. "Who dares accuse me of such lies?" Anger tightened his fists. He should have followed his base instincts. He knew the solution was too convenient, and it bothered him.

King George sat back on his throne. He stared at Max for a long minute. "What have you done with Lord Darham? Shall we discover his body too? You said in your report, he disappeared. Speak now. We would have the truth from you."

Max related all that happened in his search for the traitor. "I do not know where Lord Darham is. You closed the case, Sire, after our last discussion. You were satisfied with the conclusion. What changed your mind?"

King George rubbed his chin. "Let the witness come forward and give her testimony."

Her? Max swiveled in disbelief.

Lady Emily Roswell emerged from the crowd and

bowed low before the throne. She held a kerchief to her eyes and walked a wide circle around Max.

Max eyed the picture she presented. She looked like a schoolgirl. Her bright pink gown stopped four inches above the tops of her shoes. The neckline was high and the sleeves long. A wide ribbon around her waist drew the eye to her flat chest and tiny waist. Lady Emily's hair hung in auburn curls around her pointed face. A large bow the same pink as her gown graced the back of her head. Max marveled at the difference in her appearance.

"I first met Maximillian Rathborne at the castle when my father, Sir Harold Roswell, Lady Melissa, and I came to check on my poor crippled cousin, Lady Jane Lenwood." She dabbed her eyes and sniffed into her kerchief. "I went in search of the loo and stumbled across Maximillian arguing with a man in the library. He told the man to deliver a document to the Spanish king, or he would kill him. The document contained the location of the English Fleet."

The court gasped. Max's heart skidded to a stop. He never found the parchment. He suspected everyone but her. Max narrowed his gaze on her face. She was quiet, shy, and withdrawn, not the sort of woman capable of this kind of deceit. She used the voice of a schoolgirl, high and halting, to sway the court with her lies. She looked innocent, shy, and alone. Jane thought her incapable of deceit. He stared at Lady Emily. No, Jane's words were Emily had not taken the ring because she never left her side while she was at Rathborne. Perhaps Jane was not as fooled by Emily as he supposed.

"What did you do, Lady Emily?" The king leaned

forward to hear her answer.

Lady Emily licked her lips and glanced nervously at Max. "I told my father." Tears filled her eyes. She twisted her hands together while she talked. "The anger in Maximillian's voice frightened me. I know of his temper, and I worried if he found me in the corridor, he would kill me."

A murmur went through the crowd. Max stood stiffly watching her performance.

"Surely not," the king murmured.

"I could not eat or sleep worrying about what to do. Papa could not bear seeing me suffer. He badgered me constantly to tell him what was wrong." She wiped her eyes and drew in a deep breath as if seeking courage. "At last, I did." She bowed her head and stood quite still. When she looked up, there was a tear trail down each pale cheek. "Papa was furious. He could not understand how a lord of this kingdom could turn traitor to you, Sire."

"Quite right," King George agreed. "Quite right." He leaned back and glared at Max through narrow eyes. "Continue."

Lady Emily cleared her throat. "Papa confronted Maximillian. Maximillian threatened Papa and told him to keep his mouth shut, or he would die."

The court gasped.

"The knowledge weighed heavy on Papa, as well. He lost weight and hardly slept. He walked the floors of our home, wrestling with the knowledge. He wanted to come to London to see you, Your Highness, but the winter weather kept us away." Lady Emily took a long breath.

The king nodded again.

"Father Brown came to pay us a visit in York. Papa confessed the burden of his thoughts. The priest told Papa he would call Maximillian into confession and take care of the situation." Lady Emily glanced at Max. "Next thing we knew, Maximillian was in York. Our sentries reported Maximillian hiding in the trees around our house." She stopped. "They found Papa's body floating in the river the next morning. A week later, they found Father Brown's body. Everyone who could testify against Maximillian is dead. Everybody but me. If you had not promised your personal protection, I would not have the courage to stand before you now."

The court fell silent. Every eye turned to Max.

King George glared down at him. "What say you?"

Max looked up. "What proof does Lady Emily have? Where is this alleged document? Where is the man I allegedly gave it to? How does Lady Emily know I am the man who killed her father? He was taken by a group of men dressed in black. No one knows who murdered him. They found his body in the river. There is no evidence to support her claim, just the word of an…accomplished actress."

The king cleared his throat. "Do you have more, Lady Emily?"

A smile tugged at her lips as she looked at Max, then it disappeared. "Yes."

She turned to the king. "Maximillian's cook discovered me outside the library the day he argued with the little man. She must have told Maximillian because he came to our townhouse in York the day after my father was murdered. He told me he knew I overheard his conversation. He gave me a diamond necklace for my silence. His cook was hung from a tree in the castle courtyard the day Maximillian returned to Rathborne."

The court made the appropriate noises of disbelief. Max shook his head in amazement. He closed his eyes and thought of Jane. She was the only one who could vouch for him, her, and Lord Darham.

Lady Emily smiled. "The duke asks for proof. I have it here. "

She withdrew a diamond necklace from her pocket. The court gasped as she held it to the light. It sparkled like white fire beneath the massive chandeliers of the throne room. At least half of it did.

Max stiffened.

"If you research, you shall see this necklace is part of the Rathborne diamond collection. It proves Maximillian is the traitor."

Max swallowed the lump in his throat. He needed Jane. His gaze fell on the necklace. Lady Emily was correct. It was the one his mother wore in her portrait. He glanced sharply at Lady Emily's face. Were they all working together to destroy him? How the hell could he prove his innocence now?

"As for the document." Lady Emily batted her eyes. Her face shone with victory. She glanced at the king. "May I…. May I approach, Your Highness?" Lady Emily stuttered as if overcome with shyness.

King George motioned his guards to stand aside. "Of course, Lady Emily." His voice softened, and he leaned forward as she approached his throne. Lady Emily curtsied and pulled the parchment from her ridicule. "Here is the parchment with the details of the English Fleet sealed with the Rathborne crest."

The court was deathly quiet.

"Have you anything further to add?" the king asked Max.

His heart missed a beat. The world spun around his head. He would be hung for a traitor. "I stand by my testimony. I did not kill Sir Harold, nor did I kill my cook." He related again the events which took place. "Lord Darham had been with me constantly since my return to England. He can testify I had not the time nor the ring to make such a document. I have not betrayed you, Sire. I seek to find the one who did."

Max cleared his throat. "As I convalesced from my injuries at Rathborne, Sir Harold and his daughters came for a visit." He stared at Lady Emily. "Sir Harold bore the same tattoo as the man who stole my diamonds. Sir Harold is the traitor, and Lady Emily lies to cover the truth. I did not give her the necklace. Lady Melissa took it from the chest in my father's room the day of their visit." Max looked at the king. He had to believe him.

****

King George considered what Max said. He was correct about Sir Harold. His killer had not been located. If Maximillian were found guilty of treason, his lands would forfeit to the crown. King George opened the parchment in his hand. It damned Maximillian as sure as a bloodied sword. He rubbed his chin in his hand. The one person who could prove Max's innocence was missing. Had he made a mistake to close the case? Maximillian wanted to pursue it and search for Sir Harold's killer. He said it was too easy. The king agreed, but he had to consider Lady Emily's case, too. It was foolproof. This document nailed the last piece of Maximillian's coffin. He could not ignore the evidence he held in his hand.

He stared at Max. "You have given us much to consider." King George looked from Lady Emily to Max. "To be just, I shall give Maximillian a fortnight to prove his innocence. We shall send soldiers to York to search for Lord Darham. We shall contact the local sheriff to see if any headway has been made to find Sir Harold's killer. In the meantime, we cannot let you roam freely, Maximillian." He waved the parchment at Max. "This is enough evidence to hang you. We have taken your service to the crown into consideration. You shall be confined to your chambers under guard until we find the truth of the matter or until a fortnight expires. Whichever comes first."

****

The room shifted. *Jane!* What would she think when he failed to return? Hell, he knew what she would think. Panic clawed his insides. Jane would think the worst and leave him. Max forced the fear down and considered who he would require for his defense. "May I approach the throne?"

King George waived a hovering Lady Emily aside and motioned for Max to approach.

"I would like to send for a diamond expert," Max said in a low voice. "I require Sir Winston Whitmore. Sir Winston perfected the cut he put to my stones to track the traitor."

Lady Emily leaned forward, but Max kept his voice quiet enough only the king heard what he said.

King George nodded and waved at his soldiers. "The person you requested shall be sent for." King George dismissed Max with a wave of his hand.

"Sire," Max said. He bowed from the waist, and

then he was led away.

For two weeks, Max paced the confines of his chambers, overcome with anxiety about Jane. What must she be thinking by now? His delay would mean one thing. She would assume he had left her to rot at Rathborne as she feared. She doubted her attraction and appeal. She doubted his love for her.

A knock sounded on his door at the end of the first week. Max opened the door.

The guard indicated a thin man beside him. “This man has news of your wife. The king gave permission for you to speak with him.”

Max frowned. “I do not know this man. How does he have information about Jane?”

The man held out his hand. Jane’s wedding ring lay in the center of his dirty palm. There was blood on it. The room began to spin. Nausea rose in his throat. Rage lit his blood on fire.

Chapter Twenty-Four

Max looked at the man sharply. “Where did you get this?”

The thin man shrugged. “Yer duchess is dead, me lord. I brought her ring to show ye the truth of it.”

Max grabbed the man by his throat and lifted him from the floor. “Where is she?” His voice was hoarse with emotion. It could not be! His beautiful Jane could not be dead! He would know if she was! Somehow, his heart would know. He shook the man. The mark on the man’s head meant he was recently injured. Did his Jane do it? Max squeezed the man’s throat.

The guard stepped forward. “Let him go. The king thought you might want to ask this man questions. You cannot kill him. The king gave his word the man would be protected.”

“What is your name?” Max asked, tightening his grip. Something was wrong. Emily had to be involved somehow.

“I ain’t tellin’ ye me name, or who sent me. I wer ter give ye the ring and the message.”

The guard placed a hand on Max’s arm. “Let him go.”

Reluctantly Max complied. The man turned and hurried away. Max stared at the tiny band of gold in his hand. It could not be true! He refused to believe it. She could not be dead. Anguish tore him apart. He could not lose Jane. His sweet, beautiful girl had to be alive. She just had to. She was his only source of light. Despair tore through him. How had the man gotten Jane's ring? Why was there blood on it? He paced the confines of his chamber, overcome with grief. Agony tore his heart to shreds.

A thought struck him as he walked restlessly around the chamber. Did Jane know? Was this the vision she had the night of their engagement party? Had she witnessed the pain and agony of this moment? His stomach tightened as he considered the notion. Jane knew he would be tried for treason. She pushed him away to protect her heart. All the things she said and did now made sense. His beautiful girl knew this would happen. Had she seen her death as well? Max stopped. He would not dwell on the thought and pushed it from his mind. He must focus, so he could think of an escape. Once he was free, he would discover what happened to Jane.

When at last he stood before the King, determination, and fury screamed from every line of his taut body. He would finish this charade, whatever the outcome. Max waited while the king called the court to order. When the king motioned him forward, Max bowed and waited for permission to speak. He looked around until he caught sight of Lady Emily. He glared. Today she wore a bright red gown. Her arms were encased in long white gloves and wrapped around the muscular arm of Sir Winston, Max's own witness. Perhaps it was happenstance. Max doubted it. By God, if he discovered Emily was involved in Jane's death, he would rip her apart.

****

Emily grinned when she caught Maximillian's stare. He must be furious. He had a week alone since learning of Jane's death. A week was not long enough, in her opinion, but it was a start. As soon as Maximillian swung from the gallows and the king declared Rathborne forfeit, she planned to host a grand party. She would be well paid by her aunt, and money would no longer be a problem. She would live the life she deserved. She smiled when she thought of Jane's body decaying in the ground. Jane was selfish and self-absorbed. Not once, in all the times Emily came to Rathborne had anyone given her so much as a thought. It was as if she was invisible. No one spoke to her nor asked her opinion. No one cared if she left or if she was present. She sat in the corner and they ignored her. Well, no longer.

Emily leaned into the jeweler's lean frame a little more. She wanted Maximillian to think they were lovers. She wanted him to feel the hopelessness she did. She wanted to see him squirm, but he did not. In truth, he appeared unconcerned with her proximity to his witness and looked away as if he were bored with the whole affair. Maximillian relaxed more and more as she stared at him. Lady Emily remained undaunted. The king believed what she told him, as she planned. When she found the necklace in Melissa's jewel case, several of the diamonds were missing. Melissa sold them to fund her elaborate lifestyle. Papa kept them both penniless. He made them beg for everything. Emily had the stones in the necklace replaced with the ones Papa stole from Maximillian in York. When the constable informed her of Papa's death, the first thing she did was take the bag of diamonds from his safe. If the necklace failed to condemn Max, the document would. It should send him headlong into the hangman's noose. Once Max was in prison for treason, Emily would make a few forged signatures on several documents stating the Duke of Rathborne left his entire fortune in her hands. The king would look for someone to manage the property for him. She would convince him her fiancé, Lord Darrin Dewhurst, would make the proper overlord. Darrin had a score to settle with Maximillian ever since he killed his brother, Jonathon, in a duel. Darrin wanted revenge. With Jane out of the way, the diamond mine would be hers. Max would be dead, and her father would be avenged. Once she dealt with her aunt, it would all belong to her. Lady Emily smiled at the thought and laughed up into her escort's face. Soon she would be one of the richest women in England, maybe even the world.

****

King George looked down at Max. "You requested Sir Winston's presence. What do you seek from him?"

"I should like him to examine the diamonds in Lady Emily's necklace."

King George waved the jeweler forward. "We have established the necklace came from Rathborne. Several ladies of this court have identified it as such."

Max nodded. "The necklace is a Rathborne. However, I would like him to tell us whether the stones are the original diamonds."

The jeweler put his glass to his eye and studied the necklace. He looked for a few minutes and lifted his head. "Half of these diamonds are original. Half of them are the diamonds I cut for the Duke of Rathborne when he left for York."

Max smiled.

"Show me," the king commanded.

The jeweler showed the king the traditional cut of stone with a pointed bottom and a square shape on the top. Then he showed the king the other diamonds. They came to more of a point at the bottom and the top was round. The facets reflected the light brilliantly, outshining the other diamonds. The difference was quite remarkable.

Max waved his hand at the necklace. "I asked Sir Winston to cut my stones so I could track the diamonds I brought for admittance to the traitor's band of cowards. I find it interesting the necklace contains the stones Sir Harold stole from me in York."

Max turned toward Emily.

She changed in the blink of an eye. Two minutes before she smiled and flirted, now she shivered like a nervous child. Her eyes were downcast. She stumbled when she took a step forward. Several lords stepped forward to offer their assistance.

Max observed them through narrow eyes. She had exceptional acting skills.

One gentleman stepped forward. His brown eyes glowed with hatred. Max recognized Lord Darrin Dewhurst, older brother of Jonathon Dewhurst, the man who attacked Jane in the garden. So, that was the way of it. A lot of things began to make sense.

Lady Emily wiped a tear from her pale cheek with a shaky hand. "He lies. He gave me the necklace. He admits it belongs to him as well as the stones." She sniffed.

King George waved the jeweler away. "We have yet to find Lord Darham or Sir Harold's killer. A fortnight has not proven your innocence, Maximilian." The king shook his head sadly. "We have no choice but to pronounce sentence."

Lord Dewhurst smiled and kissed the side of Lady Emily's face.

Max stared at the king.

The king sat back on his throne and looked around the court. He turned to Max, frowning ferociously. "The parchment yet stands as evidence against you. What say you in defense?"

Max took a step in Emily's direction. He wanted to choke her lies in her throat, but King George held up his hand. "We give you this one chance to speak. Use it wisely."

Max turned to face the king. He put all thoughts of Jane aside. He took a deep breath to steady his mind. He related again, every detail of what occurred, leaving nothing out.

"The thing we cannot forgive is why you left out the part about the parchment being sealed with the Rathborne insignia when you came to us and gave your report. Why?"

Max bowed his head. "I had no way to prove my innocence without Lord Darham's testimony. The more I sought the truth, the more my witnesses died. When I could not find Lord Darham, I tracked down every person who had access to my father's ring."

"Where is the ring now?" the king asked.

"In my father's chest at Rathborne Castle," Max answered. He knew his answer damned him. "I have sent my men to search for Lord Darham, but he has vanished. Lady Emily accuses me to shift the blame for her treachery and that of her father, Sir Harold, onto me. I am an innocent man. If you hang me for treason, you will allow the true traitor to escape. We have yet to ascertain Sir Harold's killer. Father Brown threatened Lady Jane's life. He said I would not be able to protect her." Max held up Jane's gold ring. "He was correct." The words choked him. Max kept his gaze direct throughout his entire speech. "I am the last of a long line of people keeping the traitor from his goal. If you hang me, he shall win."

The king sat deep in contemplation for some time. There was not a sound as everyone waited for the king to speak.

Lady Emily wept pitifully into her handkerchief. "You have the document damning him signed with his own signet ring. What more do you require to pronounce him guilty?" Lady Emily knelt before the king. "I lay myself at your feet and beg for your majesty to be just in this matter."

The king nodded his head slowly. He stood and cleared his throat. "Lady Emily, your account is found to have more merit. The document bearing the Duke of Rathborne's seal is something I cannot overlook." He turned his gaze to Max.

"There is too much evidence against you, Maximillian. Lady Emily has proof of your wrongdoings in the form of that damning document." The king motioned toward the parchment bearing the Rathborne seal. "You give only your word." He looked Max over slowly. "I have no choice but to declare you guilty of treason. Thaddeus Maximillian Rathborne, you are sentenced to hang by the neck until dead for the crimes you have committed against the crown of England."

Max's heart dropped to his knees. He stared at King George. How the hell could this be happening? What about Jane? He swayed as dizziness washed over him. He would never have the chance to find her. He would never find her killer and make him pay. His body trembled. He would never see her again; never hear her beautiful laugh, nor would he see the red in her curls ever again. He could not breathe. His chest squeezed tight, and his whole world darkened.

"May I approach the throne?"

Max's head came up slowly. Did he imagine Jane's soft voice, or was she—He swiveled in disbelief.

Jane walked slowly toward them, her eyes on the king.

Jane was alive! Relief swept through him like a tidal wave. Max's hands trembled. His body shook. He sucked in a deep breath. His beautiful wife continued until she stood by his side. Did he wish for her so intensely he conjured her before him? He stared at her face. For more than a week, he thought she was dead. He could not believe she was here! He reached for her gold band inside his jacket and clutched it tight. By some miracle, his wife was alive and standing beside him. He would find the answers he sought, and soon.

He glanced at Lady Emily. Her eyes were wide with shock. Then, they narrowed. She knew of Jane's supposed murder. Max glared. His expression hardened. Lady Emily Roswell would pay dearly for her part in this.

****

The king passed sentence on Max as Jane entered the throne room. She walked confidently toward them. When she reached Max, she stood by his side and bowed low before King George. She did not look at Max. Instead, she focused on the king.

"Your Highness, I offer apologies for my tardiness in attending this inquisition. I was delayed in my journey. I beg your indulgence, Sire, for I have brought evidence and witnesses with me who must give their testimonies." Jane smiled up at the king.

"We were informed you were dead, duchess. We are grateful to see such is not the case." The king nodded at Jane.

"Sire, forgive me, but why should we listen to anything Lady Jane has to say? She seeks to delay justice. You have found the duke guilty, and he should hang." Lady Emily stood next to Jane. Her arms folded across her chest defiantly.

Max stepped around Jane, putting himself between her and Emily. He squeezed Jane's hand.

Jane smiled.

The king looked hard at Jane. "Lady Emily speaks truly. We have already passed sentence. Unless you give us a valid reason to hear what you have to say, the sentence remains."

Jane cleared her throat. "Sire, I have several witnesses with me. Among them is Sir Matthew's man at arms. He is willing to testify. Lord Darham is also here. He awaits your summons."

King George nodded. "We shall hear your witnesses Lady Jane."

Lady Emily opened her mouth angrily, but the king gave her a good glare. She snapped it shut and turned to Jane. "Stay out of my way or pay the consequences," she whispered furiously.

Jane smiled. She leaned around Max. "I am not one

to trifle with. Your worst shall be nothing compared to the storm you shall soon know." Emily was a traitor. She dared to touch the one person Jane cared about, Max.

Chapter Twenty-Five

"Send in Sir Edward Matthew's man at arms," King George commanded.

The color drained out of Lady Emily's face. "Why would his man-at-arms have anything of import to say?"

"Because he was in Sir Matthew's office the night the parchment with its sensitive information was taken," Jane answered.

"This is preposterous." Lady Emily took a step toward the throne.

The king waved her aside. "Let him come."

A burly man in uniform hurried forward. His mustache twitched nervously as he approached the king. He bowed low before the throne.

"Speak," King George commanded.

"My name is Miles Cardon. I am Sir Matthew's man-at-arms." He twisted his good cap in his hands and stared at the floor.

"Tell us what you know about Sir Matthews."

Mr. Cardon nodded. "Sir Matthews was responsible for keeping the information about our ships and their location secret, as you know, Sire. Sir Matthews took his job seriously, but he has a liking for…women."

King George coughed. "Continue."

"One night, a lady came asking for directions. She

knocked on the admiral's door late in the evening. The admiral tells me to see who is at the door. When I see she is a lady, I ask her to wait and report to the admiral. He invites the lady into his office. The admiral was in meetings at the House of Lords all day going over strategies. He has the new location of our fleet on his desk." Mr. Cardon cleared his throat. "One thing led to another, if you know what I mean. The admiral and the lady were intimate. When the lady leaves, the parchment was gone. She was the only one in the office beside Sir Matthews and me. The parchment was on his desk before she arrived and missing after she left."

"Sir Matthews confessed to us he allowed the document to be removed from his desk. He professed not to know the lady who took the document." He stared at Mr. Cardon. "Do you know who the lady was?" the king asked.

"I do not know her name, Your Majesty, but she is standing right there." He indicated Lady Emily.

The court gasped.

Lady Emily laughed. "Your Majesty, are you going to believe this man? Lady Jane could have paid him to make such a story up to save her husband. She does not want to admit the Duke of Rathborne is the traitor. Even Sir Matthews claims not to know this woman's identity."

"Yet his man-at-arms identifies you," the king said.

Max smiled wryly.

King George sat up. "Summon Lord Darham," he commanded his soldiers. He nodded at Lady Jane. "Now this testimony I am interested in."

"Your Majesty, I protest. The Duchess of Rathborne probably bribed Lord Darham as well. Must we listen to this drivel? She is grasping at straws. The parchment says it all. Her husband is guilty. She should accept his fate."

"Does Lord Darham's testimony frighten you?" Jane asked with interest.

King George frowned at Lady Emily. "Lord Darham is a lord of the realm. We will allow him to give testimony."

Lord Darham stepped forward and gave an account identical to Max's, and then he continued. "After Max left for Rathborne, I scoured the back of the tavern for clues on the stranger who took the bag of diamonds. His trail led me to Roswell Estate. I waited for several hours, but no one came or went. I returned to my rooms to form a plan. Sir Harold's soldiers attacked in the night. When I woke, I was face down in the alley, beaten nigh to death. I went back to my rooms and bandaged my wounds. I found a place to hide and hunkered down. I figured Sir Harold's men would be back to kill me. If I were alive, I would be able to testify against him. I was right. Sir Harold and Lady Emily have been on my trail for months now. I have been one step ahead. They planned my death many times, but I know how to conceal myself from the enemy."

King George nodded. "Continue."

"Imagine how surprised I was when a few days back, I turned around, and this beautiful lady introduced herself as the Duchess of Rathborne. She told me her husband was accused of treason, and I was needed to give testimony before the king. I believed I was well hidden, but the duchess found me. "

The king looked over at Jane. "How is it you found

Lord Darham when so many others failed?"

Jane smiled. "Maximillian left a message for Lord Darham at his rooms in York. I went there to see if Lord Darham had returned. I found him exiting the tavern through the back alley."

"But that was months ago. And why would you go around back?" King George asked.

Jane shrugged. "If someone wanted to kill me, I would not use the front door and announce my presence or lack of it."

King George smiled. "Nor would we."

Lady Emily laughed again. This time it was shrill and forced. "Jane, you go to such extreme measures. Maximillian is simply not worth it."

"There is more," Jane announced. She waved at a man in the back. "I have the jeweler who reset the diamonds in the Rathborne necklace for Lady Emily with the loose stones stolen from Max in York."

The jeweler came forward and gave his testimony. He identified Lady Melissa as the woman who brought the necklace in and sold diamonds from it a piece at a time. The jeweler indicated Lady Emily. "This lady brought the necklace back a couple of months ago and wanted me to fix the same necklace with stones she had in a leather bag."

"What does that prove?" Lady Emily challenged. "It is a Rathborne diamond necklace. He gave it to me to buy my silence." She looked Jane up and down. "Are you jealous?"

Jane shook her head. "Why would Maximillian take a necklace belonging to the Rathborne collection and reset it with stones he marked to trace the traitor?"

King George frowned at her. "Lady Emily, we

wonder the same. Do you seek to deceive your king? I now have three testimonies against you."

Lady Emily gave a tinkling laugh which echoed around the silent room. "How does Lady Jane account for the seal on the parchment?"

Lord Darham stepped forward. "Max was with me until the day he left for Rathborne. He could not have made the document. I vouch for his innocence."

Jane motioned with her hand. "A witness testifies you took the information from Sir Matthews. I have Thomas, and your lady's maid, Agatha, to explain how the Rathborne ring sealed the parchment."

The two servants walked toward them, their eyes on the floor. Jane introduced them to the king. They bowed.

"Tell us what you know," the king commanded.

Thomas gave testimony of seeing Sir Harold take the signet ring from the duke's chamber months before Max came to Rathborne. Lady Emily's maid testified Lady Emily kept it in her jewel case and later returned it to Rathborne Castle after Max arrived.

King George nodded. "Now we have the truth of it."

Lady Emily threw herself before the king. "Sire, why do you allow Lady Jane to carry out this ridiculous charade? Surely you can see she will stop at nothing to release Maximillian from his sentence. She has the wealth and power of her husband's name behind her. Few men, if any, could resist the wealth she could shower upon them."

King George glared. "This has nothing to do with wealth. We rely on the word of our lords. Maximillian was proven innocent with Lord Darham's testimony. I allowed the others to testify to satisfy my curiosity."

King George gazed at the three of them. "Lady Emily Roswell, you are under arrest for high treason against the crown. You have falsely accused my lord and are sentenced to life imprisonment." He nodded at his soldiers. "Release the Duke of Rathborne. He is an innocent man. We rescind our earlier sentence."

****

Max stood quietly and let it all sink in. Jane was alive. She came to his aid! Not only did she come when he needed her the most, but she came to defend his honor! He hardly knew how to act. What happened to change her mind about him? He turned toward her, filled with love. She was so beautiful. She took his breath away.

She smiled and tucked her hand in his arm.

Max closed his eyes and inhaled deeply. He could smell the sweet fragrance of her perfume and the rose-scented soap she used when she bathed. He opened his eyes to see King George watching him with interest.

"Your Majesty," Lady Emily began, "if I may have a private word with you, I am sure we can solve this little misunderstanding."

The king snapped his finger. "The only thing we wish to hear from you, Lady Emily, is the name of the lord you partner with."

Lady Emily paled a little. "I know no lord— "

"You give us a parchment stolen by your own hand as evidence of treason against my duke. We wonder. Did you kill your father to forward your evil design? Or is there someone else?" he thundered. "And what of Sir Matthews? We agree with Maximillian. The evidence is too tidy. Clear the court!" He pointed at Max and Jane as they turned to make their exit. “You will stay where you are.” He pointed at Lady Emily. “You, too.”

Max bowed slightly toward the king and glanced at Jane. A smiled hovered over her pink lips. His gut twisted, and his mouth went dry. It had been a long time since he had taken his little wife to bed, much too long. He stared hard at her mouth and envisioned several things he wanted to do to her, and soon. The fire of desire held him tight. His eyes glowed with heat as he looked her over again. She must have felt the flame in his eyes because she glanced at him nervously. A blush worked its way up her neck and washed across her cheeks.

The king’s voice made Jane jump.

He glared at Lady Emily. “We know you did not commit all the foul deeds associated with this parchment.” He waved it in the air. “So, we will give you one chance to name the person or persons who aided you in this grand deception. If you do, we will show forth leniency toward you.”

“I am innocent. Your traitor stands before you, aided by his lying wife. If you seek justice, hang him. In fact, hang them both,” Lady Emily said maliciously.

“Have you nothing but venom to spew?” the king asked. “This is my court. We decide who hangs.” The king’s voice brooked no argument.

Lady Emily snapped her mouth shut. She glared at Max and Jane.

“Lady Emily seeks to take Rathborne. I received this letter after you summoned my husband to London. When I refused to vacate the castle as instructed, the same man who burned your library attacked me, Sire. He took my ring as proof of my death.” Jane handed a folded missive to the king.

"What is this?" King George inquired.

"A letter Lady Emily sent. There is a grand plan afoot to destroy Max and take his fortune. I got in the way. She told me to leave England and never return. She goes on to say the Rathborne fortune, as well as my husband's mines, are being left to her. She wrote there is no hope for me. She also issued several threats should I not comply with her wishes, as you shall read, Sire." She smiled up at the king.

The king smiled back.

"A week after my refusal, a bandit crept into my home to murder me." She related the circumstances. "When I awoke, my guards were standing over me. My wedding band was gone. The bandit had escaped."

The king turned to his soldiers. "Put Lady Emily in the dungeon. Spread the word she has given us information about several persons of interest. Say we are investigating her allegations against these persons and their involvement with the Spanish king. Say she has agreed to give us more information on the morrow." The king waved the soldiers away.

"But, Sire, you cannot do this," Lady Emily screamed. "I am innocent." She turned to Max and Jane. "You shall regret this!" The guards paid her no mind. Her shrieks echoed for several minutes after they escorted her from the throne room.

Chapter Twenty-Six

Max stared at Jane. He never had his character questioned so thoroughly, nor had he been so well defended before. The fact it was Jane defending him was more of a shock to his system than the other. Jane was getting better at hiding her gift. He knew she saw Lord Darham in a vision, or she would not have found him.

Max shook his head, trying to make sense of what happened. “Sire, we do not know who killed Sir Harold. Lady Emily may have another accomplice. If she does, they will come to discover what she told the court. Her life could be in danger.”

King George agreed. “This is true. If there are accomplices, we shall catch them. We cannot have traitors among us, can we? Keep your eyes open for any visitors, Maximilian. We want to know who comes and goes to the prison to visit Lady Emily.”

Max bowed low before the King. It would be a long night, and all he wanted to do was take Jane to his chamber.

“Wedded life agrees with you Lady Jane. I seem to remember you used a cane the last time you visited the palace.” The king looked Jane over. “You are the picture of health.”

“The power of love, Your Majesty, heals much.”

****

Jane curtsied as the king dismissed them both with a wave of his hand. She felt Max's silver gaze settle on her as he escorted her from the throne room.

"My darling, it is good to see you." Max pulled her into his arms and lifted her face to his.

"It is good to see you as well," Jane answered. She allowed him one kiss and then pushed against his chest. She stepped out of his embrace.

He let her go, a frown on his face.

"May we go somewhere privately? I have much I need to speak with you about." Jane dipped her head. She worried over where to begin. She had so much to tell him and so much she wanted to explain. If she allowed more of his kisses, she would not say what she wanted to say. If only she could compose sentences which made sense.

"Of course," Max answered. "But I cannot go far, Jane. I have to watch who goes and comes so I can report to his majesty." He grabbed Jane by the hand and led her to a quiet corner where he could see the entire room and the hallway beyond leading to the dungeons. Courtiers milled about involved in their own dramas and tattling.

"I have much to speak with you about, as well. But first…" Max reached inside his jacket pocket and retrieved her gold band. He kissed her fingers one at a time and slipped the gold band on the fourth finger of her left hand. "I was told you were dead. For the last week I mourned your loss. You have no idea the torment I have been through. When I heard your voice just now in the court, I wondered if I had gone insane. I yearned to see you, to hear your voice, to hold you once more…"

Jane turned to Max, her hands twisting together as she considered what she wanted to say. "I have been in torment also."

Max took a step toward her.

Jane frowned. "You must let me say my piece."

At his nod, she took a deep breath and began. "I shall start at the beginning." She smiled as she felt her gold band. It was wonderful to have it back. She had no idea how much she twisted it when she was nervous, until it was not there anymore. "I have known for some time you would be accused of treason and hung. I saw the fate of Rathborne and all the people in it. I have been frantic these past months to find a way to save you, to save us. Try as I would, nothing more was shown to me. For the first time, my 'sight' failed me. I have been alone in this. Even the voice in my head deserted me. When you asked me the night of our engagement party, to reveal what I saw, I had no answers. I only knew what the ending would be. I have been so worried and afraid of what was to come. I have been extremely unkind to you. This is the worst of it. I should have trusted the love I have for you instead of fighting it."

Jane took a deep breath. "As I lay there after you left, I discovered the reason I was so upset was not because you left me, but because I had fallen in love with you. I marveled at the notion. I said the words aloud, and they felt so right. A peace such as I have not known for some time settled over me. I pictured you in my mind traveling to London with the wind in your hair. I rolled over and picked up your pillow. As I breathed in your scent, it happened. The vision I sought for months came to me. I let it roll over me and through me as I thought of you, and the love I have for you. Everything I needed to save you was shown to me. When I came back to myself, I was not weak as I was before. I was invigorated and happy." Jane bowed her head in shame. She had been so wrong about him. It embarrassed her when she remembered the things she said. "I found the letters Mangus wrote to you all those years ago. He gave them to my mother, but she never sent them. She hid them in the lining of her cloak." Jane's voice trailed off in a whisper.

"You have my father's letters?" Max asked incredulously. His large frame stiffened at the news.

Jane nodded. "Every one of them," she said. "I am so sorry, Max, for the way I treated you, and the things I said. Can you forgive me?" Jane's eyes filled with tears, and she dared a glance upward.

He had a strange expression on his face, his eyes unseeing as if lost in a memory. "I did not believe there were any letters. You see, Jane, I searched out my father's valet once I returned to England. I figured he would know if my father wrote to me, but he had no knowledge of any letters. All this time…your mother had them hidden. Why Jane?" Max pulled an unresisting Jane into his embrace. Then he answered her plea. "There is nothing to forgive, my love. You knew the letters were real and thought your mother sent them. You also believed I refused to answer. I figured the letters were a story made up by someone who wanted revenge, either on me, or on my father. So, I paid no real attention to anything you said about them." Max sighed. "How many letters are there? I should like to read them once we are back at Rathborne," he said quietly. "Why did your mother hide them instead of sending them?"

"I did not know until I read her diary. The workmen found it when they finished the duchess' chamber. Mrs. Patrick gave it to me when we returned from our honeymoon, but I was not interested. My mind was on saving you and Rathborne." Jane gazed deep into his eyes. "Thank you for loving me, even though I was so horrid to you."

Max kissed her cheek. "And I do love you, my Jane. Now, proceed with your story, love."

"My mother hated you. She was jealous of the time and attention Mangus gave to you and not her. She believed Mangus overindulged you, and she fought with him over the money he allowed you. Your fight with Mangus and departure from England pleased my mother a great deal. She wrote she hoped you died in the fighting because my mother inherited upon your death." Jane's voice was whisper soft again. "Perhaps inherited is not the right word. Mangus wrote a document giving her legal right to make decisions about Rathborne should you die." There were so many things Jane did not know about her mother.

"Where is this document?" Max asked. "I never knew such a thing existed."

"I saw her arguing with Mangus about it," Jane answered. "Your father hid it from her."

Jane pulled the letter from her pocket. "I followed the voices to a cell in the dungeon. I found your mother's portrait there. Mangus hid the letter in the back. He put it there before he had the castle stripped. My mother would not descend below stairs. So, it was a safe place to hide it."

Max took the letter and read it.

Jane continued. "My mother convinced Mangus to give her the letters he wrote to you. She told him she would see they were delivered to you. Then she hid them, and Mangus never knew why you did not come at his request." Tears spilled over and ran down Jane's cheeks. It hurt to think Max never knew how much his father regretted their argument and wanted him to come home.

"How did you know about the necklace?" Max asked searching her face.

"I saw the day Mangus gave the necklace to your mother. I watched as Lady Melissa took it from the chest. I witnessed Lady Emily take it from Lady Melissa's jewel case, and I watched a jeweler reset the stones with diamonds stolen from you. I saw it all."

Max nodded his head. "What about Sir Harold? Do you know who killed him?"

Jane shook her head. "There are whispers in my head. I have not been able to decipher them yet." She sighed.

"What of Lady Melissa?" Max inquired. "Is she part of all this?"

Jane shook her head. "Lady Melissa is selfish and greedy. She took the duchess' necklace to sell the stones but otherwise, she has been too busy with her lovers to pay attention to much else."

****

Max pulled Jane back into his arms. He could not believe the difference between this Jane and the one he left at Rathborne several weeks ago. He closed his eyes and thanked the gods for their intervention. Her gift saved his life. The villagers of Rathborne were right. Lady Jane was a witch, and she cast a spell over him.

He hoped it never wore off. He would need her brand of spells and the magic around him forever. He could not live without her. She enchanted him, mystified him, and held him spellbound. She carried his heart in her hands. He intended to show her how much he loved her as soon he was done with the duty the king required of him.

"If your mother wanted Rathborne and did this to ensure her rights, why did she leave in the middle of the night?" Max asked, trying to comprehend why anyone would leave his Jane alone and unprotected.

"She had a lover as you have no doubt guessed," Jane answered. "While I was busy blaming you for our poverty, my mother was having an affair with the Earl of Downing. He was privately funding my mother's jewels and gowns. They were deeply in love according to my mother's diary. He invited her to live with him at Downing castle. They were traveling to France together the night my mother left. In her diary, she speaks of how strong minded I was and how determined I was to make a go of Rathborne. Without the wealth of Rathborne, my mother had no reason to stay. She wrote Rathborne to solve her problem on what to do with me. No one would want me, for I was too plain and outspoken. I would not make a good marriage. It was better for me to wilt away at Rathborne then to be an encumbrance to her and her lover. So she left me. She held no qualms about leaving in the night with no word to me at all. She wrote she hoped she was in France before I realized what happened." Jane took a deep breath, clutching her heart.

"If she wrote all this in her diary, why did she leave it at Rathborne?" Max asked.

Jane shrugged. "My mother left in a hurry. She did not want to alert me to the fact. She planned a whole new life at Downing Castle. She left Rathborne, me, and the past behind her. I do not think she thought it important as it was well hidden. The workmen found it tucked beneath the ropes and the straw ticking."

"She does not deserve you," Max said roughly. Jane shook in his arms, and he tightened his hold around her. "I am eternally in her debt for leaving you at Rathborne for me to find," Max said huskily. He swooped down and kissed Jane passionately. Kissing first her swollen eyes red from crying, then her delicate neck where her pulse beat furiously, and finally her soft lips. He licked at the nectar of her mouth and drank deeply as if his life depended on it.

A soldier coughed nearby. Reluctantly, Max lifted his head. He glared at the man, irritated at being interrupted.

"A gentleman has requested an audience with Lady Emily in the dungeon, your grace," the soldier said, his face impassive.

Max straightened. "Guard my lady!" he commanded. "I shall return soon, Jane. I must see who this traitor is and apprehend him for the king. Stay with the soldier where I know you are safe." He handed her the letter Mangus made for her mother. "Hold on to this. We may need it."

Jane nodded and tucked the letter into her pocket. When she looked up, Max was already halfway across the room and down the stairs leading to the dungeon.

Chapter Twenty-Seven

"The king caught the traitor," Lady Phyllis Rathborne said.

"Did he hang?" The Earl of Downing asked with a smile.

"Maximillian is free. The king arrested Lady Emily," Lady Phyllis replied.

The earl struck his fist against the fireplace where he stood. He turned away from the fire and faced her. Phyllis was petite with a narrow face and two beautiful blue eyes. She had a halo of dark hair around her tiny face. She reminded the earl of a doll. "Is she talking?" he asked. Lady Emily would not be loyal now she was in the dungeon. She would barter their names to save her own soft skin. "Something must be done about her," he warned. "There is too much at stake."

"When has Lady Emily ever kept her mouth shut when she thought it could benefit her?" Phyllis asked. She rose and sauntered over to the drink trolley. She poured a shot of whiskey and resumed her seat. "The king knows Lady Emily tossed her skirts for Sir Matthews and stole the location of the fleet off his desk."

"As long as the king thinks Sir Harold is responsible, we are in the clear." The earl shook his head. "This is what comes of deviating from the plan."

Phyllis shrugged. "Lady Emily agreed to tell

everything she knows tomorrow in court."

"I figured as much," the earl replied. "Come along, my dear. I know she is your niece, but she is a danger to us. Once Lady Emily is dead, we have nothing more to fear."

"But Maximillian is still alive and so is Jane," Phyllis pouted. "You promised me you would take care of it."

"And I shall. If Sir Harold had done what I told him to do instead of getting greedy, none of this would have happened. By all rights Mauldrin Kane should have killed Maximillian in the tavern. I cannot believe his incompetence. He came so highly recommended."

The earl shook his head sadly. It was a shame. Emily would need another lesson in loyalty. He doubted Maximillian had a chance to figure the situation out, but he was no fool. Maximillian would realize Emily was not capable of doing all the killing. There was only a narrow bit of time to get in, get Emily, and get out before anyone realized what they were about. "Fetch my cape," he commanded Robert. his valet. "We are going to the palace to pay a visit."

****

Robert nodded and slipped a pearl handled blade into the Earl of Downing's pocket. The earl was getting on in years, but he was in excellent health. His lord was wickedly good with a knife. An ugly smile crossed the man's face as he started after his employer. He never did like Lady Emily. She was too good for everybody, putting on airs like she was the queen or something. But he taught her what was what, the time he caught her in the master's safe. It was either toss her skirts and let him ride her until he was done, or he would tell the Earl of Downing about her and the safe. He knew she stole from the master. He knew she stole the signet ring from Lady Phyllis, after Sir Harold brought it to her. He kept the information secret until he could put it to good use.

Robert licked his thick lips. He had one hell of an afternoon with Lady Emily. The damn woman was talented with her mouth, and one of the few women of his acquaintance who could pleasure a man in the French fashion. If she got caught in the safe, the master would punish her. He figured he did her a favor, giving her a way out like he did.

Lady Emily pretended that afternoon never happened. She avoided him whenever she came to see his master and Lady Phyllis. Robert waited for a chance to repeat what happened. He kept her under surveillance hoping for evidence to use against her. Lady Emily taunted him when she saw what he was about. He would not use her again, she warned. She made sure he knew nothing, and it infuriated him. Robert hurried to catch up with the earl, excited at the prospect of watching the uppity bitch get knocked down a peg or two. His beady eyes darted back and forth as he followed the pair to the carriage. He kept to the shadows walking as stealthy as a weasel.

****

Jane faced the door leading down to the dungeons. People sentenced to prison waited in the castle dungeon until they were transported to Newgate Prison. She shook her head over Emily. She was such a fool. Jane thought Emily resolved her jealousies. It was incredible she thought she could take Rathborne. Jane reached into her pocket and froze.

They are here. They want to kill you both. Your

mother is here.

She recognized the scent her mother wore and stiffened in surprise. She wondered how she would feel when she saw her mother again. Now it was upon her, she felt nothing. The thought surprised her. Yet it was true. Jane turned to face Phyllis Rathborne. Scene after scene flashed through her mind. There was nothing but numbness inside.

"Hello, Mama," Jane said. Too late she realized there were three of them.

Someone grabbed her from behind and pressed a knife against her throat.

"Do not make a sound," a voice said in her ear.

Jane's heart rose to her throat. The voice belonged to the Earl of Downing. He wanted to kill Max. The blackness of his soul filled Jane with terror. There was a thud as the soldier Max left to guard her fell to the ground, dead.

The weasel who tried to kill her two times before pulled a knife from the soldier's back and grinned at her. "Don't be jealous. Yer turn is coming."

Jane swallowed hard. She knew what her other power was. She could communicate with Max in her head. She called to him the night the weasel attacked her in the palace. Max heard her voice as plain as if she stood beside him. She would use it again now. Jane closed her eyes and focused.

"Max, they are coming to kill us both!"

****

Max slipped quietly along the flagstone floor of the dungeon. He stopped when he reached the end of the dim corridor and looked carefully in both directions. Lady Emily was incarcerated at the end of the corridor on the left. There was no one in sight but the two soldiers who stood guard outside her cell. Max stole along the wall until he stood outside Lady Emily's door. He motioned for the soldiers to step aside while he peered in through the narrow window.

No one was inside the dark space but Lady Emily. Her slim form lay across the narrow cot, her cloak thrown over her for warmth. Max stepped back and shut the window. "Has she had any visitors?" he asked the guards quietly.

"No, your grace." The soldiers stood at attention, their red and white uniforms gleaming in the semi darkness of the dungeon.

"No one?" Max asked.

"No one, your grace," they answered.

Max frowned. Why was he told the lady had a visitor when she had not?

"Max, they are coming to kill us both!"

"Jane?"

There was a scuffle behind him. Max turned. His heart dropped to his knees.

Lord Downing came toward him in the dimly lit corridor. He had a sneer of contempt on his handsome face. He held Jane in front of him like a shield, a knife at her throat. They stopped several feet in front of Max.

Rage roared through Max's veins.

Jane's face was as pale as the first snow. Her eyes bored into his begging him to help her. The Earl of Downing was a dead man.

"Good evening Rathborne," the earl drawled. He held the advantage while his knife was pressed against Jane's throat, and they both knew it.

"Downing." Max returned, his voice cold and

deadly. He motioned for the two guards behind him to put down their swords. If they rushed the earl, Jane would die.

"I have come for Lady Emily."

"Let my wife go," Max said. "This is between you and I." He smiled into Jane's eyes to calm her down. She was terrified. Her hands trembled where she clutched them together in front of her.

The earl laughed. "I want Emily, and you want your wife. What are we to do?" He stared at Max. "I have waited forty years for this moment, and I intend to savor every second. If only Mangus were here to watch the final destruction of his name and legacy." He took in a huge breath of air. "I can smell victory. What do you smell, Rathborne?"

Max smiled and folded his arms across his broad chest. He leaned back against the cold, stone, dungeon wall as if he had all the time in the world. "I smell a traitor." The Earl of Downing was the mastermind and the traitor Max searched for. "Why did you do it?"

The earl laughed aloud. "I knew you would figure it out. There is a lot of money to be made in times of war. I saw an opportunity."

He tightened his hold on Jane. "I intend to kill your wife and then you." He chuckled. "This is such a joyous moment. I told Mangus I would make him pay if it was the last thing I did. He had no right to marry Margret. She belonged to me until Mangus stole her. I swore I would take everyone he loved in repayment for what he did. I told him I would destroy everything." He chuckled. "It should have worked when you were eighteen. Catherine did a magnificent job. She had you convinced you were in love." He chuckled again. "You offered for her hand! We could have taken Rathborne and all her wealth right beneath Mangus' nose. Then you had to ruin it and run away. I was devastated. Mangus had to suffer the way I suffered. I had to come up with a different plan. I had a hard time getting in again until Phyllis came along. Once I saw how much Mangus loved Phyllis, I knew what I had to do." He smiled over Jane's head. "I took her away from Mangus. I gave her jewels and clothes. I took her to Paris and Vienna. I even bought her a racehorse. She would tell Mangus some lie or other to explain her absence. He never suspected. You have no idea how exciting it is to bed your enemy's wife in their bed. I had an affair with her right beneath his roof." The Earl of Downing laughed long and loud. "One day Mangus came home and caught us in her chamber. I will never forget the look on his face! He was furious. I escaped out the window and retreated to Downing Castle. Mangus tore Rathborne apart and burned everything in the castle. He knew Phyllis married him for his wealth and title. Since she betrayed him, he took it away from her. It was a grand victory! Mangus destroyed everything and saved me the trouble."

"You talk too much, darling. Just cut her throat and be done with it." The sultry voice came from behind the earl. Jane's mother strolled into view a few seconds later.

Max glanced at Jane to judge her reaction.

She did not look up. "Do you care so little, Mama? I am your flesh. You are supposed to love me." Jane lifted her gaze. "Why did you leave me?" Her terrified whisper stabbed his heart.

The Earl of Downing chuckled again. "Tell her, my

love."

"You were an incumbrance, darling. I deserve luxury and wealth. Thomas could provide it." She walked around the earl where she could watch Jane's face.

"Your mother came to me to escape that dreadful place. We figured Rathborne would crumble to the ground around you and be no more," the Earl of Downing added. "When we learned of your…accident and deformity…we added a little spice to your life."

"Father Brown," Jane said.

"Yes, Father Brown. He made sure no one talked to you, and he kept you at Rathborne. Sir Harold checked on you and kept us up to date on any news of Maximillian," her mother chimed in. She smiled as if quite pleased with herself. "He was supposed to find the document Mangus made for me giving me Rathborne. He failed, so I killed him."

"Why accuse me of treason?" Max knew the answer. He stalled for time. With every minute they kept the earl talking, it was another minute Jane lived. Phyllis moved closer. She was within striking distance.

"Come now, Rathborne. You are the continuation of Mangus. You must die. If you live, part of Mangus does too. I cannot allow it," the Earl of Downing drawled.

"And I cannot have Rathborne while you live. So, you see, there is no other choice," Phyllis said.

"Then, let Jane go. She has nothing to do with this." He spoke calmly, his eyes calculating the distance between them. Max leaned a little further.

A thin little man paced behind the earl. The man was the human version of a weasel. His eyes darted back and forth as if looking for a means of escape, his hands clenched and unclenched as he paced. He was the same man who told him of Jane's death. He was the one who attacked Jane at Rathborne, for he still had the mark Jane made with the candlestick. According to Jane, he was the same man who tried to burn her alive in the palace, the night of their engagement. It all made sense. Max assessed the distance between his opponents.

"It must have been a disappointment to you when you discovered your man had not killed Jane as you ordered." Max did not spare Jane a glance. He could not afford to take his eyes from the snake who held his wife.

The earl glanced behind him. "Robert and I shall sort it out as soon as I am done with you. I *was* surprised to see Jane standing in the corridor upstairs." He shrugged. "She was supposed to be dead. It does not matter, for she shall still die. She gave me the advantage just now with you, but it shall all end the way I planned."

The little man behind the earl tripped up. So the earl was unaware the weasel failed until he met Jane upstairs. It must have surprised Emily as well. He remembered the look on her face when Jane entered the throne room.

Phyllis strolled over to Jane and took the letter from her pocket. "It was marvelous of you, Jane darling, to find this pesky little paper for me. I was ecstatic when I realized what it was. Maximillian told you to hold onto it." She laughed. "Then, I recognized Mangus' signature. He was such a coward to hide it from me." She lifted the letter and sniffed. "It smells of him." She gazed at Max. "No matter. I have it now and that is all that matters. I shall have everything my heart desires as soon as Thomas kills you."

Max studied Phyllis, his mind putting the pieces together. "You are the woman Sir Harold met in the black carriage. What is your connection to the monastery?"

Phyllis laughed. "You ask too many questions, Maximillian. But I suppose it does not matter, now. In a few minutes you will be dead." She played with the necklace clasped around her neck. "I am a patron of the monastery. I give them gold and they do little errands for me." She laughed at Max's expression. "Do not be so shocked. The bishop and I go way back. We have been…friends forever." She glanced at the earl.

The earl dropped his smile. "Enough of this idle chat. If you do not order Emily's release this instant, I shall slit Jane's throat." He tightened his grip on Jane and pressed the knife into her flesh.

To Jane's credit, she did not make a sound even as a trickle of blood ran down the smooth white skin of her neck.

Max breathed in slowly to steady his racing heart. He needed all his wits and could not be distracted by Jane's terror. He could feel it so palpably it was a taste in his mouth. "The king alone commands the release of Lady Emily," Max answered. His posture appeared relaxed, but he was strung tight, adrenaline pumping furiously through his body, ready for the fight ahead.

The earl took a step backward, disbelief in his eyes. "Are you stupid, man? You barter with your wife's life so recklessly. Do I do you a favor by killing her? Are you tired of her crippled body? I admit you intrigue me,

Rathborne. Most men would not watch their wives die with such enjoyment." He glanced around. Not one of the soldiers moved.

Max did not move either. His eyes calmly assessed his enemy, a smile upon his face.

****

The Earl of Downing was furious. "You should be on your knees before me pleading for your wife's life. This is not the scene I envisioned when I saw the duchess in the corridor with only one soldier to guard her. Two things happened. I realized Robert failed me again. I also realized you waited in the dungeons below. You are not complying as a husband should, especially a new one." He spit on the ground.

"I changed my mind, Rathborne. I planned to let this bitch go if you begged for her life and got on your knees before me. I shall kill you both, regardless. Once you are dead, I shall release Emily. We shall take your diamond mine and your castle. Together we shall see to it every evidence of your existence is exterminated. Soon all the world shall fear me. My wealth and power shall be unimaginable, while you and your twisted duchess rot in your graves with Mangus. This is the end of Rathborne. I have won at last."

Jane drew in a deep breath. She thought Max was unaffected by the blood trickling down her throat. Then she saw his clenched jaw, and the pulse pounding furiously in the side of Max's neck. She smiled. Max would kill the earl, and everything would be all right.

Trust him.

I do. I trust him with my life, my heart, and my soul.

Max stared at her.

When I move be ready....

His voice played clearly in her head. Jane nodded slightly, to let him know she understood.

"Robert will pay for failing me. Jane must die. I have no choice but to—" The earl never finished the sentence, for at the same instant he moved the knife along Jane's throat, Max struck.

Max knocked the knife away from Jane's neck and shoved her backward so suddenly, the earl never saw it coming. Jane hit the wall with a thud.

Max snapped the weasel's neck and knocked Phyllis toward the soldiers. He had Downing on the ground with his sword above the man's heart in the next instant. The two soldiers who stood outside Lady Emily's cell were still reaching for their swords when it was all over. They blinked at each other and shrugged. Nobody saw the duke move until it was over.

Phyllis screamed and reached for one of the soldiers' swords.

Bind her," Max commanded. "The king will want to question her."

The soldiers caught her wrists and bound them together.

Max looked down the sharp edge of his long sword poised above the earl's heart and smiled. "Apologize to my wife for hurting her."

The earl opened his mouth to protest when the tip of Max's sword sliced through his skin and stopped at the bones protecting his heart. He screamed with pain.

"Apologize," Max commanded.

"Max, I am all right." Jane pushed against the dungeon wall where she landed and got slowly to her feet.

Max did not look up. “No, Jane. He hurt you. He will apologize, or he shall die slowly and painfully. He was dead the second he touched you, but he was too caught up in his own stupidity to recognize it for what it was. He chose to hide behind your skirts, and for this he must pay.”

Jane shivered at the deadly calm of his voice. Max meant every word he said.

“I apologize—” The earl died the next second. The point of Max’s sword pierced his heart even as he said the words.

Phyllis screamed again. She lunged at Max, but one of the soldiers caught her.

“Max…” Jane began, her hands pressed tightly against her mouth. She hated the sight of so much blood. Nausea rose in her throat.

Max nodded at the two soldiers behind him. “Take the traitor out of here and see Lady Emily is closely guarded. I must report to the king.” He stopped. “Take her to the throne room.” He indicated Phyllis Rathborne with his chin.

They nodded and began the task of dragging the earl from the dungeon.

Jane hurried toward the stairs. She must have fresh air and a cool breeze on her face. Dizziness assailed her. She grabbed the wall for balance. It was too much to take in at once. Her mother left her for the Earl of Downing. She was a few hours ride away all this time. She knew about Jane’s knee and did nothing. She paid Father Brown to incite hatred against her. *All this time she blamed Max, and it was her mother who was responsible!*

Two strong arms picked her up and held her close

as Max bounded up the stairs from the dungeon. Several long minutes later, Jane was laid back against soft satin sheets and a mound of feather pillows.

Max kissed her brow gently. A maid handed him a clean cloth soaked in warm water, and Max carefully washed the blood from her neck. He tied a soft cloth loosely around the wound, allowing her to breathe. "Are you all right, my love?" Max asked softly as he stroked the auburn curls from her damp brow.

Jane opened her eyes and gazed up into his. A smile touched her lips. "I am always all right when you are with me," she sighed. A wave of nausea took her by surprise. She leaned over the chamber pot on the other side of the bed until the sickness passed. She must be overtired from her long journey to London. Jane laid back and closed her eyes once more. Now Max was safe, and the real traitor was dead. Everything would be all right after all, and she could have some much-needed sleep.

****

Max frowned at Jane's pale face and closed eyes. "Are you feeling sickly? Perhaps I should take you outside for some fresh air," he suggested. Why was she still so ill? They were no longer in the dungeon with the blood and the smell. He clasped his hands behind his back and paced. He went over everything in his mind but could come up with no good reason for her illness other than a weak stomach. Jane was not used to seeing so much blood. Surely, this must be the reason. She was such a conundrum, part warrior and part princess. Perhaps a little rest was in order. Brightening at the notion, he approached the bed.

"Jane…" he began.

She looked up and smiled. His heart squeezed tight in his chest at the sweetness of her smile. God, he loved this gentle, beautiful woman. He yearned to hold her against him and tell her of his love until the terror of the last few weeks vanished from his mind.

"Go to the king, my love. I shall be right here waiting for your return."

Max bowed slightly and turned toward the door. The sooner he told the king his news the sooner he could return to Jane.

Chapter Twenty-Eight

Jane's gift strengthened daily. Admitting her love for Max opened her to her true potential. Not only could she communicate through her mind, but she heard other people's thoughts, as well.

Max caught her on several occasions arguing with an unseen source.

Jane did not know how to answer his questioning look. So, she shrugged and pointed to her head. He would smile and nod as he walked away.

When Max returned to their chamber after speaking with the king, he cradled Jane in his arms. "I have something to tell you, love." He frowned. "The king sentenced Lady Phyllis to life imprisonment for treachery. Her cell is next to Lady Emily's."

Jane nodded. She already knew. She had to walk in the gardens and sing to drown out her mother's curses.

Lady Phyllis hung herself the next morning. She could not bear to live without her life of privilege and would rather die than live behind bars.

Jane informed Max of her mother's demise before the guards found her body. Jane heard Lady Phyllis' last thoughts before she tied a sheet around her neck and stepped from the cot in her cell. She had no idea her mother harbored such hatred and violence.

Lady Emily lingered in Newgate Prison alone and abandoned. No one came to visit. Lady Melissa refused to soil the soles of her new shoes with the prison's dirt, and Lord Dewhurst promptly broke off the engagement following Lady Emily's sentencing. He courted the daughter of a baron instead. Jane's head burned with the heat of her malice.

It was a solemn two weeks before they returned home. Jane spent much of the time over the bedpan in their chamber. Her sickness had not improved.

Max informed her she required the fresh air of Rathborne and placed her gently in his carriage for the long ride home.

They stopped often, so Jane could breathe in the fresh air and stretch her legs. A week later, they turned onto Rathborne land.

Jane muttered beneath her breath as their carriage wound through the forest toward the castle. Suddenly, she sat up.

Danger approaches.

Jane stilled, holding a hand to her stomach.

Death waits beneath the trees ahead.

Jane glanced at Max. "I must have some fresh air. Please ask the driver to stop."

Max stared at her. "Are you ill again, love?" He tapped on the roof of the carriage with his cane to alert the driver to stop.

Jane shook her head. "I have something I must see to."

As soon as the carriage slowed, Max jumped out and assisted Jane to the ground.

"Stay here," she said and walked forward. She held her head high, her gaze on the trees in front of her.

The growl of the alpha wolf rumbled from the forest. His yellow eyes glowed beneath the dark, twisted trees.

"Come out," she commanded.

The wolf snarled and trotted out to the middle of the forest road. His pack appeared behind him.

Max sprang to her side, grabbing his sword. "For God's sake, Jane. Get behind me."

Jane kept eye contact with the alpha male. She placed a hand over Max's. "Let me go, dear. This is between him and me." She indicated the wolf with her chin.

Max stilled.

She could tell he meant to jump in front of her. "Max," she said softly. "Trust me. He shall not hurt me." She felt the tension in him. "Trust me," she said again.

Max released her arm.

Jane stepped in front of him and focused her energy on the wolf.

The alpha was black as a moonless night. He stared at her and took another step forward.

"Leave," Jane commanded.

"This is my forest," the wolf answered. *"This is my territory. I have claimed it. My pups are hungry. We shall kill you all."* He snarled, showing his razor-sharp teeth.

Jane narrowed her gaze. She put every ounce of strength into her command. *"No! This forest belongs to me. You must go back to your old hunting ground. If I see your sign after today, I shall kill your mate and every member of your pack with my magic. This is your warning."*

The alpha wolf backed up. He stared at her for another second and then disappeared into the trees. The rest of the pack followed.

Jane smiled. Life was much easier with magic.

****

Suddenly, Max had her in his arms, striding back toward the carriage. "For God's sake, Jane, do not take chances like that again. How did you know the wolves were here? How did you know they would listen to you? Where did they go?"

Jane tightened her arms around his neck. "I sent them back to Scotland." She gazed at up him and smiled. "All is well."

He swallowed his fear. He lost several years of his life when he looked past her and saw the wolves. "Do not ever frighten me so again." He wiped the perspiration from his face with his kerchief and stopped. "How did you make them go?"

Jane shrugged. "I commanded him, and they left."

Max stared at her. "How did you know it would work?"

She kissed his pale cheek. "I just did."

It took several minutes for his hands to stop trembling. God almighty, he could not endure any more surprises like that.

It was early evening when they arrived at the castle. Max kept a close eye on Jane for the next few weeks. She was ill off and on the entire time. The illness was more difficult to control in the mornings, and Jane tired easily. When she started taking naps in the afternoons, Max feared for her in earnest.

"What if she has acquired the same sickness my mother had?" Max asked Mrs. Patrick one afternoon when he found Jane sleeping on the sofa in the library.

"Och, I am just as sure she has, your grace. But not

the same illness which took her life." Mrs. Patrick hurried to reassure him. "Nay, this illness resolves itself at the end of nine months."

Confused, Max wondered if his housekeeper had gone daft in his absence.

Mrs. Patrick patted his arm and said, "Dinna worry, your grace. 'Tis a babe. The duchess is with child!"

Max's heart burst inside his chest. A babe! He was going to be a father! So, this was the secret she harbored. Wonder dropped him to his knees beside her. He placed his palm gently on her stomach. Max considered the tiny life there and smiled with pride. Leaning over, he kissed his duchess' soft lips. He wondered if the voice in her head told her the joyous news or if she guessed. His worry over her illness vanished into thin air. It was the last thing he expected to hear but the best news by far. He stared at Jane in awe. She carried his child!

****

Jane opened her eyes and smiled. Her hands moved down and covered Max's. Happiness filled her heart as she sat up. Her gaze sought the silver gleam in his. "Are you pleased?" she asked sleepily.

Max took her in his arms and kissed her thoroughly. "I am more pleased than it is possible to be."

Mrs. Patrick went out, closing the door softly behind her.

"So much has changed since I stumbled inside Rathborne's gates ahead of the wolves. I had no idea I would end up here with you in my arms."

Jane stroked his face with the tips of her fingers. "I was not sure how to act with such a handsome man in my dungeon. I worried about the coming winter and food. I had nowhere to turn and no friends or family. Then you came along. You were so confident and commanding. You frightened me."

Max chuckled. "I was in the dungeon. You could have tied me up and had your way with me." He winked suggestively.

Jane laughed. "I suppose I could have, but food was a more pressing concern." She looked him over from head to toe. "Now, however…" She wrapped her arms around his neck and brought his mouth to hers once more.

Max got up and swung her into his arms. He strode to the master chamber and placed her carefully on the large bed. He locked the door, and neither one of them emerged until the next day.

****

Max's life had taken such a turn in the last few weeks it was hard to imagine how different things were now from then. The letters from his father healed a place inside him he did not know existed until he read his father's words. Then the emotions flowing through him rocked him to his soul. If only he received the letters years ago and made amends with his father, things would have been different.

It was Mrs. Patrick, once again, who came to his rescue. "If you went back and changed how things were, things might not be how they are now. Are you sure you wish to change the past?"

Max thought about what she said and had to agree. He would not change what he held now for all the diamonds in Brazil.

Months later, Max's eyes settled on Jane, sleeping

soundly in the large bed, her auburn curls spread out on the pillow beneath her. Her white, naked shoulder peeped out from under the brocade coverlet. She slept with a smile on her soft sweet mouth.

Max tucked his shirt into his breeches and headed for the door. A soft baby sound caused him to stop. He walked slowly over to the cradle next to the large bed and gazed down at his little daughter. Her red hair curled riotously around her tiny face. Her bright blue eyes looked up with innocence and trust. The baby gurgled again, a smile splitting her round face. Two chubby hands reached toward him.

Max leaned forward. The baby touched his hand, and Max saw the image of the castle lake in his mind. Two beautiful white swans glided across the silvery water. He looked at his daughter in surprise. "You want to go see the swans?"

Elizabeth smiled and held her arms up for him to take her.

Max knew the power the Lenwood women shared. Jane's special ability was speaking through the mind. She never told him how her knee healed. He suspected Lady Aldetha had something to do with it.

Her grandmother made the journey north for the birth of their daughter. Lady Aldetha laughed aloud when she touched the child and announced she was special. At Max's inquiring look, she said, "You shall see. You shall see."

And he did. Elizabeth had her opinion on where they should walk and what she wanted to see. She was not shy about letting him know it, either.

Jane would not let anyone take her daughter out of her sight. Her daughter would be drawn in rather than shut out, as she was. So, the baby slept in an elaborate cradle next to her mother's bed.

"Come along, Elizabeth." Max scooped the child into his arms and tucked her blankets firmly around her. "Let us go for a walk while mama sleeps. Shall we?"

Elizabeth touched his cheek showing him the swans again.

"Yes, my love. We shall visit the swans."

Max took one more look at the beauty sleeping in his bed. Jane bewitched his life, possessed his soul, and enchanted his world. Settling the baby into the crook of his arm, Max walked away, telling the red-headed nymph the most ridiculous stories involving princesses, dragons, and knights in shining armor. He made sure to mention the prince never rescued the princess until well after the princess turned forty and seven. No princess would be allowed to leave her papa before then, because to do so, would break his heart into so many pieces he would not be the same again. Max looked forward to each new day with his two beautiful witches and all the wonder which came with them. Life was perfect, Max decided, wonderfully, bewitchingly, magically perfect.

A word about the author…

I have been married to my best friend for thirty-nine years. I have two dogs and enjoy knitting, crocheting, and quilting. My favorite flower is the rose. I love everything about them. At one time I had over a hundred rose bushes and enjoyed spending time outside working with them.

I have worn many hats over the years including, daughter, sister, friend, wife, mother, hostess, housekeeper, EMT, lieutenant, supervisor, lead, and now I am adding my dream hat, author! I am so excited to be here!

Thank you for purchasing
this publication of The Wild Rose Press, Inc.

For questions or more information
contact us at
info@thewildrosepress.com.

The Wild Rose Press, Inc.
www.thewildrosepress.com

www.ingramcontent.com/pod-product-compliance
Lightning Source LLC
LaVergne TN
LVHW020531100826
845148LV00010B/1420

* 9 7 8 1 5 0 9 2 3 7 9 6 8 *